# LOUISE M. GOUGE

## Cowboy Homecoming

HARLEQUIN® LOVE INSPIRED® HISTORICAL

Recycling programs
for this product may
not exist in your area.

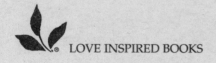

LOVE INSPIRED BOOKS

ISBN-13: 978-0-373-42519-8

Cowboy Homecoming

Copyright © 2017 by Louise M. Gouge

All rights reserved. Except for use in any review, the reproduction or utilization of this work in whole or in part in any form by any electronic, mechanical or other means, now known or hereinafter invented, including xerography, photocopying and recording, or in any information storage or retrieval system, is forbidden without the written permission of the editorial office, Love Inspired Books, 195 Broadway, New York, NY 10007 U.S.A.

This is a work of fiction. Names, characters, places and incidents are either the product of the author's imagination or are used fictitiously, and any resemblance to actual persons, living or dead, business establishments, events or locales is entirely coincidental.

This edition published by arrangement with Love Inspired Books.

® and TM are trademarks of Love Inspired Books, used under license. Trademarks indicated with ® are registered in the United States Patent and Trademark Office, the Canadian Intellectual Property Office and in other countries.

www.Harlequin.com

**Printed in U.S.A.**

## Laurie's bright blue eyes shone with kindness.

Could she see his inner turmoil? He dipped his head to hide his face.

She moved forward as if about to jump down from the rail, and Tolley hurried around his horse and grabbed her waist to lift her down. Once her feet touched the barn floor, he didn't want to let go. Marrying this pretty little gal would have all kinds of benefits, not simply gaining the Colonel's approval. That selfish thought, so like his old way of thinking, broke his grip like a bee sting. He stepped back. "Those city shoes might turn your ankle if you jump. They'll sure as anything get messed up if you tromp around these stalls."

"I suppose so." She sounded a bit breathless as she blinked those big blue eyes at him.

He started to chuck her under the chin like he used to but resisted the urge. Such a gesture might offend her.

"One of our cowhands can take Gypsy back to Four Stones."

"Thanks." He secured his carpetbag to the back of the saddle and mounted up. "See you later, Laurie."

She reached up and squeezed his hand. "Welcome home, Tolley."

How did she know those were the exact words he'd needed to hear?

Florida author **Louise M. Gouge** writes historical fiction for Harlequin's Love Inspired Historical line. She received the prestigious Inspirational Readers' Choice Award in 2005 and placed in 2011 and 2015; she also placed in the Laurel Wreath contest in 2012. When she isn't writing, she and her husband, David, enjoy visiting historical sites and museums. Please visit her website at blog.louisemgouge.com.

## Books by Louise M. Gouge

### Love Inspired Historical

#### Four Stones Ranch

*Cowboy to the Rescue*
*Cowboy Seeks a Bride*
*Cowgirl for Keeps*
*Cowgirl Under the Mistletoe*
*Cowboy Homecoming*

#### Lone Star Cowboy League: The Founding Years

*A Family for the Rancher*

#### Ladies in Waiting

*A Proper Companion*
*A Suitable Wife*
*A Lady of Quality*


*Love Thine Enemy*
*The Captain's Lady*
*At the Captain's Command*

Visit the Author Profile page at Harlequin.com for more titles.

Man looketh on the outward appearance,
but the Lord looketh on the heart.
—*1 Samuel* 16:7b

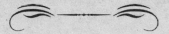

This book series is dedicated to the intrepid pioneers who settled the San Luis Valley of Colorado in the mid to late 1800s. They could not have found a more beautiful place to make their homes than in this vast 7500-foot-high valley situated between the majestic Sangre de Cristo and San Juan Mountain ranges.

Thanks go to my beloved husband of fifty-two years, David Gouge, for his loving support as I pursue my dream of writing love stories to honor the Lord Jesus Christ.

# Chapter One

June 1885
San Luis Valley, Colorado

*At last!*

Tolley Northam struggled to keep from laughing with unfettered happiness as the Denver and Rio Grande train descended onto the vast San Luis Valley plains, picking up speed after its laborious climb over La Veta Pass. After wiping what must be a foolish grin off his face, Tolley glanced around the Pullman car at his fellow passengers, especially the couple who'd sat across from him since the train left Walsenburg early this morning.

"Almost home." The middle-aged woman gave him a maternal smile, reminding him of Mother.

"Yes, ma'am." When they'd asked about his travels, he'd told them about attending college in Boston to become a lawyer and how he now headed home to open his practice and help run the family ranch. "My whole family will be at the train station. They always come out in force to welcome home family members who've traveled."

"As it should be." The husband nodded his approval. "We expect our son and his family to be waiting for us in Alamosa."

The two years in Boston had seemed like an eternity, but at last Tolley would be back on the family's ranch doing the work he loved. Of course he'd honor his father's wishes and set up a law practice, as befitted his Harvard law studies. He'd even purchased a shingle that should please the Colonel, as everyone called his formidable father. Gone was the mischievous boy who'd caused more than his share of trouble. Tolley vowed to be the perfect son so maybe, just maybe, the Colonel would at last approve of him.

He'd pictured this day in his mind for the entire two years. He'd kiss Mother first, of course. Shake hands with his brothers and brother-in-law. Kiss his sister and sisters-in-law on the cheek. Embrace his nieces and nephews, some of whom he'd never met. But his imaginings always stalled over how he'd greet the Colonel. Maybe the old man would reach out to shake his hand and Tolley wouldn't have to decide. But then, their bitter parting had been fueled by anger on both sides. He could only pray the Colonel had mellowed.

Tolley gulped back the fear that always tried to consume him when he recalled the night his father ordered him to leave, ordered him to Boston to become a lawyer and finally make something useful of his sorry self. After all he'd done as a boy and youth, Tolley couldn't deny he'd needed correction, but if he ever had a son, he'd guide him with a loving hand, something he'd learned about from an elderly Boston pastor. Yet all of old Reverend Harris's paternal kindness didn't change Tolley's desperate need for his own father's approval.

He shook away his thoughts. If nothing else, the rest of the family would welcome him home, and Tolley could get back to Thor, his Thoroughbred stallion he'd raised himself.

The train chugged to a stop, and the conductor called out, "Alamosa, Colorado."

"Here we are." The couple stood and gathered their belongings, and Tolley stood in deference to their age.

"Best wishes for your homecoming." The man shook Tolley's hand.

The woman reached up and patted his cheek. "Blessings, dear boy."

Touched by their kind wishes, Tolley reclaimed his seat and watched through the window as they disembarked. Sure enough, a young family greeted them with hugs and kisses, all the things Tolley looked forward to upon his own imminent arrival at home.

"All aboard!"

The conductor waved his white signal flag to the engineer and then hopped up into the passenger car. The train picked up speed and chugged over the seventeen miles to Esperanza. With every mile, Tolley's heart seemed to inch closer to his throat. In spite of his pleasant conversation with the couple, by the time the engine screeched to a halt at the yellow-and-brown depot building, Tolley could barely control his shaking, inside and out. He grabbed his carpetbag, followed the other five passengers to the door and descended the three steps to the platform.

The empty platform.

And all the emptier as the other passengers gathered their baggage and went about their business, leaving him alone.

Tolley swallowed hard. He'd written Mother to let her know when he'd arrive. If his father and brothers weren't eager to see him, she, at least, should've come. Perhaps he should get back on the train and keep traveling. But where would he go? This town, this community, held everything he knew and loved. Apparently his love wasn't returned. Perhaps his youthful mistakes were too much even for these kindhearted people to forgive.

Laurie Eberly drove the box wagon through the dusty streets of Esperanza as fast as she dared, being out of practice driving the two-horse conveyance. She dreaded the chore ahead of her. Knowing Tolley, he'd pout and bluster over no one being at the station to meet him, and it would all fall on her shoulders to soothe his crossness. Well, it wasn't Laurie's fault. She wouldn't have chosen to take on this responsibility if it weren't for her love for the rest of the Northam family.

The thick leather reins tugged against her cotton-gloved hands, causing her fingers to ache. In the past two years while she studied at the Denver Music Conservatory, a friend or beau always drove her around so she could protect her hands from strain that might interfere with her piano playing. Now she must reclaim her former skills learned on her family's cattle ranch.

The windy day sent dust whipping up around her, soiling her yellow gown. She hadn't had time to change clothes after Nate Northam asked her to fetch his spoiled youngest brother from the train station while the entire Northam family tended a more important matter.

As she'd feared, the moment she turned off Main Street into the depot yard, the Denver and Rio Grande train pulled out of the station and headed west toward Del Norte. After the last car sped past her, she could see Tolley standing alone beside two trunks and a carpetbag. The hunched-up look of his shoulders made him seem angry, just as she'd expected.

Or was it something else? The word *forlorn* came to mind, but she quickly dismissed it. Brash, know-it-all Tolley Northam could never be accused of having such a wounded disposition. He'd always done most of the wounding.

She set the brake and climbed down from the wagon, taking care that her new high-topped white shoes didn't slip on the narrow step. As she walked toward Tolley, remembering to take small, ladylike steps as she'd learned at the conservatory, he caught sight of her and gave her a smile of recognition.

Something slammed into her chest. She stopped walking and reached up to see what had struck her. Nothing. Not even a stray rock whipped up by the train wheels or blown by the wind. It was his smile, the one that sent all the girls into a swoon. Even Laurie fell for it as a young girl. But no more. She'd known Tolley all her life, and she'd never let him have her heart, no matter how devastating his smile. She exhaled crossly. A troublemaking young man simply shouldn't be that handsome.

Continuing her walk toward him, she hurried to mend her attitude. No matter what he'd done in the past, even Tolley Northam didn't deserve to hear bad news delivered in an unkindly manner.

Tolley's heart began to race. He could hardly believe the beautiful vision gliding toward him with the grace of a skilled ice skater on a frozen pond. Little Laurie Eberly. My, how her gait had changed from the stride of a cowhand to that of an elegant lady. How she'd grown into a lovely young woman in two years. Her face had the slender lines of a Greek sculpture. Her posture exuded confidence and refinement rivaling any Boston debutante's. In all of his boyhood mischief, he'd never flirted with girls, but this beautiful woman's appearance tempted him to try.

Nonsense. The Eberly girls were like sisters to his brothers and him. Of course, the Colonel always wanted at least one marriage between the two families. Maybe he should marry this little gal. Then the Eberly family would turn out to welcome him home next time he traveled.

"Good morning, Tolley." Laurie offered no smile, and her eyes held a guarded look as she approached him.

"Morning, Laurie." Tolley smiled, which only made her wince. "If you're meeting somebody, I'm afraid they didn't arrive or went off before you got here." He should've talked to more of his fellow passengers to see if they knew any of his friends. But he'd spent most of his travel time talking about himself to anyone who'd listen. Another failure on his part.

"I came to meet you." Laurie touched his arm, and a spark shot clear up to his shoulder, raising gooseflesh on his neck. "Nate asked me."

He had no time to examine his response to her *or* his bitter disappointment. Before anger could take hold of him over his family's careless neglect, tears shone in her eyes, and fear crowded into his heart. "What is it? Mother?" Three years ago, Mother and the Colonel went to Italy for her health. Did her heart finally give out?

Laurie shook her head, and her sunny red curls bounced around her face. "It's your father, Tolley." She gripped his arm more firmly. "Doc says it's apoplexy."

For countless moments, Tolley couldn't move, couldn't breathe. Finally, he managed, "I-is he—?"

"No, he's not gone." The words *not yet* hung in the air between them.

Laurie stared away for a moment, then gazed up at him with sweet compassion. "Your family is with him now. I know your mother will be glad to see you." She waved a hand toward a box wagon he recognized from the many times he'd visited the Eberly place while growing up, the ranch next to his own family's spread. "Maybe we can find someone to help load your trunks." She glanced around the area.

"I can get them. Just drive the wagon over here. No, wait. I'll get it." In the past, the Eberly girls would've considered his gentlemanly offer offensive, being capable cowhands themselves.

This new Laurie simply smiled. "Thank you."

Tolley quickly loaded his trunks and took the reins. As he drove, he and Laurie didn't speak. His mind disoriented, he couldn't even think of what to ask about his father's illness.

The familiar sights of Esperanza, along with the newer buildings, filtered past his numbness. Mrs. Winsted's mercantile. Williams's Café. The barber shop. Across the street sat the bank, the sheriff's office and two empty buildings. At the corner where they turned south, the Esperanza Arms, his sister's hotel, loomed over the town with its three towering stories, shops lining the south side and a narrow portico on the east.

Tolley guided the team of horses around the corner headed south and urged them to a brisk trot. Down one side street, he spied Mrs. Foster's boardinghouse. On another street stood the high school Tolley helped to build. Would anyone remember that good deed?

The more important question? Would he see the Colonel before he died?

Laurie clung to the side of the driver's bench, sure she'd tumble to the ground if they hit a bump. Tolley drove with understandable urgency, but he also skirted around the worst of the ruts and dips in the road. He obviously hadn't lost his driving skill while in Boston. Aching sympathy rose up within her, accompanied by a pinch of shame over her poor attitude about coming to town to fetch him home.

While she couldn't say for sure, it appeared Tolley had changed. Even before she delivered the bad news about the Colonel, Tolley's gaze in her direction appeared softer, gentler than before. His countenance exuded some quality she couldn't name. What she'd first regarded as belligerence in his posture now appeared to be vulnerability, especially in light of his father's condition.

"What happened?" His question startled her out of her reverie.

"Nate said they found him unconscious in the barn

last evening. I didn't press him for details because he needed to get back to the ranch."

Tolley kept his eyes on the road and gave her a curt nod. "Doc's with him?"

"Yes." Her brother-in-law, Doc Henshaw, was the most capable doctor in the San Luis Valley.

"If anyone could help the Colonel, it's Doc." Tolley smiled, and Laurie's heart warmed at his attempt at problem-solving. But then, he'd always been that way, from trying to fix her broken corncob doll to trying to figure out how to build a bridge over Cat Creek. Once again, shame pinched at her conscience for assuming the worst about him. Since Tolley's childhood, his father had heaped condemnation on him, sometimes warranted, sometimes not. Laurie needn't add her own disapproval.

Four Stones Ranch lay about six miles south of Esperanza. Even at a brisk trot, it took over twenty minutes to traverse the distance. Tolley turned down Four Stones Lane and drove into the barnyard at the back of the house. His brother Rand, an older version of Tolley and second oldest of the four Northam children, came out to meet them just as Tolley jumped down from the wagon.

"Tolley!" Rand shook his brother's hand and slapped him on the back as if nothing was wrong. "Good to see you. Welcome home."

Tolley gave him a shaky grin. "I wish it could be under better circumstances."

"Rand, is there anything I can do?" Laurie remained on the driver's bench, knowing what his answer would be but still needing to offer. Her pa had come over here once they got the news of his old friend's illness, but he must've left already, for his horse wasn't tied to the back hitching rail.

"Thanks, Laurie, but no. The whole family's inside. You've been a big help by bringing this maverick home."

Did he even notice Tolley's wince at his teasing? Probably not. His own face bore a worried look. The two men unloaded the trunks and said their goodbyes.

"We'll be praying for you all." Laurie took up the reins and guided the team toward the lane. A glance back toward the house revealed two dejected brothers heading inside, shoulders slumped with sorrow.

Tolley *had* changed. She just knew it. And even if no one else noticed the difference in him, she'd try her best to help him find his place in the community. "It'll have to be pretty fast, Lord." She glanced up at the clear blue sky. "I'm going back to Denver in September, so please help me be the friend Tolley needs until then."

As always when she discussed the subject of returning to Denver with the Lord, an uneasy feeling crept into her chest. She dismissed it, *as always*. Of course the Lord wanted her to return to that lovely, growing city. As the daughter of a successful cattle rancher, she'd fit into Denver society like a hand in a glove, and she could hardly wait to begin her teaching career at the conservatory.

Leaving his hat on a peg in the mudroom, Tolley moved through the house in a daze. Familiar smells met his senses: fresh-baked bread, leather, Mother's roses. His seven-year-old niece, Lizzie, grabbed him around the waist and cried out a weepy welcome. He bent down to return her hug. The other children were nowhere in sight, but they wouldn't know him anyway. His oldest brother, Nate, came downstairs and shook Tolley's hand. Their sister, Rosamond, embraced him and sobbed briefly on his shoulder. His two sisters-in-law and one brother-in-law each greeted him. From their warm if subdued responses, he thought he'd said the right thing to each one.

He climbed the front staircase on wooden legs, fearing what he'd find at the end of the second-floor hallway. Gathering courage, he nudged the door open.

Mother rose to greet him. "Tolley." She spoke his name as if he'd only come in from milking the cows, at the same time moving between him and the four-poster bed where the Colonel lay. But Mother was too short to hide Tolley's view of the motionless figure lying there, his full bush of dark hair shot through with far more strands of white than when Tolley left home. He pulled her into a gentle embrace and kissed the top of her head.

"How is he?" He whispered the question, even though the Colonel appeared beyond hearing. The old man's eyes were closed, and his complexion, weathered to a deep tan by a lifetime in the sun, bore a gray pallor.

She sniffed and dabbed her cheeks with a handkerchief. "Still with us. Doc gives us hope—" She choked on the word.

A movement on his right caught his attention.

"Welcome home, Tolley." Doc Henshaw stepped near him and reached out to shake his hand. "Let's go out to the hall." Still gripping Tolley's hand, he urged him out of the room as though he had no right to be there. "I've reason to believe he can hear, so it's best to discuss his condition out here," he whispered.

Breaking away from Doc, Tolley couldn't keep anger from his voice. "Are my brothers and Rosamond allowed to see him?"

Doc gave him a sad smile, but didn't answer.

"Why can't I see him? If he can hear, can't I tell him I'm home?"

"Soon enough. I'm still assessing his condition." Doc clapped him gently on the shoulder. "Why don't you settle in? You must be tired from your trip."

Every instinct told him to force his way back into the sickroom so he could see for himself how his father fared. But instinct had been his worst enemy while he grew up, getting him into more scrapes than he could remember. Old Reverend Harris in Boston taught him to be more thoughtful and to take more time to make decisions.

"All right." He turned away from the now-closed door. Didn't Mother even want to see him? To welcome him home with more than a brief embrace?

He walked down the hallway to his bedroom and opened the door.

"Shh." Rita, the family housekeeper, rose from a rocking chair and hurried toward him. "The little ones are sleeping, Senor Tolley." Whispering, she waved a hand toward two small heads at rest on his pillow and a cradle holding a red-haired doll that must be Rand's new daughter. "Senora Northam uses this room as the nursery now. The children often come here."

Tolley's knees threatened to buckle. So he couldn't even find refuge in his old bedroom. Even his belongings were nowhere in sight. "I see. Very well." He backed out into the hallway and made his way downstairs to the front parlor, where the others had gathered.

His brothers had made no move to bring his trunks inside. In fact, the moment he entered the room, they traded guarded looks. Nate cleared his throat.

"This all happened very suddenly, Tolley. Last night, when we heard about the Colonel's…illness, Rand and I agreed we needed to move our families here so we can run the ranch and our wives can run the house. Then Mother won't have to worry about a thing. We moved here this morning and, as you can see, it sort of makes for a full house."

Rosamond, always the protective big sister, came over and looped her arm in his. "We expected you to stay in Boston for another year." Compassion filled her voice, making him uncomfortable. "To finish your schooling."

"I did finish." He lifted his chin defensively and continued before they could ask questions. "I wrote to the Colorado attorney general in Denver. Judge Thomas sent me the paperwork, and based on my performance at Harvard, he's accepted me into the Colorado judicial system. That's more than a whole lot of so-called lawyers achieve all over the West where there's no accountability. A lot of men hang out a shingle without even having any training."

Why did he always feel the need to defend himself, despite being twenty-two years old? It didn't seem to matter how much he'd accomplished; they still treated him like the baby of the family. Wouldn't they ever let him grow up? "I wrote to Mother about coming, but I asked her not to say anything. I wanted to surprise everyone else."

Silence filled the room. His brother-in-law, Garrick, joined Rosamond and took her hand. "Sweetheart, let's have Tolley stay at the hotel until everything returns to normal." His English accent no longer irritated Tolley, but his suggestion needled him. Moving to the hotel would be another way to separate him from his family during this terrible crisis.

"Maybe Mrs. Foster has an empty room." Marybeth spoke up. She'd lived in the widow's boardinghouse before she married Rand. "It'll be much homier than the hotel." The pretty Irish lady gave Tolley a warm, sisterly smile, and the red curls around her ivory face momentarily reminded him of Laurie Eberly. Right now, he'd appreciate having Laurie around. At least she'd welcomed him home.

Because Marybeth meant well with her suggestion, Tolley couldn't fault her. Yet he remembered both she and Susanna actually employed deceit with the entire family when each one first came to Esperanza. Of course, after considerable turmoil in both cases, they'd ended up marrying his brothers, but not until after each one asked for forgiveness. Why could they be forgiven for their wrongdoing, but he couldn't? Why was he always the one on the outside?

"Sure." He infused his voice with as much energy as he could. "I'll go into town right now and see if Mrs. Foster has a room." He headed for the back door, where he'd dropped his carpetbag. He'd saddle Thor to ride to town and leave his trunks for the cowhands to bring later. For now, he couldn't wait to get away. No matter how his heart ached over his family's rejection, he'd do what was best for everyone.

He strode across the barnyard toward the weathered barn. A tiny figure in a blue gingham dress stood outside the main corral. Little Lizzie peered through the slats at the horses milling about. At least Lizzie had given Tolley a heartfelt welcome when he arrived.

"Hey, sprout, what's up?" He started to tousle her hair, but that would mess up her perfect blond braid. Instead, he patted her head.

She looked up at him, her face streaked with tears. "Uncle Tolley, is Grampa going to die?"

Tolley swallowed hard. "Naw. He's too tough. Say, have you learned to ride yet?" He grabbed her waist and lifted her up to sit on the top rail, which brought on a bout of giggles, just as he'd hoped.

"No, sir." Lizzie's blue eyes turned sad again. "Mama says I'm too young."

"Too young?" Tolley stroked his chin thoughtfully. "Aren't you about twenty-five?"

"Uncle Tolleeeee!" She giggled again, as he'd hoped she would. "I'm seven."

"My, my. All grown up."

"Besides, nobody has time to teach me." She sighed and looked at him with those big blue eyes.

"You little rascal." Tolley laughed for the first time since he'd gotten off the train, a true belly laugh. "Maybe I'll have time to teach you." Especially since his family didn't seem to need him for anything else.

"Would you please?" Lizzie launched herself off the rail and flung her arms around his neck, almost knocking him to the ground.

He laughed again and managed to catch her up in a firm hug without falling down.

"Hey, what's going on here?" An angry male voice accompanied the thump of boots on the hard-packed yard.

Still holding on to Lizzie, Tolley turned to see Seamus O'Brien, Marybeth's brother and the Northams' ranch foreman, stalking toward him, fists bunched at his sides. As Tolley set Lizzie down, Seamus stopped and blinked.

"Tolley? Well, of all things. I'm glad to see it's you. I was worried somebody was about to carry off our little Lizzie." He reached out and shook Tolley's hand.

"Uncle Seamus, you're so silly." Lizzie spied one of the barn cats and danced away to catch it. "Here, kitty."

"How're you doing, Tolley?" Seamus gave him a respectful smile, no longer looking at him as if he were a troublemaking youngster. Which, of course, he had been, driving all the cowhands crazy with his pranks and dragging a few of them into trouble with him.

"Not bad." He couldn't exactly tell this man his family had just the same as run him off. Being Rand's brother-in-law, he'd deny it…or make excuses for them. "I thought I'd saddle Thor and ride him into town."

"Um, I see." Seamus's face crinkled up with perplexity.

"What's going on? Has something happened to my horse?" Tolley's stomach turned. He doubted he could stand any more bad news.

"Nothing like that." Seamus shrugged. "Last month the Colonel sent him over to the Eberly place for stud purposes. George wants some of that Thoroughbred blood in his herd."

Tolley sagged with relief. The Colonel and George Eberly had settled here at the same time with plans to help each other build their large spreads. The Colonel made it no secret he wanted Nate or Rand to marry one of the five Eberly girls. When they'd married other ladies, all such talk ceased, of course. Once again, the idea that he should marry Laurie crept into his thoughts. Of course, he could only offer her a marriage of convenience, but— *No*, he must stop such foolish thinking, even if it would give him one more way to impress the Colonel when…if…he recovered.

Tolley forced his thoughts in another direction. "Seamus, if my old saddle is still in the barn, I'd like to ride over and visit Thor." *And Laurie*. But he wouldn't say that out loud. "You tell me which horse I should take."

"How about Gypsy?"

Tolley winced. He owed the bay mare a big apology. Maybe he could make amends to her today. Did Seamus remember what Tolley did to her? "Gypsy's fine."

The Irishman grinned. "You remember how to saddle a horse?"

"I think I can manage." *If* Gypsy would even let him near her after the last time he put a saddle on her.

Laurie tried to peel the potatoes, but the dull kitchen knife sliced too deeply. She dried her left hand and reached for the whetstone on the shelf beside the table.

"Now, now." Ma grabbed the slender stone and gently took the knife from Laurie. "You gotta take care of those hands, darlin'. I can peel the vegetables."

Laurie hid her quiet sigh of frustration. In the two weeks since she'd returned home, if she worked here in the kitchen or dusted the parlor or washed her laundry, either Ma or Georgia moved her aside and took over. Why did they pamper her as though she were a delicate doll who needed protection?

At least she'd been allowed to drive into town and fetch poor Tolley from the train, but only because she

and Pa were the only ones around when Nate arrived
with the sad news about the Colonel. Pa hurried over to
Four Stones Ranch to see his friend while Nate helped
her hitch up the team. She'd had no trouble driving.
True, her hands still ached from wearing cotton gloves
instead of leather, but they weren't really hurt.

How could she keep from boredom for the entire
summer on this busy ranch if she wasn't permitted to
lift a finger to work? In Denver, the ladies with whom
she'd socialized did charity work when not engaged in
teas or parties. At the least, they sewed for the poor,
another thing Ma wouldn't permit. "Why don't you go
practice piano?"

The perfect diversion. Laurie loved to play and
looked forward to giving concerts when she returned
to Denver. Seated at the piano by the parlor's front window, she found the simple act of practicing her scales
helped to work some of the ache from her fingers. Then
she thumbed through her hymnal and practiced her favorite hymns to refresh her memory in case Mrs. Foster asked her to play for church.

A movement outside the window caught her eye.
To her surprise, Tolley rode down the lane toward the
barnyard. What could he be doing here?

Her heart skipped, then dropped. Did he bring bad
news about his father? But wouldn't they send a cowhand instead of a family member if Pa's dear friend
had died? Wouldn't the family want to gather together
and comfort one another?

Laurie dashed through the house to the back door,
seeing through the glass that Tolley had dismounted
and tied his horse to the back hitching rail. Her heart
pounded, no doubt from the short run. After all, in

Denver she'd never run. Ladies didn't, *after all.* And of course her haste accounted for her inability to breathe as Tolley approached the house.

She flung open the back door. "Tolley! Is everything all right?"

He gave her that dangerous smile, which surely gave *other* girls palpitations. Not her, of course, because she knew him too well. As he came closer, she saw the pain in his eyes, and all thoughts of his good looks disappeared, replaced by the compassion she'd felt for him on the ride from town.

"Tolley, what is it?"

"Aw, nothing. Just wanted to get reacquainted with my horse. Is he in the barn or out in a pasture?" His false good humor didn't fool her.

She touched his arm. "Is everything all right at home?"

His smile slipped. "If you call having to find someplace to live because there's no room at the ranch for me 'all right,' then yes, everything's fine."

"No place to live in your family's home?" She couldn't keep the indignation from her voice. "Why on earth?"

There was that smile again. "Aw, it's all right. Doc says the Colonel is likely to recover, so I don't need to stay close in case he—" He cleared his throat. "My brothers and their wives need to be close by to help our folks, so it takes up all the bedrooms. Besides, I need to live in town so I can set up my law practice."

He didn't fool her. His hurt feelings were obvious. But she wouldn't contradict him. "So, your sister's hotel or Mrs. Foster's boardinghouse?" She punctuated her words with raised eyebrows and a silly grin, something she never would've offered any Denver acquaintance, either gentleman or lady.

He responded with a genuine laugh. "You know our town." And offered a charming shrug. "I'll try Mrs. Foster's first. More homey. Better cooking."

Laurie returned a gentle laugh. "So true. Although you may want to try Chef Henrique's French cuisine at the hotel."

"No, just give me a juicy steak or chicken and dumplings any day." He closed his eyes. "Mmm-mmm."

A hint? The aroma of cooking chicken wafted through the open window. "You can stay for dinner."

"Naw, I'd better head into town and find out where I'll be staying tonight. But thanks."

"Well, then, let's find Thor."

The stallion grazed in a near pasture, and she sent a cowhand to fetch him. The horse pranced majestically on his lead rope, but when he spied Tolley, he whinnied and broke away, cantering toward them. Lowering his head and rubbing against Tolley's chest, the magnificent beast acknowledged his master and friend. Eyes closed, Tolley pressed his head against Thor's.

The meeting between horse and man moved Laurie to tears. Maybe Tolley's family had no room for him, but his faithful horse gave him a welcome any cowboy would envy.

He needed a friend, so she'd be that person. Only she mustn't revive her foolish childhood affections for him. She'd noticed romances couldn't be successful if built on sympathy. Besides, she'd found her place in Denver and would return there in the fall, so she must keep her heart reined in.

That bothersome, undefined reservation about Denver crept into her mind, but as always, she dismissed it. It was her dream, after all.

# Chapter Two

Tolley led Thor and Gypsy to the barn to curry both horses and move his saddle from the mare to his stallion. Laurie tagged along just as she used to as a pesky little tomboy wearing braids and trousers. Only this time, instead of finding her presence annoying, he found it comforting. And helpful. She brought him a currying brush and pointed to stalls where he could work on the horses, but her being there helped most of all.

Thor needed a good brushing, and he leaned into the stiff-bristled brush, whickering his appreciation. While working on the magnificent beast, Tolley felt his heart lighten in an unexpected way. This is where he longed to be, working with horses and raising prime beef. Not sitting behind a desk in a dull law office pushing papers around and making sure his clients filed the right land forms or got their fair share in business deals. He certainly wasn't interested in defending outlaws.

"You missed a spot." Laurie, who'd climbed up to sit on the stall's top rail, pointed to Thor's left side. Her impudent grin sent a warm feeling through his chest.

He walked around Thor and saw the thick patch of hair. "Why don't you grab a brush and help me out?" He nodded toward the wall where brushes and tack hung on pegs.

To his surprise, she sighed. "Ma made me promise not to work with the horses." She held up her hands. "She's afraid I'll ruin these for playing the piano."

"Huh. That's odd." He shrugged. "I never figured any of the Eberly girls would turn out to be—" *Dainty* came to mind, not a word usually associated with these cowgirls.

"Useless?"

"Not at all." He swiped the brush over Thor's side. "Do you miss it?"

"Not so much the work, but I do miss feeling useful."

*I know how you feel.* But he wouldn't say that. Instead, he gave her a sympathetic smile as he brushed out the last of Thor's coat and cleaned the clump of hair from the currying brush. "There you go, boy." He patted the stallion's rump and moved over to the next stall.

Was it his imagination, or did Gypsy eye him nervously? He wouldn't blame her if she did. She'd been fairly docile when he saddled and rode her here, no longer a lively horse. Was that his fault?

"Here you go, beauty. Let's make you comfortable." He threw the left stirrup over the saddle, loosened the cinch and let the girth fall, then lifted the saddle and blanket off her back.

"You need a fresh blanket?" Laurie waved toward the tack room where multitiered racks held blankets and saddles.

"Yeah, I guess that's a good idea. This one's damp

and needs airing." Another homey feeling swept through him. Their families always helped each other, knowing they'd get their own things back in due time.

He grabbed a fresh brush and worked on Gypsy's coat. His fingers swept over a dark, shallow dip on her back where the saddle had sat, and a chill plunged clear down to his belly. This was where he'd wounded her two years ago by slipping a large burr between blanket and horse to keep Garrick from winning the Independence Day horse race. He'd expected Gypsy to throw Garrick. Instead, the mare raced her heart out, every stride digging the burr deeper into her flesh. She and Garrick finished only a half-length behind Tolley and Thor.

Later, during the dance, Tolley picked a fight with Garrick, earning himself the Colonel's sentence of banishment to Boston. And all because the Colonel had shown favor to the Englishman such as he'd never shown Tolley. Even now, shame vied with jealous anger. While he'd made friends with Garrick when he and Rosamond came through Boston on their honeymoon and had been forgiven by the man, now his brother-in-law, he'd never understand why his own father seemed to despise him. Or worse, never gave him a second thought, as though he didn't even exist unless he got into trouble. And now maybe the Colonel would never know all Tolley had done to try to earn his favor.

"Tolley?" Laurie's bright blue eyes shone with kindness.

Could she see his inner turmoil? He dipped his head to hide his face.

"Yeah?" He moved away from Gypsy and fetched

a fresh blanket from the tack room, then smoothed it over Thor's back.

"You sure you don't want something to eat before you go to town?"

He placed his saddle on the stallion and reached under his belly to grab the girth. "No, thanks. I'll grab a bite at Miss Pam's." After cinching the girth, he looked over Thor's back at Laurie. "She still runs the café, right?"

"Yes. And still makes the best pies and cakes."

"I seem to recall all of you Eberly ladies are mighty fine cooks, too."

"We try." Laurie moved forward as if about to jump down from the rail.

Tolley hurried around his horse and grabbed her waist to lift her down. Once her feet touched the barn floor, he didn't want to let go. Marrying this pretty little gal would have all kinds of benefits, not simply gaining the Colonel's approval. That selfish thought, so like his old way of thinking, broke his grip like a bee sting. He stepped back. "Those city shoes might turn your ankle if you jump. They'll sure as anything get messed up if you tromp around these stalls."

"I suppose so." She sounded a bit breathless as she blinked those big blue eyes at him. "You sure you won't stay for dinner?" she repeated.

"Still no, but thanks." He started to chuck her under the chin like he used to but resisted the urge. Such a gesture might offend her.

"One of our cowhands can take Gypsy back to Four Stones."

"Thanks." He secured his carpetbag to the back of the saddle and mounted up. "See you later, Laurie."

She reached up and squeezed his hand. "Welcome home, Tolley."

How did she know those were the exact words he'd needed to hear?

As Tolley rode away, Laurie shook her head. No matter how fond of him she used to be, she also remembered his boyhood mischief and the way he'd hurt many people. Besides, despite how attractive he was, she refused to fall for a San Luis Valley man, especially one who wanted to settle here. Her future lay in Denver.

After picking at her noon meal, she tried practicing piano again. But she kept looking out the window to see if Tolley would ride by. A silly idea, of course, because he'd be in town at Mrs. Foster's boardinghouse or Rosamond's hotel.

Maybe she could spend time with Maisie and help with baby Johnny. One day Laurie hoped to have children, too. Oddly, all she could picture were pint-sized cowboys learning to ride on one of the tamer old cow ponies on the ranch. Another silly idea, because her children would live in a Denver mansion and attend boarding schools.

"Ma, if I promise not to work too hard, may I visit Maisie for a few days?"

"Why, what a wonderful idea." Ma plunged the dinner dishes into the hot soapy water and began to wash them.

"I'll dry the dishes first." Laurie grabbed a tea towel.

"Oh, no, you don't." Ma tugged the towel away from her. "You go on and pack a bag. I'm sure Maisie will welcome the visit. George, you be sure to saddle Laurie's horse, you hear?"

"Yes, ma'am." Seated at the kitchen table, Pa grinned and winked at Laurie. At least he didn't treat her like a fragile flower. "I'll take care of it, sunshine."

By the time she'd changed clothes and packed, Pa had Little Bit saddled and waiting by the back door. He'd also put her rifle in the saddle holster as protection against possible encounters with coyotes or rattlesnakes.

She took her time riding the nearly five miles to Esperanza. The warm, sunny day had just the right amount of breeze wafting over the landscape. Birds sang or chirped in the shallow marshes along the road, and in the distance she saw rabbits out for an afternoon stroll. Or so her Denver friends might think. Laurie itched to shoot the critters to take to Maisie for supper. But that would involve skinning and gutting them. Maisie might not have time, and Ma would throw a fit if Laurie used a hunting knife to do the job.

At Maisie and Doc's two-story house, she tied Little Bit's reins to the front hitching rail beside another horse and the undertaker's hearse. One of Doc's patients must have died, and others needed his care. He must have returned from Four Stones Ranch after tending the Colonel.

Seated on settees and chairs along the wall in the front hallway, folks awaited Doc's help.

"So glad you came, sis." Maisie handed her infant son to Laurie and whispered, "If you can tend Johnny for a bit while Doc finishes up with the dead fella, I'd appreciate it."

"I'd love to." Laurie adored the chubby little rascal who'd thrown his tiny arms around her neck. She and her sisters looked enough alike that Johnny seemed to accept her without reservations. "Who died?" Like Maisie, Laurie kept her voice to a whisper.

"Dathan Hardison." Maisie sounded sad, as though that varmint's death wasn't a relief, since he'd lingered near death since before Christmas. All that time, she and Doc tended him, valuing his life as much as any upright citizen's.

Laurie had her own feelings about Hardison. He'd shot their sister Beryl during a bank robbery attempt. According to their sister Grace, the other outlaw, Deke Smith, repented and came to the Lord…right before he shot Hardison to keep him from killing Grace, Reverend Thomas and Marybeth Northam. Then poor old Deke died, too.

"Did Hardison ever…?" She let the question hang in the air.

Tears eased down Maisie's cheeks as she shook her head. "Don't think so. Doc and I did try to persuade him."

Laurie sighed and hugged Johnny closer. In spite of all the evil Hardison had done, she couldn't shrug off the dreadful thought of his eternal destination, one of his own choosing.

The surgery's pocket doors slid open, and Doc appeared in the hallway carrying one end of a stretcher. Deputy Gareau, whose first name, Justice, was appropriate for his work, held up the back end. Mr. Macy, the undertaker, trailed behind. A white sheet covered a body so thin it seemed nearly flat. A murmur went through the waiting area, some saying, "Good riddance."

Maisie faced the group. "Folks, as soon as I can clean the surgery and Doc finishes up with Mr. Macy, we'll take care of you." She entered the room and slid the pocket doors shut.

Dismissing her dismal thoughts about the lost outlaw, Laurie gave Johnny another hug. Maisie needed help, so she'd make herself useful. In Denver, she'd missed the sisterly camaraderie the five of them shared. Had missed lifelong friends, even a rascal like Tolley Northam. Would miss them again when she moved back to the city for good. Of course, she only felt sad about leaving because she loved them all so much. Once back in the city teaching at the conservatory and giving concerts, she'd be happy again. Of course she would.

Mrs. Foster welcomed Tolley like a long-lost son but asked for time to prepare his room, so he spent the night at the hotel. When he returned the next morning, she showed him to his room.

"I have only two other boarders," Mrs. Foster said, "but other than mealtimes, they mostly keep to themselves. Mrs. Runyan is the milliner, and Mr. Parsley is a watchmaker. Their shops are over at the hotel."

"Thank you for the room, ma'am." Tolley glanced around the spacious, modestly furnished chamber. "You let me know if I can help with anything."

"Why, I'll do that, Tolley. Such a kind offer. Adam Starling does a bit of work for me, but he has other jobs around town, so he's not always available. He's supporting his family, you know."

"Yes, ma'am. I know." Yesterday had been the hardest day of Tolley's life, but at least money wasn't a problem. With a sick father, seventeen-year-old Adam bore a heavy load as the man of his family. Tolley's own father lay ill, too, but nobody needed him to step in and take charge. Nobody needed him at all.

That afternoon, boots off and jacket hanging over the back of a desk chair, he lay on his bed. A warm, pleasant breeze blew in through the open window, fluttering the frilly white curtains and making him drowsy. He'd never realized how tiring travel could be. He'd spent five days and nights on various trains as he crossed the country. With the added emotional shock of the Colonel's illness and his own exile from home, he felt as beaten down as if he'd walked all the way from Boston. Sleep beckoned, and he relaxed into the comfortable feather mattress. After all, no one needed him. No one even wanted him. Maybe when he set up his law office…

A hard thump, followed by a scream, woke him with a start.

A weak voice called out, "Lord, help me."

"Mrs. Foster!"

Tolley shook off sleep and dashed from the room. At the bottom of the back staircase, Mrs. Foster lay in a heap, a tin bucket beside her and water covering the stairs and the lady's skirt. She groaned softly. Taking care not to slip, Tolley descended, soaking his socks in the process.

Mrs. Foster's eyes filled with tears as she cradled one arm in the other. One black high-top shoe stuck out at an odd angle from beneath the hem of her black muslin skirt.

Heart in his throat, Tolley forced away his horror. "Dear lady, what can I do to help? Shall I carry you up to your room?" Painfully thin, she'd make a light burden.

She shook her head. "Let me catch my breath." Trembling, she stifled another whimper. "I think my arm is broken."

"Then I shouldn't move you. Will you be all right while I fetch Doc Henshaw?"

Biting her lip, she nodded.

Coatless, hatless and bootless, Tolley didn't bother going upstairs to retrieve his garments. He hurried out the back door and across the yard, taking a shortcut through gardens and over fences until he reached Doc Henshaw's kitchen door, his feet muddy and sore. Unlike in Boston where everyone came to the front door, in Esperanza people generally came to back entrances, at least at the homes of their friends. While he pounded on the door, he realized his mistake. If Doc was home, he'd be working in his surgery at the front of the house.

To his surprise, Laurie opened the door, a red-haired baby on her hip. She looked a bit frazzled and beyond adorable. But he mustn't waste time on such foolish thoughts.

"Tolley, what on earth?"

"Mrs. Foster fell down the stairs." He paused to catch his breath. "She thinks her arm may be broken."

"Oh, no!" Laurie thrust the infant into his arms and hurried from the room.

The baby gave him a startled look and then burst into tears, his cries reaching a high pitch any Boston soprano would be proud of.

"Um, uh, there, there. Shh, shh." Tolley bounced the little one and gave him a silly grin, which did nothing at all to calm the child.

Maisie entered the kitchen, worry written across her pretty face. "Thank you, Tolley. Here's Mommy, my sweet darlin'." She took her son. His wailing ceased, but he eyed Tolley with a wary look. "Doc and Laurie went out the front door." She glanced toward the door leading to the rest of the house.

Suddenly embarrassed, he gave her a sheepish grin. What had the neighbors thought of a man running through their backyards? "Thanks, Maisie. I'll walk around the house so I won't track up your floors."

As he stepped off the back porch, Maisie called out, "Welcome home, Tolley."

Appreciating her kind words, he grinned and waved over his shoulder.

"Laurie, will you get some towels?" Doc knelt beside Mrs. Foster, tending her ankle.

"On the table." Mrs. Foster waved her uninjured hand toward the kitchen, then grabbed her other arm and bit her lip.

Laurie hurried to do as Doc asked. A stack of neatly folded ivory linen towels sat on the kitchen table. This must be laundry day at the boardinghouse, because other clean items filled a wicker basket nearby, probably awaiting ironing. Did Mrs. Foster do laundry for her boarders? Ironing? The thought didn't sit well with Laurie. She picked up three of the large towels, thinking of the work involved to make them so fresh-smelling and spotless.

In the hallway, Doc gently examined Mrs. Foster's foot. "Wrap a towel around her." He covered her bare foot with another one.

Following his orders, Laurie sat on the bottom step and pulled the shivering woman into her arms. Even though wetness seeped through her own skirt, she hoped her body heat would help warm her dear friend. "What happened?"

"I've made a mess of things." Mrs. Foster released a shaky laugh. "Was taking water upstairs to clean the floors before my boarders come home in another hour."

Laurie noticed the bucket. "She shouldn't be carrying full buckets up these stairs."

Doc shook his head. "I've tried to tell her."

"What you didn't tell me is how I'm gonna take care of my boarders if I don't—"

"That's the last bucket you'll carry." Tolley appeared in the doorway to the front hall. "From now on, I'll take care of hauling water." He gave Laurie a gentle smile.

Her heart popped right up into her throat. Because of his kind offer, of course, not because of that smile.

"Hey, Tolley." Doc spared him a glance as he continued his assessment of Mrs. Foster's injuries. "Good thing you happened along when you did."

"You want me to carry Mrs. Foster upstairs?" He stood there in his bare feet and with muddy socks dangling from one hand.

"I want to stabilize her injuries first."

Mrs. Foster sighed, and her pale cheeks turned pink. "I'm so sorry to be such trouble."

"Now, now," Doc said. "You're no trouble at all. Tolley, would you go back to the surgery and ask Maisie to send over a large and a small splint?" He gave Tolley a quick grin. "You could put something on your feet first."

Now Tolley's cheeks took on a little color. "Sure thing." He made his way to the front staircase, and the sound of his bare feet running up the steps came through the walls and ceiling.

If Mrs. Foster's situation weren't so dire, Laurie would've giggled. "Is there anything else I can do?"

"How about some tea?" Doc's forehead creased slightly. "Wait. Mrs. Foster, would you like for Laurie to help you into some dry clothes?"

"Y-yes, p-please." She shivered again despite the warm day.

Laurie didn't need further instructions. Within ten minutes, she'd fetched a dry gown and underpinnings for the lady and helped her change while Doc made tea in the kitchen. Tolley returned with the splints, then disappeared upstairs while Doc secured them to Mrs. Foster's leg and arm. Doc also gave her the tea.

"I'm sorry to say the arm is broken, but I think your ankle is only sprained. The willow bark in your tea should help a little with the pain, but be sure to tell me if you need something stronger." He lifted Mrs. Foster and began the trek up to her room. With Tolley and Laurie helping, they soon settled her in her four-poster bed.

"Oh, dear." The usually calm lady fluttered her un-injured hand over the quilted coverlet. "How will I care for my boarders?"

"Don't you worry for a minute." Laurie gently grasped that fluttering hand and patted it. "I'll move in and manage everything for you." Even Ma would approve of her taking care of the lady who'd taught Laurie to sing and play the piano.

"Would you, my dear?" Mrs. Foster's eyes grew moist again. "I'd be so grateful."

"I'll be here, too." Tolley gave Doc a doubtful look. "If you think it's all right."

"Most folks are pretty understanding when a need

arises like Mrs. Foster's. And, after all, another unattached lady and gentleman live here, and no one has considered it improper."

"Good to hear." Tolley grinned, his relief apparent.

Laurie considered what to do next. "I'll see what I can find in the kitchen for supper."

"I planned fried chicken, dear," Mrs. Foster said. "Would you mind— Ow, oh, dear…" She gripped her injured arm with her free hand.

"Ma'am," Doc said, "if you don't object, I'm going to give you a dose of laudanum. A good rest will help you to heal."

"Oh, my." She gave him a doubtful look. "I suppose so."

"Fried chicken coming up." Laurie hoped her cheerful tone would encourage Mrs. Foster. She hadn't cooked in two years, but it should be like riding a horse. Once in the saddle or, in this case, the kitchen, everything should come back to her. Or so she hoped.

Doc gave Mrs. Foster her laudanum and instructed Laurie on subsequent doses. Then the three of them left her to rest and went downstairs.

"I know you'll manage things here, sis." Doc patted Laurie on the shoulder. "I'll send Maisie over to check on you later this evening."

"I'll be fine, although I do need to let Ma and Pa know where I'm staying. Maybe Georgia could pack more clothes for me and bring them to town."

"When Adam Starling comes by to see if we need anything, I'll send him out to the ranch to arrange it." Toting his black satchel, he headed for the front door.

"I guess I'd better see about supper." Laurie glanced through the large opening to the parlor, where she'd spent countless days taking piano lessons from Mrs. Foster. The old upright piano still sat in the corner, an embroidered linen runner protecting its mahogany top. The house appeared spotless. How did Mrs. Foster do all the cooking and laundry and also clean her boarders' rooms? Laurie moved toward the kitchen door. "First I should clean up the stairs."

"What should I do?" Tolley followed her.

"Peel some potatoes and—"

Before she could finish, the front door opened, and Mrs. Runyan walked in. The short, middle-aged woman set her parasol in the hall tree by the door and took a step toward the staircase. Seeing Laurie and Tolley, she stopped and gasped, her brown eyes wide with shock.

"What on earth is going on here?"

Behind her, a well-dressed gentleman entered the house. "Who are you people?" He removed his black bowler hat, narrowed his already beady eyes and glared at Laurie first, then at Tolley.

Tolley stood so close to her she could feel him bristling. The boy she'd grown up with had a quick temper, so the accusatory looks in the boarders' eyes might easily set him off. She stepped in front of him.

"Mrs. Runyan, how nice to see you. And you must be Mr. Parsley." She reached out to the short, slender gentleman. "How do you do? I'm Laurie Eberly. This is Bartholomew Northam."

"Indeed!" The man moved back and stared at her hand like it was a rattlesnake. A growl rumbled in Tolley's throat, and even Laurie battled with her temper. But an angry retort wouldn't solve anything.

"Mrs. Foster had an accident. We are her lifelong

friends, and we came to help." She could hear the snippiness in her own voice at his suggestion of impropriety.

"Indeed?" Mrs. Runyan looked at her up and down, then did the same to Tolley. "Am I to understand you two unattached young people will both be residing here to assist her?"

Laurie bit her lip. Apparently the woman had no interest in learning what happened to Mrs. Foster.

"Yes, we'll be residing here." Tolley moved toward Mrs. Runyan, towering over her, and gave her a deceptively charming smile. "Like you and Mr. Parsley."

Mrs. Runyan gasped. "Why, you impudent young man. I am a respectable widow and a gifted milliner. The wealthiest ladies in town patronize my shop. I am above reproach."

After looking down his long, pointed nose at Mrs. Runyan, Mr. Parsley lifted his equally pointed chin. "*I* am an important businessman." He sniffed with indignation. "People come from all over the San Luis Valley and beyond to engage my watchmaking services."

"Well," Laurie chirped. Apparently neither of these newcomers knew the Eberlys and Northams were the founding families of Esperanza. "Now we all know who we are. What are we going to do to help our dear Mrs. Foster? Mrs. Runyan, would you be so kind as to help me prepare supper? And Mr. Parsley, perhaps you could bring in some firewood?"

Although obviously not friends, the two boarders gasped together as if they were a Greek chorus.

"Help you? The very idea!" Mrs. Runyan placed a hand on her chest and stepped back. "I pay for my room and board in this establishment, and I expect my supper to be served promptly at seven."

Barely able to comprehend the woman's hauteur, Laurie looked to the man.

"As I have already informed you, I am a watchmaker. Do you have any idea how delicate my hands are? How I must protect them?" He clutched the appendages to his chest and huffed. "Carry wood? How insulting." He marched up the front staircase, stopping halfway. "Friends of Mrs. Foster or not, rest assured I shall watch you two young people. One small inappropriate step, and I shall vacate the premises and move to the hotel."

"Humph." Mrs. Runyan began her own march up the stairs, but obviously couldn't permit the watchmaker to outdo her with his arrogance. "Breakfast at eight a.m. Supper at seven sharp. My room is to be cleaned weekly, and I expect clean linens every week, or I shall find other accommodations. Is that understood, Miss Eberly?"

"Why, you—" Tolley lifted a scolding finger.

Again, Laurie stepped in front of him, this time elbowing him hard in the ribs. She covered his startled "oof" with "Why, of course, Mrs. Runyan. Breakfast at eight. And tonight, supper at seven sharp." She barged through the swinging kitchen door, trying to quell her anger at the two selfish boarders. Did they have no compassion? Didn't they know people out here in the West took care of one another?

"Why'd you do that?" Tolley followed her into the kitchen, one hand on his rib cage. "You have sharp elbows."

She rolled her eyes as she spun around to face him. "Don't you be giving me trouble, too."

He held up both hands in a pose of surrender. "Hey, take it easy. This isn't all on you, y'know. I'll help with the chores."

She exhaled in relief. "Thank you. That's what I needed to hear. Now, while I start the chicken, would you please peel the potatoes and then clean up the back stairs?"

"Wait. What? I didn't mean I'd do women's work."

The puzzlement on his handsome face would be humorous if he hadn't just dashed Laurie's hopes of getting real, actual help in making sure Mrs. Foster's boarders didn't move out. If they did, how would her dear friend support herself?

Couldn't Tolley see how selfish he was being?

## Chapter Three

"This chicken is burned to a crisp." Mr. Parsley dropped his fork with a clatter. "These potatoes are barely cooked. I'm paying good money here, and I won't stand for this kind of tasteless fare."

Seated at one end of the dining room table, Tolley glanced at Laurie, who sat nearest the kitchen.

Strain showed on her face, but she forced a smile. "I'll do better with breakfast."

"I certainly hope so. This is terrible." Despite her complaint, plump Mrs. Runyan continued eating. "If I have to purchase my breakfast at Williams's Café, you can be sure I'll deduct the cost from my rent."

"Now, see here, Mr. Northam." Mr. Parsley aimed his tiny, bespectacled eyes in Tolley's direction. "Exactly what will you be doing tomorrow? What I mean is, will you be staying here with Miss Eberly, with your only chaperone in this house a sick old woman upstairs in her bedchamber?"

Tolley nibbled a bite of dry, grainy but edible meat he'd located beneath the burned crust and skin of a chicken breast. This man sure got under his craw, but as

Laurie requested, he'd try not to get mad at the old coot. "Well…" He drawled out the word. "I thought I'd go over to the bank and see if they'll rent me one of their empty Main Street buildings to set up my law office."

"Law office?" The small man's scoffing tone almost earned him a boxed ear. "Why, you couldn't possibly be old enough to be a lawyer. Why would you expect people to trust an untrained boy with their legal matters?"

Tolley breathed in and out slowly. "I wouldn't expect them to." He also wouldn't say another word in his own defense. His pastor friend in Boston urged him to let his work speak for itself. Instead, he mashed the hard potatoes into an almost edible consistency and poured gravy over the whole thing, the least he could do for Laurie, who'd obviously done her best to please these two boorish people. He might say something to her about improving her cooking, though not in the hearing of the older folks. He wouldn't entirely discount marrying a gal who couldn't cook very well, but she'd have to possess a powerful lot of other attributes to make up for it.

Why did he entertain such foolish thoughts? Probably because fatigue crept into his bones and he couldn't think straight. Yesterday and today had been the longest two days of his life. He'd spent the night before last at the hotel in Walsenburg, ridden the train over the Sangre de Cristo Mountains, found out his father nearly died of apoplexy, spent the night in the Esperanza Arms, moved to the boardinghouse and rescued poor Mrs. Foster when she broke her arm. Not to mention having to eat a poorly cooked supper. Things like that wore a man out. He'd sleep well tonight.

"If you folks will excuse me." He rose from the

table and set his napkin beside his plate. "I think I'll hit the hay."

"But—" For a moment, Laurie looked like a lost waif. Then she frowned. "Good night, Mr. Northam."

What set her off? He was too tired to ask. Besides, Mrs. Runyan and Mr. Parsley would probably find it scandalous if Tolley even walked into the kitchen when Laurie worked in there alone.

He'd brought in the wood for cooking supper, and tomorrow he'd carry the water upstairs so Laurie could do whatever cleaning Mrs. Foster had intended. Maybe in the morning he should feed the chickens, too, the least he could do for his childhood friend.

While washing the dishes, Laurie let a few tears splash into the dishpan, dissolving some of the bubbles Mrs. Foster's lye soap had generated. What a disappointment Tolley turned out to be. He hadn't even helped her clear the table. But then, growing up in a family with a housekeeper and a sister to help his mother in the kitchen, no wonder he regarded housework as women's work. Still, understanding him didn't make it any easier to shoulder all of the chores herself. After all, she and her sisters had learned to do both housework and ranch work.

A soft, cool evening breeze blew in through the window, bringing with it the merry chirp of a robin. Laurie brushed away her tears and smiled. How silly. Only yesterday, she'd resented having to fetch Tolley from the train depot. What made her think he'd changed? Still the same selfish boy she'd always known. And what of her own resentment over not being permitted to work around her parents' house and ranch? Well, now her hands were more than full, and she thanked the Lord for it. If she must endure the eccentricities of Mrs. Foster's self-centered boarders, so be it.

Supper had failed because she'd forgotten Ma's lessons. As promised, breakfast would be better. She'd dried and put away the last dish when a cross "meow" sounded at the back door. She hurried to let Mrs. Foster's black-and-white cat inside. He rubbed against her skirt and looked up at her. His next "meow" definitely had a question mark at the end of it.

"Mrs. Foster is upstairs, Pepper." Fortunately, she'd left Mrs. Foster's door slightly ajar so she could hear if her friend called for help. "I'm sure she'd welcome a visit from you."

The cat scampered from the room as if he'd understood her words. Laurie laughed. She'd always enjoyed playing with the barn cats at her family's ranch and had missed having them while in Denver. Chatting with Pepper would brighten the days ahead. He knew her and always answered when she spoke to him.

After checking the downstairs, Laurie headed upstairs to turn in for the night. With the clothes Georgia brought her earlier, she could stay as long as needed. Six bedrooms lined the two sides of the center hall, which opened onto a balcony that extended over the front porch. Mrs. Runyan and Mr. Parsley had the two front rooms, Tolley and Mrs. Foster the middle two. She'd settled into the smallest bedroom at the corner of the house close to the back staircase and over the kitchen, with one empty room across from hers. Several times during the night, she tiptoed into Mrs. Foster's bedchamber to tend to her needs but still managed to get a few hours of sleep.

In the morning, she slipped downstairs quietly and fixed breakfast without disturbing the boarders. As she'd promised, breakfast was a success. The bacon crisp, the biscuits light, the eggs scrambled to perfection. The coffee tasted slightly bitter, but the boarders didn't seem to notice, for they put copious amounts of sugar and cream into their cups.

With a final warning to Laurie and Tolley concerning proper behavior, the two older boarders made their exits, traipsing off to their respective shops. Tolley lingered over a third cup of coffee and helped himself to another biscuit, slathering it with butter and raspberry jam.

Feeling a bit smug over breakfast, Laurie propped the swinging kitchen door open and noisily cleared the table. Maybe Tolley would get the hint and decide to help her after all. Or maybe he'd leave so she could shake out the tablecloth and see if she needed a fresh one for supper. A sigh escaped her at the thought of all the laundry involved in keeping boarders, especially grouchy ones. Mrs. Foster probably couldn't afford the Chinese laundry.

"Breakfast tasted mighty fine, Laurie." Tolley lounged back in his chair and called through the open door.

"Glad you liked it." In her morning prayers, she asked the Lord for patience, so tests would surely come. The first? Mrs. Runyan's comment about the biscuits needing sugar. Where did the woman come from to think sugar belonged in biscuits?

Carrying the last dish, except for Tolley's plate and cup, into the kitchen, she gently nudged the door closed. Within five seconds, he opened it and stood in the doorway, resting his large frame against the door-jamb while continuing to eat his biscuit.

"I've been thinking."

"Uh-oh. Sounds ominous." She pumped cold water into the dishpan in the sink, added soap flakes and la-dled in hot water from the tank above the stove. "Say, weren't you going to open your law office today?" She didn't have time to listen to whatever he wanted to yammer about.

He grinned that grin of his, and a saucer slipped from her hands into the tin dishpan. She gasped softly. It wouldn't do to break Mrs. Foster's lovely china. To her relief, the saucer rested safely on the bottom of the metal pan.

"What this house needs is a bathroom." Tolley popped the final bite of biscuit into his mouth and walked to her side, his arm brushing against her shoulder as he slid his plate into the dishpan on top of the saucer. "Upstairs, of course."

A pleasant shiver streaked up Laurie's arm. Her five feet four inches had never felt short, but now it did. At over six feet, Tolley stood tallest of the Northam boys… men. My, how her heart began to flutter. She had only one defense against such silly feminine feelings.

"So, are you going to wash the dishes?" She waved a shaky hand over the sink.

He snorted. "No, but I will feed the chickens." He walked toward the back door. "Where's the feed?"

The instant he moved away from her, she managed to relax. Why did she respond to his presence this way? This was her old friend, knows-it-all, obnoxious Tol-ley. "In a tin tub on the back porch. You'll find a bas-ket for the eggs, too."

"I'll be back shortly." He stepped out and then poked his head back inside. "Be thinking about that bathroom." The *shoosh-ping* of feed being scooped from the bin and into a tin pail came through the open door.

She watched out the window over the sink as he crossed the wide backyard, his long stride quickly eating up the distance. He unlatched the gate to the chicken pen, and the hens flocked to him. She could hear his baritone singsong call beckoning any strays from the henhouse to come and get it. He certainly hadn't lost his ability to work with critters while in Boston.

Once he ducked his head and disappeared into the structure, she shook herself. She really must get over these foolish reactions. What did he say about a bathroom? Here? The hotel had bathrooms, but to her knowledge, none of the houses in Esperanza boasted such a luxury. Perhaps Nolan Means, the banker, and his new wife, Electra? Would such a thing even be possible?

Tolley's thoughtfulness softened her annoyance over his refusing to help with housework. In coming up with such an unselfish idea for Mrs. Foster, maybe he'd changed more than Laurie thought.

Showing the pugnacious rooster who was boss with a harmless shove of his boot—twice—Tolley took his time feeding the chickens and gathering the eggs. No sense in hurrying back to the kitchen, where Laurie would try to lasso him into washing dishes by batting those big blue eyes at him. In their younger years, he'd never noticed how pretty all the Eberly girls were. Now he regarded Laurie as prettiest of the lot, maybe because of that sassy little dimple in her left cheek. Without too much trouble, she could probably get him to do just about anything. Except washing dishes or doing any other housework. He must stand firm about that.

A quick glance at the garden let him know it didn't need watering, for dew still sparkled on some of the leafy plants. For a moment, Tolley stood in the middle of the grassy yard, breathing in both the familiar musty smell of chickens and the invigorating scent of country air. Mrs. Foster's house lay close to the outskirts of town, but even in the center of Esperanza, the air was fresh and clean. Another reason to be thankful for being here. Sometimes the city smells of Boston had almost choked him.

Despite his exhaustion from the two previous days, he hadn't slept well last night. He kept waking up from dreams of his father dying, of Mrs. Foster lying helpless at the bottom of the stairs, of Laurie looking like a lost waif with all the work before her. Yet when he awoke early this morning, the water situation bothered him most. When Laurie returned to Denver—a day he didn't look forward to because he would miss her friendship—Mrs. Foster would have to take care of her boarders by herself. It didn't make any sense for her to carry heavy buckets of water up that curved back staircase with its narrow treads.

The obvious solution? A bathroom. If his sister and brother-in-law could install bathrooms in their hotel three blocks from Mrs. Foster's house, why couldn't Tolley install one here? Boston had boasted water and sewage systems for almost forty years, so why shouldn't Esperanza step into the modern world? Maybe not right away, but in the near future. For now, he'd have to figure out all the details for a single house. The more he thought about it, the more excited he got. Laurie hadn't seemed interested, but he'd convince her. Now to figure out the details.

Back in the house, Laurie no longer worked in the kitchen, so he left the basket of eggs for her to tend. Although he hadn't done that chore in a long time, he remembered how to tell which hens were brooding. He supposed Mrs. Foster sold her extra eggs at Mrs. Winsted's mercantile. If he wasn't mistaken, Mrs. Foster's flock should increase by eight or ten in a week or two, which in turn would increase her income. Later today he'd muck out the chicken pen and pile the droppings in the wooden compost bin by the back fence.

He wanted to discuss the bathroom with Laurie, but maybe he should visit Nolan Means and see about renting that empty office space two doors down from the bank. The idea made him smile.

He'd wash his hands in the dishwater, but Laurie might come downstairs and think he'd changed his mind about washing the dishes. Instead, he returned to his room by the front staircase and used the cold water from his pitcher.

Yep, this house needed a source of water on the second floor. This morning, Laurie had carried pitchers of hot water upstairs for everyone. Tolley admired her willingness to work hard and give up her time to help a needy widow. Admired a lot about her. But for now he needed to concentrate on his own part in helping Mrs. Foster. He'd done a lot of building in his life, even helped dig a few wells. But piping water up to a second floor and digging a cesspool at the back of the property might raise unique challenges.

He must not fail at this. Maybe his brother-in-law could offer suggestions. Despite his wealth and position, Garrick had participated in every part of building his hotel. Tolley hadn't gotten along with the Englishman when he came to Esperanza, but when he and Rosamond visited Tolley in Boston on their honeymoon, they'd put the past behind them.

Dressed for business in the suit he'd worn on the train, he emerged from his room just as Laurie came from Mrs. Foster's chamber, her arms laden with laundry.

"I'm going to the mercantile. Do you need anything?"

Those big blue eyes blinked with obvious surprise, and something twanged in his heart like a cowboy plucking his guitar.

"Let me think." She walked toward him, chewing her lower lip thoughtfully.

He'd never noticed how pretty and smooth and plump her lips were. Sure would be nice to—

"You could take the wash to Chen's Laundry," she whispered. "Don't tell Mrs. Foster, though. I'll pay for it."

"Laundry again today?"

She nodded. "It never ends. Apparently she does towels and kitchen linens on Wednesday and the boarders' clothes and sheets on Thursdays."

"Whew. That's a lot of work for a little old lady." Tolley didn't know where toting laundry fell on the list of women's or men's appropriate chores, but he'd do it this once until he found out. "I'll take it."

He waited by the front door while Laurie gathered the guests' laundry and bedding. She dragged it down the stairs all bundled up in a sheet. When he slung it over his shoulder, the weight made him wince. What a heavy load for a little gal like Laurie. How much harder for old Mrs. Foster.

"See you later."

Laurie held the door open, and he stepped outside as Doc Henshaw rode up from the south.

"Hey, sis, Tolley." He dismounted and came to the front door carrying his black bag. "I want to look in on Mrs. Foster. How is she?"

"In pain." Laurie's delicate eyebrows bent into a worried frown. "And a little dizzy. I gave her another dose of laudanum in the middle of the night, as you said, but she wouldn't take any this morning."

"Probably best." Doc eyed the laundry and clapped Tolley on his free shoulder. "Glad to see you're helping out. Good for you."

An odd and foolish sense of satisfaction swept through Tolley. He admired Doc, so his approval meant a great deal. If his father had ever once said anything like that—

As if he'd heard Tolley's thoughts, Doc continued. "I was out at Four Stones just now. The Colonel is doing as well as can be expected. I'm optimistic about his recovery. Pray for him and for your mother. She won't leave his side."

"Thanks." Tolley's suddenly raspy voice held more emotion than he wanted to reveal. He cleared his throat. "See you later." He lumbered off down the street, feeling the weight of his burden like the ragmen he'd seen carrying similar loads in Boston, where they scoured the streets for cast-off cloth to sell to the paper mills.

In spite of Doc's approval, Tolley could only picture

his father lying still on his bed, face immobile, a face that might never show approval for Tolley. A selfish thought, of course. Poor Mother sat beside her husband day and night. That was her way. He'd even admit to harboring some pity for his father. Yet if the Colonel recovered, Tolley wanted to have a long list of accomplishments to show him so he'd no longer be ashamed of his youngest son. Or, at the least, so he could no longer ignore Tolley's very existence.

The residential areas of Esperanza had grown since Tolley left for Boston, with numerous new houses on every street. More businesses had come to town, such as the six shops lining the south side of the Esperanza Arms, his sister's hotel. With a bank, a mercantile, many other small businesses, even an ice cream parlor, now the community would be able to boast about having its own lawyer.

After depositing the washing at Chen's Laundry on the east side of town near the railroad tracks, Tolley strode up Main Street to the bank. Then he cooled his heels in the lobby for a good half hour, wondering whether the banker would refuse to see him. But why? Nolan Means owed him for helping to thwart a bank robbery four years ago. That should give him some favor in the man's eyes.

*Don't be defensive. Trust the Lord to bring about His will for you.* Remembering Reverend Harris's wise words soothed Tolley's growing uneasiness, and none too soon.

Nolan entered the lobby through a door beyond the teller's cage and strode across the space, hand extended. "Good morning, Tolley. It's good to see you back in town. Let's go into my office."

"Thanks." After shaking his hand, Tolley followed him into the well-appointed room. The banker's polished mahogany desk and chair didn't show a speck of dust. Oil paintings adorned the walls, and several figurines graced the bookshelves and side table. Tolley could imagine his own office furnished this lavishly, as befitted either a banker or a lawyer. "Thank you for seeing me."

Nolan chuckled. "Would I ever refuse to see a Northam?"

Tolley grimaced. Echoing Nolan's question, would *he* ever earn respect without relying on his family name? Fortunately, Nolan was making his way around the massive mahogany desk and didn't notice Tolley's involuntary reaction to his rhetorical question.

"Have a seat." Nolan sat and waved toward one of the brown leather chairs in front of his desk. After they'd exchanged general news—Nolan's recent marriage, the Colonel's tenuous health, Mrs. Foster's accident—he asked, "What can I do for you?"

"I understand the bank owns that building on the other side of the sheriff's office. I'd like to rent it."

"Ah." Nolan sat back and steepled his fingers. "So you're a lawyer now."

A statement, not a question. Tolley smiled, but not too broadly. "Yessir. I have my credentials from Harvard and a letter from Judge Thomas, the Colorado attorney general, welcoming me into Colorado's judicial system." In his own ears, he sounded a bit of a braggart. Or a boy reciting his lessons.

Nolan apparently thought no such thing. His eyebrows arched, and he gave Tolley a broad smile. "Congratulations. That's quite an achievement for—"

"A former troublemaker?" Tolley wanted to bite his tongue. What had Reverend Harris said about not criticizing himself?

Nolan chuckled. "I was going to say for such a young man."

"I turned twenty-two last month." And no family there to celebrate with him. Uh-oh. Self-pity. Another habit the good reverend warned him against. "Twenty-one is the minimum age to practice law here in Colorado...legally, that is." He grinned.

"A clever bit of wordplay, eh?" Nolan laughed aloud. Tolley could grow to like this former stuffed shirt. Maybe his recent marriage had mellowed him. "So you'd like to hang out your shingle next to the jail, not in your sister's hotel?"

Now Tolley laughed. "It's the only way I can show my independence."

"I know all about that," Nolan said. "It's why I moved here from New York. Out here in the West, a man can make his own reputation."

Tolley grunted his agreement. Yes, he could easily see becoming friends with this man.

Nolan dug into the center drawer of his desk and pulled out a key on a metal chain. "Here you go. Rent is five dollars a month."

Tolley's lawyer instincts sent out an alert. "No contract?"

"Absolutely a contract." Nolan stood and stuck out his hand. "A handshake and a good man's word is contract enough for me."

"Thank you, Nolan." As they shook hands, Tolley appreciated the respect this man showed him. He took the key and made his exit. Once he'd checked his new office, he couldn't wait to get home and tell Laurie about this milestone in his professional career.

Home? Laurie? Where did that thought come from? Mrs. Foster's boardinghouse wasn't his home. And he should want to tell his family first, not Laurie. Except, he couldn't bear to go back to the ranch only to be sent away again. Anyway, his family didn't seem interested in what he was doing. Laurie did.

Marriage hadn't been in his immediate plans, but he kept thinking marriage to Laurie would be a real feather in his cap, an accomplishment the Colonel could neither disapprove of nor ignore when…if…he woke up.

Laurie thought her back might break from putting fresh sheets on the beds, toting water up the stairs, scrubbing the rooms and weeding and watering the garden. In all her years of visiting this house, why hadn't she noticed how hard Mrs. Foster must work to keep body and soul together? Her widow's pension from the War must be pitifully small.

Before noon, she started a pot of beans and fatback for supper. The two older boarders always ate dinner at the hotel, so she needn't prepare a midday meal for them. Tolley would probably dine at Williams's Café, but she still prepared enough soup to include him.

"Vegetable soup. My favorite." Mrs. Foster grimaced in pain as Laurie helped her sit up. After Laurie placed the tray on her lap, Mrs. Foster tried to use the spoon with her shaking left hand but only managed to dribble the soup down the front of the apron Laurie had put on her. "Oh, dear."

"It's all right." Laurie dabbed up the spill with a napkin and took the spoon. "Let me feed you."

Tears formed in Mrs. Foster's eyes. "What a mess I've made of things."

"Now don't start that again." Laurie gave her a teasing smile. "I'm grateful Doc says you've only sprained your ankle. We'll pray you'll be back on your feet soon."

"My broken arm won't heal any time soon." Mrs. Foster viewed her splinted right appendage. "I won't be able to play the organ for a long time. Or even show my students proper piano technique."

Laurie had already decided what to do about both situations. "You leave those to me. Your job right now is to get well."

Mrs. Foster gave her a sad smile. "But, my dear, what about your position at the conservatory this coming fall?"

"*My* dear, haven't you always told me to take no thought for tomorrow, as the Lord said?" Laurie struggled with her own fears about losing her teaching position, but nothing could be done about it. She must do right, which meant helping Mrs. Foster. "Besides, we have all summer for you to get well before I go back to Denver." While her brother-in-law said the bones of older folks took longer to heal, Laurie would pray for the best, more for her mentor's health and comfort than for anything to do with herself.

That afternoon, when she thought she'd earned a short rest, Seamus and Wes arrived from Four Stones Ranch with Tolley's trunks, so she guided them upstairs to his room. Shortly after they left, she greeted Mrs. Foster's six piano students. By the time she'd finished the last lesson, she needed to make the corn bread and cook the tender turnip greens she'd harvested from the garden.

She'd grown up on a ranch and known hard work all her life. But at home, many hands made light work. While she'd never abandon Mrs. Foster, this day wore her out. How had the dear lady managed all of this work, plus helping Laurie achieve her dream of becoming a conservatory teacher?

In spite of her encouraging words to Mrs. Foster, Laurie knew she must get back to Colorado's capital city in the autumn. Otherwise her position would be given to someone else, and Laurie would be forced to say goodbye to her dreams forever. Which made her prayers all the more urgent. Perhaps even desperate.

# Chapter Four

"A bathroom?" Mrs. Foster's weathered face crinkled with puzzlement as she sat against her pillow. "Why, who ever heard of such a thing?"

"I think it's *just* the thing." Laurie sat in the bedside chair and patted the lady's uninjured arm.

"Same here." Tolley stood at the foot of the bed, hands in his pockets, feeling like a schoolboy who wanted to please his teacher.

"But I can't afford—"

"We aren't going to talk about money." Tolley playfully wagged a scolding finger at her and grinned, but he meant it. Several years ago, his family had made the final payments on this house, the least they could do for the widow of Major Foster. If Foster hadn't stepped in front of the Colonel at Gettysburg, taking a bullet himself, Tolley might never have been born. The old major suffered the rest of his life from the injury, finally passing away six years ago.

"Oh, dear, I don't know."

"We do." Laurie's blue eyes sparkled, and her smile brought out that dimple. My, she was pretty today.

Every day, in fact. "All we need from you is your permission, and we'll get started."

Tolley could see she enjoyed this as much as he did. Having a partner would help greatly, especially this partner, especially since no one in his family cared for his company. But he mustn't think about such things now. "What do you say, Mrs. Foster?"

The lady set her hand against her cheek and gave him a wobbly smile. "I won't turn down such a generous gift, my boy." Her eyes watered, and she dabbed at them with a linen handkerchief. "But where will you put it?" She peered toward the open door as if trying to envision the new room's placement.

"We can convert the smallest bedroom, the one I'm in now," Laurie said. "I can move to the empty one next to you."

"Since the smaller room is at the back corner and over the kitchen, the plumbing will be easy." Maybe not *easy*, but Tolley relished the challenge of installing the required pipe system.

"Oh, my." Mrs. Foster fluttered her good hand over the quilt covering her lap. "Seems so complicated. Are you sure you can do this?"

"Yes, ma'am." Tolley had prepared himself for questions. "I learned that Nolan Means installed the first bathroom in Esperanza even before Rosamond built the hotel. I asked him for advice, and he sent me to the workmen who dug the leaching field to handle the drainage. They'll do that for us, and I'll handle the rest, the interior part."

"With my help." Laurie gave him a challenging smile.

"Yep. Your help." He wouldn't argue in front of Mrs.

Foster, but before they got started, he'd have to set some rules so Laurie would help, not get in his way.

"Then let's get busy." Laurie stood and bent to kiss Mrs. Foster's cheek. "Would you like your book?"

"Why, yes. Thank you, dear."

Laurie handed her the volume. "If you need anything, ring the bell." She nodded toward the brass bell with a wooden handle sitting on the bedside table. The old schoolmaster who'd once boarded here had left it behind.

"It's so loud." Mrs. Foster clicked her tongue.

"Yes, ma'am. All the better to hear it." Tolley laughed. "Laurie, let's get busy."

Laurie took the last of her dresses from the small wardrobe and moved them across the hall to the larger room. Later, Tolley and Adam Starling rearranged the furnishings for her.

"Are you sure this is where you want the vanity?" Tolley's voice held an edge, though Laurie couldn't imagine why.

"Well…" She tapped a finger against one cheek thoughtfully. "Another twelve inches or so to the left."

He rolled his eyes, but Adam chuckled. "Makes sense to me."

"Don't encourage her." Tolley scowled at Adam.

Adam shrugged. "It's awful close to the stove. Might warp the wood."

These two back rooms were heated by small woodstoves, unlike the four front bedrooms, each of which contained a fireplace built back-to-back with the adjacent room and aligned with those on the ground floor to share the house's two chimneys.

"Thank you, Adam." Laurie gave him her sweetest smile and noticed a hint of red beneath the tan of his cheeks. Tolley frowned at her. Did he think she was flirting with Adam? Even if she were, which she wasn't, it was none of his business.

"All right, let's move it." Tolley gripped one side of the oak vanity. "Careful of the mirror."

Once they placed it, Laurie gave them a firm nod. "Perfect. Thank you. Now, I'd better get busy with supper, or I won't have it on the table at seven sharp."

While Tolley chuckled, Adam questioned her with one raised eyebrow.

"Don't ask," Tolley said, but added, "Grumpy boarders."

"Ah." Adam nodded his understanding.

With all of the people who employed him for odd jobs, Laurie had a feeling he knew plenty about grumpy people.

"Off you go." She herded the two from her new room and hurried down the back stairs. She'd have to put her personal belongings away later.

Tonight's stew simmered in the cast-iron Dutch oven. She retrieved the peeled potatoes and carrots from the icebox and added them to the meat. Next came the dinner rolls. Earlier, she'd made the dough, so she needed only to shape it into balls to rise again on the baking sheet. That done, she double-checked the cooling apple pie she'd made earlier from last year's fruit. Mrs. Foster had harvested the green apples from the tree in her yard, then sliced and dried them so she could provide this dessert to her boarders all year long.

After her first disastrous attempt at cooking supper, Laurie quickly learned to manage the stove. She figured out how to adjust the flue and how to move the wood around to control the heat for both the oven and the stovetop. Although Mrs. Runyan and Mr. Parsley remained hard to please, their complaints often seemed petty, perhaps even an attempt to outdo each other with displeasure. Laurie knew some cowboys here in the San Luis Valley who competed on anything from horse races to eating pie. At least Tolley offered compliments about the food, as did Mrs. Foster when Laurie carried her meal up before serving the others.

That evening, according to their plan, Tolley offered the blessing for supper and then introduced the subject of the bathroom to the other boarders. It took a moment for either one to grasp the idea. Then the comments began, as she and Tolley expected.

"Why, the very idea!" Mrs. Runyan served herself a large portion of pot roast.

"Humph! Never heard of such a thing." Mr. Parsley ladled gravy over his potatoes.

"There goes modesty out the window." Mrs. Runyan waved her fork in the air to emphasize her complaint. "Where I come from, bathing in a tub is considered indecent."

"You'd better not make noise and disturb my rest."

"You'd better not work on Sundays."

As the meal progressed, they continued to make disparaging remarks, seeming to vie for the most indignant expression of outrage.

She could see Tolley clench his jaw as he struggled to control his temper, so she sent him a meaningful glare. He'd promised her he wouldn't answer the others' insults. They both needed to remember Mrs. Foster didn't want to lose her boarders.

"Well!" Mrs. Runyan shot a cross look at Laurie and then Tolley. "At least you'll be too busy to get into mischief."

Mr. Parsley blinked and sputtered, clearly outdone. After a moment, he took his last bite of potato. "Miss Eberly, I do hope you have dessert for me. My room-and-board payment includes dessert after every supper."

Laurie could hardly keep from rolling her eyes.

"Yes, of course, Mr. Parsley." She stood and began to clear the empty plates. "It'll only take a moment to whip the cream."

She carried the stack of plates toward the kitchen and backed through the swinging door. But she couldn't miss his comment. "Don't take too long. You should have—"

She let the door swing closed, cutting off the rest of his complaint. Taking the cold bowl of cream from the icebox, she whipped it vigorously with Mrs. Foster's new rotary eggbeater, taking out her annoyance on the hapless liquid. This wasn't funny anymore. Pleasing these grumpy boarders seemed impossible. Only Tolley's presence kept her calm.

"What do you think?" Early Saturday morning, Tolley stood inside the small room, Adam at his side as he considered the layout of the bathroom. "Any ideas about where to start?" He already had his own plans but wanted to hear the younger man's opinions.

"Seems your water pipes will need to come up about here." Adam pointed to a spot a few feet from the west window and close to the small cast-iron stove. "Drainage over there." He indicated another spot close to the same wall. "And the vent pipe directly above it."

"We should take out this west window and board up the hole. Otherwise, it'll be pretty cold in here for bathing."

"No, you don't." Laurie appeared in the doorway. "We need the ventilation."

Tolley shook his head. "There's your ventilation." He pointed to the open north window, where frilly white curtains fluttered in the breeze. "That'll be enough. In the winter, the cross breeze would freeze the water in the fixtures."

"Cross ventilation works better to keep mildew from forming."

Tolley looked at Adam for support.

Adam shrugged. "Don't suppose the window needs to be boarded up. That woodstove should keep it warm enough."

Laurie gave Tolley a triumphant smile.

"Aren't you supposed to be fixing breakfast?" His stomach had growled for a good half hour.

"It's in the oven and will be ready at eight o'clock sharp." Another triumphant smile.

Something kicked up inside of Tolley's chest. She looked awful cute when she smiled that way, with that sassy dimple making a rare appearance. If she kept on looking at him, he might just give her whatever she wanted. Except he'd built a house and a high school and knew far more than she did about such things. He pulled out his pocket watch.

"My, my, look at the time." He showed her the time-piece, which read seven fifty-seven. "This is set to railroad time."

"Oh! I thought—" She hurried from the room.

Adam appeared to hide a chuckle, then sobered. "Mr. Northam, do you mind if I make a suggestion?"

"You have some advice for dealing with females?"

Now Adam laughed out loud. "No, sir. I don't know nothing…anything…about females. But I did help out a bit over at the hotel when they were putting in the washrooms."

"Ah, very good." Tolley looked at the youth with a new appreciation. "What's your suggestion?"

"First, you gotta make sure the structure can bear the weight of a water-filled tub." He waved a hand over the bare floor. "We should probably pull up a board or two and check the strength of the wood underneath."

Tolley nodded. The idea made sense. "Shall we get started?"

"I wish I could, sir." Adam shook his head. "This being Saturday, lots of folks come into town, so Mr. Russell needs me over at the livery stable." He cast a worried look at Tolley. "I can help on Monday…unless you want to find someone else to work for you today?"

Tolley clapped him on the shoulder. "Nope. I'll need your experience, so I can wait until Monday."

"Thank you, sir." The relief on Adam's face touched something deep inside of Tolley. Maybe this project wasn't only about helping Mrs. Foster.

Later, as Tolley sat at the desk in his room sketching possible layouts for the bathroom fixtures, a knock sounded on his door.

"Tolley, Rosamond and Garrick came to see you," Laurie called. "They're downstairs."

*Rosamond!* His family hadn't entirely deserted him. "I'll be right down."

He quickly donned his suit jacket, mainly to look good for his always well-dressed English brother-in-law, and started for the door. On a whim, he grabbed the sketches. Maybe Garrick could give him some advice about adapting the room.

Halfway down the stairs, another thought struck him. Had they come with news of the Colonel? Had his father died?

"Tolley!" Rosamond rushed into his arms and held him fast.

As he enfolded her in a firm embrace, his sketches fluttered to the floor.

Over her shoulder Garrick wore an unreadable expression. But then, he was English, so most of his expressions were unreadable.

Tolley squeezed his sister before moving her back to arm's length. "I-it's good to see you, sis. What brings you here?" He stilled his racing heart, preparing for bad news.

"Tolley, we've all been so taken up with Father's illness." She wiped away tears. "He's doing as well as can be expected. But this morning as we were getting ready to move back to the hotel, I realized how we'd barely acknowledged your homecoming." She hugged him again. "I'm so sorry. I've missed you terribly. We all have, especially Mother. She sends her love."

He patted her back and swallowed the unexpected riot of emotions her words caused. So the Colonel still lived, thank the Lord. And Mother hadn't entirely forgotten Tolley. "Thanks. Did the family get word about Mrs. Foster's fall?" He needed to move to a safer topic so he wouldn't break down in front of Garrick. Or Laurie, who stood nearby. He didn't mind her being here, but a man had his pride when it came to emotional matters, especially in front of other people.

"Yes, Doc told us." Rosamond moved to Garrick's side. "We'd like to see her, if she's well enough."

Doubt crowded out his growing joy. They'd come to visit Mrs. Foster, not him.

"I'll go check." Laurie skipped up the stairs, her light footfalls as dainty as any Boston belle's.

At least Tolley could count on her friendship, even if he did have to put up with her prickliness.

"I say, old man." Garrick clapped him on the shoulder. "What've you done with yourself these past few days?" He picked up the sketches and gave them a cursory glance before handing them to Tolley. "Building something?"

"Yes. An upstairs bathroom." As much as he wanted to feign indifference, Tolley couldn't keep the eagerness from his voice.

"Absolutely brilliant." Garrick inspected the pages.

Rosamond moved to Tolley's other side and did the same. "How exciting. Tell us all about it."

"Laurie and I—" he paused, savoring for a moment the partnership they'd formed to take care of the elderly lady "—we think it's ridiculous for our Mrs. Foster to carry water upstairs any longer, so we decided to turn the smallest bedroom into a bathroom."

"Oh, Tolley." Rosamond's eyes filled with tears, and she gripped his arm and gazed up at him with sisterly admiration that brought a homesick ache to his heart. "How good of you."

He gulped. "I have to do something to fill my time before my law practice picks up."

"Brilliant. Absolutely brilliant." Garrick continued

to study the drawings. "Where did you plan to get the fixtures?"

"Mrs. Winsted's Montgomery Ward catalogue has tubs and sinks for sale. Not sure about the commode."

Rosamond grinned at Garrick, and he nodded.

"Well, old boy, you don't want to wait for a delivery from Chicago. We have the items you need in our hotel storeroom."

"Do you mean it?" Tolley laughed in surprise. "Why, we can have the whole thing installed within weeks."

"That's very generous." Smiling, Laurie descended the staircase. "I know Mrs. Foster will be pleased. By the way, she's waiting for you both to visit."

"Very good." Rosamond's voice held a hint of her husband's English accent. "Let's go."

While she and Garrick ascended the stairs, Laurie peered at the sketches. "So does this mean you plan to put the tub in this corner?" She pointed to the page.

"Yes." Tolley tried not to sound defensive. After all, Garrick said the plan looked "brilliant."

"I think it should be here by the stove so we don't need to carry the hot water across the room."

"All six feet?" Tolley rolled his eyes.

She lifted her perfect little chin. "Still a long way for Mrs. Foster. Our purpose is to make things as easy for her as possible."

Tolley briefly clenched his jaw. "The design isn't complete yet."

"By the way, as much as I'm pleased by Garrick's offer of a porcelain tub like those at the hotel, they're pretty large. Have you seen them? One of them might not fit the room along with the other fixtures and the woodstove. We should probably order a smaller copper tub through Mrs. Winsted."

Tolley exhaled crossly. "Why postpone the installation? Let's use what we have."

"A small tub will require less water to fill than the larger one… Less for Mrs. Foster to heat."

Tolley folded his sketches. As annoyed as he felt over her disagreements with almost everything he said, part of him agreed with her reasoning. But he would pay for this endeavor, would do the hands-on work. The final decisions would be his. Before he could figure out a way to tell her as much, Rosamond and Garrick descended the stairs.

"Mrs. Foster wasn't up to a long visit," Rosamond said. "But she did look pretty well, considering such an awful accident at her age." She looped an arm around Laurie. "Is there anything we can do?"

They stepped into the parlor, obviously wanting to keep their discussion private. Tolley grabbed this opportunity for some private discussion of his own.

"Say, Garrick, how large is that bathtub you offered?"

His brother-in-law shrugged. "I'm not certain. Why?"

"Need to be sure the floor will hold it."

"Good thinking." Garrick nodded.

In the past, Tolley would've taken the praise. Now he gave credit where due. "Adam mentioned it. Said he helped put in the plumbing at the hotel."

"Adam's a good lad. Smart. Hardworking."

"That he is."

Garrick clapped him on the shoulder again. "You're doing a good thing, Tolley. I'll help any way I can."

Pleased at his approval, Tolley grinned. "Thanks. I'll be calling on you."

And he'd be calling on the Lord to help him overcome this desperate need for approval. He'd try to recall his Boston pastor's last words to him: *serve God and leave the results to Him.* While that attitude had sounded good on the train platform in Boston, it was turning out to be much harder to adopt than Tolley had expected.

## Chapter Five

Laurie carefully cut a few of the tender beet greens for this evening's supper, making sure to leave enough to nourish the tiny beets below the ground. In a nearby row, Pepper chased a small garden snake, so Laurie tossed a rock beyond the cat to distract him.

"Pepper, snakes help you keep the field mice out of our garden. You can't catch them all yourself."

Pepper meowed indignantly but stopped his chase and pranced over to her side.

"Come along." She gathered her harvest in her apron and stood. "Let's get these washed and ready to cook."

Tolley stood inside the back door as if waiting for her. Under his arm he clutched a long package.

"I'm going over to my office to hang my shingle. Do you need anything from Mrs. Winsted's?"

Laurie's heart warmed at his thoughtfulness *and* his beguiling smile. He could be helpful when he wanted to be. "Yes, but first I want to see your sign."

That boyish look she'd grown fond of spread over his face. "You don't want to wait until it's hung?"

"I'd love to be the first to see it." She slipped past

him and walked through the small back porch and into the kitchen, where she dumped the greens into the sink. "If it won't be too much trouble."

Pepper scooted inside with her and now tangled himself in her skirt.

"No trouble at all." Tolley placed the package on the empty worktable and began to unwrap it. Pepper now rubbed against his trousers and meowed as if curious about the package. "Not like this annoying cat." He gently shoved the creature aside with his foot as he untied the string.

"Pepper?" Laurie gave him a sidelong look. "Why, he's adorable. Right now he's listening to the crinkling of the paper. Can you tear off a corner and wad it up for him to play with?"

"And waste good paper we can reuse?" Tolley snorted. "Besides, cats belong outside." He peeled the paper back and studied his sign with a critical eye. "I haven't seen it since picking it up at the sign painter's in Boston. What do you think?"

Pepper batted at the twine hanging from the table, then grabbed it and dashed toward the back stairs, the long string trailing behind him.

"Hey!" Tolley lunged for him, but only managed to step on the string. "Ha! Got it."

Pepper returned, staring up at Tolley and meowing while batting at the string as Tolley attempted to roll it into a ball.

Laurie giggled. "See? He likes you and wants to play."

"As I said before, cats belong outside." Brow furrowed, he started to rewrap his sign.

"Wait. Let me see it." Laurie folded the paper back

to reveal a painted tan board. A black silhouette of a man's head in a top hat graced the upper left corner. In the center, the words Bartholomew Lincoln Northam, Esq. were written in black script, and underneath, Attorney at Law.

"It's beautiful. Just perfect." He'd always hated his Christian name. Maybe he'd changed his mind while in Boston.

"The sign maker did a good job. Can't wait to get it hung." In spite of Pepper's antics, he managed to rewrap it and tie the string around the package. "You wanted something from Mrs. Winsted's?"

"Not from. To. The eggs for sale are in the basket and ready to go. Can you carry the sign and the basket?"

Still grinning, Tolley stared down at her, and her heart did a silly little hop. "Of course."

He gathered the two items and, using one broad shoulder, shoved his way through the swinging door and disappeared into the center hallway.

A warm feeling settled inside her as she went about her Saturday chores. Tolley seemed to have grown up quite a bit over the past two years. Instead of doing what would bring him the most favor and praise from other people, he selflessly spent his time caring for Mrs. Foster.

Laurie pumped water into the sink and washed the greens, then let the dirty water out through the pipe leading to the garden. After placing the greens in a pot, she returned to the sink and pumped more water to scrub her hands so she could start the supper biscuits.

Ma wouldn't be happy to see the dirt under her fingernails, but when Laurie had sent word she'd stay in town to take care of Mrs. Foster, Ma had approved. She'd taught her five daughters to set priorities in life. First came the Lord, next the family, then those who couldn't help themselves. Mrs. Foster's situation certainly qualified as the latter.

Then Tolley's handsome face came to mind. But why? He didn't need her help. Did he?

Tolley stepped down from the ladder and stood back to view his sign hanging above the door and perpendicular to the front of the building. For a moment, as a breeze gently caused the sign to sway in an appealing way, pride welled up in his chest at the professional appearance of his new office's entrance. He cast a self-conscious glance over his shoulder to see if anyone was watching. No one. In fact, most of the people he'd seen, those who'd known him since his childhood, offered at best a tepid greeting.

At least Laurie admired the sign. And Mrs. Winsted welcomed him...or at least welcomed the eggs he'd brought so she could sell them for Mrs. Foster. Then when he'd purchased the hooks, nails and short lengths of chain, the kindly storekeeper offered the use of her hammer and folding ladder. The understanding in her eyes seemed to say more than her words, but he didn't ask why. Not until he felt the chill of being ignored by other townspeople did he wonder at her apparent acceptance.

When he returned the borrowed items, he thought to engage her in conversation, maybe ask why she treated him so kindly. But too many customers filled her mercantile and clamored for her attention. As soon as he saw the clerk, Homer Bean, between customers, he quickly hailed him.

"Morning, Tolley." The slender man hurried across the store. Like Nolan Means, he seemed eager to serve a Northam. "What can I do for you?"

"I set Mrs. Winsted's ladder and hammer at the end of the counter. Will you give her my thanks?"

"Sure thing." Ever the salesman, Homer beckoned Tolley over to a display. "Now you'll need a broom and some cleaning rags. You'll be wanting to wash those front windows, so you'll need a bucket and some vinegar."

"Vinegar?" Tolley tilted his hat back and scratched his head. "I'm opening a law office, not making pickles."

Homer guffawed and slapped Tolley on the back. "Vinegar will make those windows shine. See what I mean?" He pointed to the mercantile's display windows. "First thing I do every morning before I open the store is shine the glass with vinegar water."

Tolley listened to Homer's detailed instructions, for the first time realizing that if he cleaned his own office, he'd be doing women's work after all. He just wouldn't mention it to Laurie, or she'd want him to do the same at the boardinghouse. But a clean window would be essential to presenting a professional appearance, so what choice did he have? After making the purchases Homer suggested, he clutched the items and strode back across the street, dodging people, horsemen, carriages and wagons. He felt a little kick in his chest when he saw his shingle.

His front door opened into a ten-by-twelve-foot reception area, behind which lay a hallway leading to two offices, each one furnished with an oak desk and chair. The larger room at the end also held an oak filing cabinet that had seen better days, along with pine book-shelves under the front window. Cobwebs stretched across many open areas. Dust covered everything, no surprise for any building in the San Luis Valley, where the wind blew sandy soil across the landscape nearly every day.

He swept the dirt from the back office floor and then dusted the room, only to discover sandy powder cover-ing the floor anew. *Bother.* Exactly why housecleaning was women's work. They knew all about when to do what. By the time he'd dusted and swept the entire building and whisked the sand out the back door, his dark trousers were covered with the evidence of his work. He beat at the fabric to get rid of it, only to find the floor where he stood needed to be swept again.

How did women keep up with it all? When Tolley was growing up, men's work and women's work were clearly delineated. He and his brothers helped the Col-onel run the ranch. Mother and Rosamond, along with the family housekeeper, did the women's work in the house. He remembered the house was always spotless. Did the women clean every day? If the chore took as much effort as cleaning this office, maybe he should relent and help Laurie take care of Mrs. Foster's house.

No, his jobs—the men's work—were putting in the bathroom and starting his law practice. Besides, Lau-rie seemed to have his mother's gift of being able to do it all. He'd continue to take care of the yard and the chickens and of course this office. Which wouldn't be finished until he washed the front windows.

Now, what had Homer said about vinegar water?

With his rags full of dust, he decided they'd do more harm than good. He rinsed them out at the pump in the courtyard behind the building and hung them over the back hitching rail. Tomorrow was Sunday, so he'd have to wait until Monday to shine the windows.

He sure did need someone to clean this place so he could stick to more important tasks.

Before going to the church early to practice the hymns, Laurie fed the boarders, washed the dishes, made sure Mrs. Foster had everything she needed and put a roast and potatoes into the oven to bake for dinner. At the church, she found her sister Grace setting out hymnbooks, one hand on her round belly. By October, the family would be blessed with another baby.

"Hey, sis." Grace greeted her with an awkward hug and went back to her work.

"Hello, Laurie." Her brother-in-law, Reverend Micah Thomas, waved to her from the podium, where he wrote on a tablet, no doubt revising his sermon notes. "Thank you for taking on the music duties. I put a list of the hymns on the organ."

"It's my pleasure." Laurie noticed a loving look passing between Micah and Grace. Who'd have thought her next-older sister, who'd served as the rough-and-ready deputy of Esperanza for three years, would be the one to nab the attractive minister, previously the object of many a young lady's pursuit?

"Sure is a nice sunny day." She set her reticule and parasol beside the organ and brought Grace another pile of hymnbooks from the shelves in the cloakroom. "Let me help you."

"Thanks." Grace put a hand on her lower back and stretched. "All that bending makes Junior kick like crazy."

After they'd distributed the books, Laurie sat on the organ bench and pumped the bellows with her feet. When the instrument had enough air, she warmed up her fingers by running scales before opening her music.

As she practiced "Immanuel's Land," she noticed Tolley entering the church. After shaking Micah's hand and speaking quietly with him for a moment, he sat in the back pew and turned his gaze—and that appealing smile—toward her. Her fingers slipped, and a noisy discord filled the room. Heat rushed to her face.

"Oops!" Grace laughed, a hearty sound so like her. "Good thing you came early to practice."

"Sounds like a bawling calf," Tolley called out.

"That's enough out of you." Laurie wrinkled her nose at him. Same old Tolley, always teasing. She grinned and shook her head.

Standing next to the organ, Grace looked from Laurie to Tolley and back again, eyebrows raised, eyes widened.

"Uh, *no*," Laurie muttered. "Don't you dare suggest anything."

"What?" Tolley called.

"Nothing," Grace said.

"Nothing," Laurie said with a little more emphasis.

A very handsome man, Tolley would be pursued by plenty of young ladies in the congregation. While the thought didn't sit well with her, she wouldn't be among them. No, indeed, she would not. She knew him too well ever to fall in love with him.

* * *

Glad he came early, Tolley watched as Laurie prac-ticed the hymns. She looked mighty pretty sitting at the organ. Competent, too. The restful music put him in a worshipful frame of mind. Laurie played even better than Mrs. Foster, probably due to her two years at the conservatory. Music added so much to a church service. Added to the atmosphere of a home, too. He should encourage her to play at the boardinghouse. Maybe music would improve the other boarders' dis-positions.

The objects of his thoughts entered the church sep-arately and took seats on opposite sides of the room. Their obvious dislike for each other was both sad and funny.

He watched for his family to enter, but no Northams joined the eighty or so parishioners who filed into the pews before the worship service. With some effort, he turned his thoughts away from his disappointment and decided to sit back, enjoy the music and take in whatever Reverend Thomas said. Though young, the minister had the same kind, accepting character as old Reverend Harris. Tolley wished he'd listened to Rev-erend Thomas as a youth. Might've kept him out of trouble. Maybe if he'd… No! *Maybe* he needed to take Reverend Harris's advice: forget the past and reach to-ward being like Jesus. Tolley couldn't remember the verse exactly.

Before he could open his Bible to search for it, a hand gripped his shoulder.

"Scoot over." His oldest brother, Nate, grinned and gave him a little nudge as he moved into the pew.

Tolley felt a burst of joy. As his face grew warm, he

covered the bothersome surge of emotion by peering around Nate. "Where are Susanna and the children?" And the rest of the family?

Nate seemed to understand his unspoken question. "I expect Rosamond and Garrick shortly. They've moved back to the hotel, although Rosamond will probably come out to the ranch every day. Everybody else is staying at the big house for now." He gave Tolley a sidelong glance. "They all send their best. We're proud of you for helping Mrs. Foster."

"It's the right thing to do. How's the Colonel?" He should have asked right away.

Nate shrugged. "The same."

Memories of a family tradition surfaced, and Tolley gathered courage to ask, "What about the usual big Sunday dinner?" Pride kept him from outright begging for an invitation.

Nate shook his head. "We're trying to keep things as quiet as possible."

Tolley nodded, even as he noticed the contradiction in his brother's words. With three little grandchildren running around the house and a crying baby, how did they keep things quiet? Instead of confronting Nate about it, he lifted the hymnbook from the pew. "Speaking of being quiet, you aren't going to sing, are you?" Notoriously tone-deaf, Nate was good-natured about it.

"Of course I am." Nate smirked. "Couldn't appreciate the words near as much if I didn't."

Tolley grimaced and shuddered comically. Before he could add another quip, Rosamond and Garrick moved into the pew beside him. As he greeted them, the preacher stood up in front of the congregation, welcomed everyone and announced the first song. The

strains and poetry of "Immanuel's Land" filled the
sanctuary, and Tolley concentrated on the words.

While he looked forward to going to heaven one day,
he had a lot of living to do, a lot of proving himself to
those he'd hurt or disappointed, a lot of proving himself to God. Revered Harris had told him, *Men look
on the outside, but God looks on the heart*, so Tolley
trusted the Lord knew how much he regretted his past.
But he couldn't let go of the idea that actions would
prove it to Him and to everybody. He could use more
of the old minister's counsel. Now he'd have to figure
these things out for himself.

As the song continued, Tolley noticed Nate didn't
sound half-bad today, mainly because he didn't sing
as loudly as he used to. Would their family appreciate
Tolley's changes as much as they surely appreciated
Nate's improvement? But if he couldn't go to the ranch,
he'd never have a chance to prove himself.

After announcements and prayers, including one
for Colonel Northam, Micah began his sermon. As
he spoke, Laurie noticed a change in his demeanor.
His usual cheerful optimism disappeared, and his eyes
grew red as he announced the death of Dathan Hardison last Wednesday. Laurie had been so involved in
her own activities she'd forgotten the unrepentant outlaw who'd caused much grief to the people of Esperanza. He'd been buried on Thursday with no one to
mourn him. While many folks said, "Good riddance,"
Micah reminded them God was not willing that any
should perish.

He went on to speak about the Christian's future
in heaven, seeing departed loved ones again, being

free from fear and pain and, most of all, seeing Jesus
Christ face-to-face. He read from 1 Corinthians 13:12–
14: "'For now we see through a glass, darkly; but then
*face to face*: now I know in part; but then shall I know
even as also I am known. And now abideth faith, hope,
charity, these three; but the greatest of these is charity.'

"So, beloved—" Micah gazed around the room
"—go forth this week in faith and hope and especially
in love for one another."

The service ended with an invitation to salvation, a
prayer and the stirring hymn lyrics "My hope is built
on nothing less than Jesus's blood and righteousness."
By the last verse, most congregants were smiling and,
as they filed out of the pews, shared hugs and kind
words with one another.

Laurie continued to play softly so as not to drown
out the conversations. After Micah's message, her heart
felt full and her mind enriched. With only a few parishioners left in the room, she closed her hymnbook
and gathered her reticule and parasol.

Ma and Pa came forward to hug her and say how
much they'd missed her.

"Seems like that conservatory was worth the
money." Pa's eyes twinkled with pride.

Ma patted his arm. "Don't talk about money,
George." To Laurie, she said, "You're doing a fine thing
to take care of Mrs. Foster, honey. Just be sure to take
care of those hands, too." Before Laurie could pull on
her gloves, Ma gripped her hands and studied them,
clicking her tongue over their redness. "When you go
to bed, use that cream I sent and put on an old pair of
gloves to keep 'em soft."

"Yes, ma'am." She followed them up the aisle, out

the door and into the late-morning sunshine. After they'd chatted for a few minutes, her parents climbed into their surrey and headed home.

"May I walk you home?" Tolley stood beneath the nearby cottonwood tree and twirled his black Stetson in his hands. He seemed subdued, perhaps as moved by Micah's message as she.

"You may." She raised her parasol under the bright sunshine.

Although she guessed Tolley wanted to talk before they reached Mrs. Foster's house, he remained silent. Maybe he merely wanted some company.

"I thought you'd be going home with Nate. Isn't your family having their usual Sunday dinner?" She'd seen him chatting with Nate, Rosamond and Garrick after the service.

"Nope."

"Is there any change—" She didn't know how to finish the question. Surely if the Colonel had taken a turn for the worse, Micah would've said something during the service. After all, the Colonel and Pa had founded this community, so everyone cared about his health.

She waited for an answer, but none seemed forthcoming. *Lord, what can I do to help him?* If all else failed, maybe a bit of teasing would cheer him.

"Since you'll be eating at the boardinghouse, it's a good thing I'm cooking an extra-large pot roast." She injected a bright tone into her words. "And plenty of potatoes and gravy."

He gave her a little grin. Though small, it caused her heart to trip. More with sympathy than admiration, of course.

"Could you check on Mrs. Foster while I put dinner on the table?"

"Huh?" He blinked, as though lost in thought.

"Mrs. Foster." Laurie giggled. "Check on her so I can serve dinner?"

"Oh. Sure." His stomach rumbled softly. He shot her an embarrassed glance and laughed. "Yeah, you get dinner on the table. I'll check on Mrs. Foster."

Laurie laughed, too, but sadness lingered for her childhood friend. While their families were always close, they'd also been different. Pa and Colonel Northam were both successful ranchers, but she and her sisters never had to earn Pa's approval. The Colonel seemed harder to please. Had Tolley's childhood mischief been an attempt to earn that approval? She'd seen such behavior in some of her students in Denver. While the parents of those children usually ignored their antics, the Colonel had responded by sending Tolley away. Though he'd returned home, the whole family held him at bay. Could she do anything to help him?

*If so, Lord, please show me the way.*

# Chapter Six

Tolley rose early on Monday to take Thor for a workout. He'd missed these daily morning rides and wanted to be sure the stallion didn't mind being stabled instead of pastured. After their run, Tolley brushed him and fed him oats.

"I could do that, Mr. Northam." Adam leaned over the top rail of the stall, worry creasing his forehead. "I take care of the horses boarding here at Mr. Russell's."

"I know. You do it very well." Tolley gave him an easy smile. "I need to remind Thor who I am. I raised him from birth."

"Yessir." Adam's face relaxed. "I understand."

"Say, if Ben can spare you for an hour, could you come over to Mrs. Foster's and help me evaluate the floor, as you suggested we do?" Tolley couldn't wait to get started. "In fact, I'm hoping you can help me install the bathroom. I'll pay you for all of the time you work for me, of course."

Adam perked up. "Yes, *sir*. I'm almost caught up here, so I'll be there. I've been hoping to get more work. Thanks, Mr. Northam."

"Call me Tolley." He finished grooming Thor and cleaning his saddle. "See you soon, Adam."

After breakfast, using a crowbar he found in Mrs. Foster's barn, Tolley managed to loosen and lift two four-foot floorboards. He considered the three splinters in his fingers both annoying and a sort of badge of honor. In Boston, he'd done some carpentry work to help at Reverend Harris's Grace Seaman's Mission. He'd also driven a buggy from time to time. In spite of those activities, his hands had become too soft for his liking over the past two years. Time to start building new calluses.

By the time he'd removed the boards, Adam arrived to help him assess the strength of the supports below the floor. With him came Mrs. Foster's pesky cat, which promptly jumped into the hole in the floor. While Adam burst into laughter, Tolley plopped down on the floor and grabbed at the animal. It paid him no mind, instead moving into the musty depths, sniffing the wood and sneezing from the dust. Only its tail remained visible, swishing back and forth like it was hunting mice. Tolley learned his lesson early in life about grabbing a feline's tail, so he resisted the urge to retrieve this one that way.

"Come here, you stupid cat!"

Laurie appeared in the doorway. "What's going on?"

"C-cat—" pointing at the hole, Adam could hardly speak for his laughing "—under the floor."

Laurie gasped. "Don't hurt him."

Tolley glared at her over his shoulder. "I don't plan to hurt *it*, but—" He reached as far as possible into the hole, but the critter seemed determined to avoid his grasp. Instead, it disappeared into the dark.

"I'll be right back." Laurie left the room and soon came back with a three-foot length of white ribbon. "Here, use this."

Tolley took it in hand and dangled it in the hole. "Here, kitty, kitty." He tried to copy the silly, high-pitched tone Laurie used when she called the critter.

Adam snorted with laughter, and Laurie giggled.

"You look like you've done this before." Laurie knelt beside him. "If you can get him close, I can grab him."

The cat jumped out of the darkness, pounced on the end of the ribbon and dug in its claws. While Tolley dragged it closer, Laurie cupped a hand under its considerable belly and pulled it up.

"There you are, you silly boy." She cuddled the cat and caressed its dirty back, sending a flurry of dust into the air. "What am I going to do with you?"

"You'd better put it outside where it belongs." Trying to tamp down his irritation, Tolley sat up and brushed dirt from his clothes and hair. "I'm not playing silly games to coax it out every time it jumps in there."

"My, my." Laurie held the cat up with its nose to hers. "He's such a grouch, isn't he, Pepper?" She flounced out of the room, cooing to the pest as she went. "Let's go visit Mrs. Foster."

All the while, the cat meowed in varying tones as if it understood her words. Tolley shook his head. "Stupid cat."

Adam leaned against the doorjamb, crossed his arms and continued to snicker.

Tolley glared at him, trying to stay cross but at last surrendering to a few chuckles. "Enough of that. Too bad the little beast couldn't tell us what those joists look like." He pointed to the small worktable he'd brought into the room. "Hand me that lantern."

"Yes, boss."

"None of that 'boss' nonsense." Tolley grinned. For a young man carrying the weight of a family on his shoulders, Adam sure had a good attitude.

After lighting the lantern and using it to illuminate the sixteen-inch space between the floorboards and the first-story ceiling, they decided the joists were well placed and strong enough to support the porcelain bathtub Garrick had offered. Garrick had also offered the services of his water maintenance man for the fixture installation. With no experience in plumbing except for helping his family dig a well years ago, Tolley had readily accepted. He'd drawn plans for the placement of the fixtures so the man would know where to install the water and vent pipes. Once the pipes were in place, Tolley and Adam would cover the wooden floor with tiles before helping the plumber install the fixtures Garrick had donated.

For today, however, he must finish setting up his law office. After cleaning up, he bade Mrs. Foster goodbye and went downstairs to let Laurie know not to hold dinner for him. He found her in the kitchen stirring batter in a large tan crockery bowl. The scene and aromas reminded him of Mother mixing up her culinary wonders in the kitchen at home, and a strange feeling tugged at his heart. He dismissed the melancholy and cleared his throat.

"What's cooking?" He picked up the egg basket he'd filled earlier to take to Mrs. Winsted. "Smells good."

"Why, thank you. It's a cake for tonight's supper." She sent him a sweet smile, which caused her dimple to appear. She'd piled her red hair up into an elegant style, but one curly strand lay against her ivory cheek, giving her a winsome look.

Now his heart kicked up something fierce. She sure did look pretty. He really should marry her. The Colonel would approve of the match. Maybe even show some approval for Tolley himself when he recovered. And a wife this pretty would be an asset with the townsfolk. But first things first. He must set up his law office and make himself worthy of taking a bride. In the meantime, he liked sharing responsibilities with Laurie as they took care of Mrs. Foster. The three of them almost made up a family. Almost.

"I'll have dinner at Williams's Café, so don't hold any for me."

"Oh." She blinked those pretty blue eyes. "All right." She went back to work.

"Have a nice day." Why couldn't he simply turn around and walk out? But his feet refused to move.

"Bye." She sent him another quick smile over her shoulder.

My, what a fine sight. Tolley swallowed hard. With no little difficulty, he shook off his inconvenient reaction and headed out the door, walking the three blocks toward Mrs. Winsted's.

As he turned the corner to head down Main Street, he glanced toward his newly installed shingle from a distance. To his dismay, it hung from one hook, dangling dangerously over the wooden boardwalk where it could fall on anyone passing by, should the wind hit it the wrong way.

Great. Just great. Instead of impressing the citizens

of Esperanza with his professional-appearing sign, he might end up injuring one of them, or worse.

For some reason, disappointment filled Laurie because Tolley wouldn't be home for dinner. She might as well admit to herself she enjoyed his company. While he could still annoy her, especially when it came to poor sweet little Pepper, his conversation was no longer filled with sarcasm and angry grievances as when he was younger. Instead, he'd begun to compliment every meal she prepared, making sure Mrs. Runyan and Mr. Parsley heard him.

In spite of his kind words, the other two boarders continued their complaints, hinting she could never match Mrs. Foster's cooking. So Laurie decided to use tried-and-true recipes from her landlady's handwritten recipe book. To practice, she fixed a smaller portion of a special chicken recipe for herself and Mrs. Foster.

"This is delicious, Laurie." Mrs. Foster used her uninjured left hand to hold her fork. It was an awkward endeavor, but she insisted upon feeding herself. "Who'd ever think to mix cabbage, potatoes, onions and peppers to stewed chicken?"

"You, that's who." Laurie laughed. "It's your recipe. And I noticed your comment on the recipe page that Mrs. Runyan particularly likes it." She spoke cheerfully, hoping not to add to Mrs. Foster's difficulties by mentioning her boarders' complaints.

"Ah, yes, now I remember. As for Mrs. Runyan, she's Irish, you know, and the Irish do love their cabbage." She chuckled. "If you ever run out of things to talk about at supper, ask her about her girlhood in

Ireland." She dabbed her lips with her napkin and set it on her tray, indicating she'd eaten her fill.

"I will." Laurie lifted the tray. "Ring the bell if you need anything."

On the way downstairs, she considered Mrs. Foster's idea. Perhaps this evening, she could direct the conversation to topics they might care about. Anything to keep them from staring back and forth between Laurie and Tolley with those accusing eyes.

Tolley's handsome face came to mind, especially his quirky smile and twinkling eyes when he teased her. If she weren't returning to Denver in the fall, she could permit herself to care for him as more than a friend. But she *would* return to Denver, where her dreams would be realized. And that was that.

And yet, as she worked in the garden, dusted and swept the house, taught three piano students and prepared a larger recipe of cabbage chicken, Tolley continued to creep into her thoughts.

After making sure the sign wasn't damaged and the hooks were securely closed, Tolley felt confident it wouldn't fall again unless an unusually strong wind blew it down. Once again he'd borrowed Mrs. Winsted's ladder and tools to complete the task. When he took them back, no customers shopped in the store. Approaching the store owner, Tolley ventured to ask a question nagging him since Saturday.

"I appreciate your generous help, ma'am." Tolley offered a grin. "And your friendliness." He added a chuckle to soften his words as he forced out the hard truth. "Seems like most folks around here can't forget what a rascal I used to be."

Mrs. Winsted stopped folding bolts of material and gave him her full attention. "I can't answer for anybody else, Tolley, but I believe in giving people second chances."

Her steady gaze into his eyes emphasized her words and brought a lump to his throat. His family hadn't given him a second chance. But her comment answered his unspoken question. She was one of the few who forgave and accepted him.

"I appreciate it, ma'am." He turned to leave, but she touched his arm to stop him.

"We're all praying for the Colonel. Please tell your mother."

So she didn't know about his banishment from the family. He sure wouldn't mention it because it would sound like a plea for pity, the last thing he wanted or needed. He'd have to be very careful whom he told about his unwanted estrangement.

"Yes, ma'am." He tipped his hat and left the mercantile, then made his way down the street to the newspaper office.

As he entered, the bell over the door jangled, summoning Fred Brody from the composing room in back. "Tolley Northam! Welcome back to town. Saw you across the sanctuary at church yesterday." He offered a hearty handshake. "What can I do for you?"

"Howdy, Fred. I need a small sign to announce my hours over at my law office." Tolley pulled a folded paper from his suit jacket. "Here's what I want. Can you print this?"

Fred studied the page. "Sure thing. Congratulations on your new career, by the way. Would you like to purchase an advertisement for me to print in the *Esperanza Journal*?"

"Hadn't thought about it, but it's a good idea."

They discussed the wording and design of both the advertisement and the sign, and Fred said he'd print the sign by the next day. Tolley paid the required amount and shared another friendly handshake with the newspaperman.

On the way back to his office, an unwelcome suspicion crept in. Maybe both Mrs. Winsted and Fred Brody were so friendly because they wouldn't dare snub a Northam. The same family wealth that kept Tolley's share of the ranch profits in his bank account and cash in his pocket assured that folks in business wouldn't jeopardize their own profits by turning him away. He wished he didn't think so little of human nature. At this point, he trusted only Laurie's friendship, at least when she wasn't being prickly.

As he neared his office door, George Eberly approached from the other direction. A nervous impulse seized Tolley. Maybe his return to the Valley's high altitude had finally caught up with him. He slowly breathed in and out to steady his nerves.

"Morning, George." He spoke cheerfully and reached out a hand. The Colonel's old friend hadn't exactly ignored him yesterday after church, but he hadn't bothered to speak, either. His curt nod showed Tolley George's opinion of him. "How are you?"

George merely glanced at Tolley's hand before tilting his head toward the office door. "We need to talk."

"Sure thing." This wasn't a good beginning to whatever George planned to say.

As he unlocked the door, an all-too-familiar fear

gripped Tolley. Did this man bring news about the Colonel? Once inside, he led the way to the back office, where a new layer of dust covered everything. He grabbed one of the cleaning rags, now dry and stiff, and did his best to wipe off a chair for George.

"Have a seat." He waved toward the ladder-back chair across from his own leather one behind the desk. "What can I do for you?" He doubted George needed his legal services.

George sat and crossed his arms over his barrel chest. "I don't like you living in the same house as my daughter. Why aren't you staying at Four Stones?"

Tolley managed to swallow both anger and hurt. "The house is pretty full right now, and—"

"What's the matter with the bunkhouse? You've spent many a night out there planning mischief with some of the worthless cowboys who were hired for seasonal work."

"My family didn't want me on the ranch." The words came out before Tolley could stop them, at least carried on a tone of resignation instead of self-pity.

George's jaw dropped. He stared at Tolley for several seconds. "I never heard of such a thing. What do you mean they don't want you?"

Tolley did his best to lighten his voice as he quickly described his failed homecoming. Before George could respond, he addressed the man's other concern. "I'd never do anything to harm Laurie's reputation. We're very careful about propriety. She and I are doing our best to take care of Mrs. Foster, so you can see the Lord worked it all out." Despite believing that, he felt uncomfortable mentioning the Lord to bolster his assertion.

"Huh." George stared out the window.

The dirty window, Tolley noticed. He desperately needed to find someone to keep this place clean…and soon.

"Sir, I've made some changes in my life since all that boyhood mischief—"

"Mischief?" George's blue eyes blazed. "You call burning down one of my haystacks simple mischief? Almost burning down my barn? Mistreating one of your pa's best mares? Cheating in the Independence Day horse race? Letting Mrs. Wilson's chickens out of the pen to get killed by a coyote? Should I stop now, or do you want to be reminded of the rest of your malicious deeds?"

Tolley swallowed hard. Despite what George thought, he hadn't meant to start the fire. An Eberly cowhand offered him a freshly rolled cigarette, and when Tolley tried to smoke it, he had a violent coughing spell. He didn't even remember dropping the burning cigarette onto the hay. All he recalled was the haystack igniting into an inferno and his own desperate attempts to put it out. If the Colonel hadn't brought several wagonloads of Northam hay to replenish George's winter supply, Eberly horses and cattle would have gone hungry. As for the horse race, he had no excuse for trying to win at all costs.

"No, sir. Those were more than mischief, and I can't tell you how sorry I am. But I'm working real hard to change, to make up for all of it. In Boston, I attended a Bible-teaching church every Sunday and listened real hard to the sermons. I worked hard to get good grades at Harvard, and I've been admitted to the Colorado judicial system." Tolley couldn't stop his pathetic self-defense, even though he wished he were addressing the Colonel. "I even—"

"That's enough." Scowling, George stood and stepped toward the door. "You make sure you don't do anything to hurt Laurie. As anybody with eyes can see, you two ain't children anymore." He slapped his hat on his head and marched from the building.

Tolley rested his arms on his desk and his head on his arms and breathed out a long, deep sigh. If George Eberly, one of the founders of Esperanza, wouldn't trust him with his daughter, that boded ill for his future here. If the Lord weren't using him to help Mrs. Foster, he'd pack up and leave. He didn't know where he'd go, but surely someplace in this world would grant a man a new beginning.

That evening, seated at the kitchen end of the dining room table, Laurie ladled out the chicken stew and passed the first bowl to Mrs. Runyan.

"Mrs. Foster tells me this is one of your favorites." Laurie smiled at the woman. "Of course it won't be as good as hers, but I hope you'll enjoy it. We Irish do like our cabbage, don't we?" Perhaps being both chummy and self-effacing, she could forestall any complaints.

Mrs. Runyan's eyes widened. "Why, yes, we do. I didn't know you are Irish." As she spoke, the brogue she'd never used before crept into her words.

"Yes, ma'am." Laurie served bowls for Tolley and Mr. Parsley and passed them down the table. "You can see it in the red hair my sisters and I inherited from our Irish ma."

"She's the Irish one, you say?" The woman took a

bite of her chicken stew. "Not bad, though I think it needs a dash of pepper."

Pleased her strategy worked, Laurie glanced down the table at Tolley. He'd been awful quiet since coming home. In fact, he'd gone to his room until time for supper. Now a little smile crept over his face, though it didn't quite reach his eyes.

"Say, Mr. Parsley." Tolley handed the basket of rolls to the man. "My watch needs to be cleaned. Could you look at it tomorrow?"

Mr. Parsley stared at Tolley as though surprised by the request. "I shall have to consult my schedule. I am currently making a watch for an important client, and he expects it to be completed by the end of this week. Then I have other clients…"

"Of course." Tolley caught Laurie's gaze and shrugged. "Fit me in where you can."

She made sure the others weren't looking her way before rewarding him with a wink. Oddly, Tolley frowned and gave a little shake of his head. Did he mean she shouldn't wink, as they'd always done? She sighed. Now that they were grown-ups, would she and her sisters lose all of their fraternal camaraderie with the Northam brothers?

"Miss Eberly." Tolley gave her a bland look. "Would you grace us with a piano performance this evening?"

Why did he act so formally, as though they hadn't grown up together like brother and sister?

Mr. Parsley perked up. "I do miss Mrs. Foster's lovely playing of an evening. While I doubt your performance could match hers, I should greatly enjoy such entertainment."

When Mrs. Runyan echoed their request, Laurie could only acquiesce. After all, if it brought unity among the boarders and improved the atmosphere of the house, she'd gladly do it. Of course, that generated an important question. If she spent an hour or so entertaining them, would any of them help her afterward with cleaning up the kitchen and taking care of Mrs. Foster? Quite unlikely.

As she retrieved the applesauce cake from the kitchen and served it to the others, she struggled against resentment. Ah, well. This situation wouldn't last long. Summer would end, and she'd return to Denver, where she could concentrate on the career the Lord had set before her.

Seeing the distressed look on Laurie's face, Tolley would've bent his rule about women's work and carried some of the dishes to the kitchen, but he couldn't be alone with her in a room with the door closed. Neither of the other boarders gave any indication they'd changed their minds about helping. But George's angry charge made Tolley determined to avoid any hint of impropriety. Even sharing winks, something he'd done all his life with the Eberly girls, must now cease. The same went for sociable banter. Yet if he couldn't enjoy his friendship with Laurie, he'd feel more alone than ever in a town full of people who shunned him.

After dessert, Mrs. Runyan and Mr. Parsley settled themselves in the parlor and watched expectantly, even impatiently, through the arched doorway into the dining room while Laurie cleared the table. Arms loaded with dishes, she pushed through the kitchen's swinging door, and soon the clatter and clink of plates and silverware reached Tolley's ears.

He couldn't help her, and he couldn't bring himself to join the others in the parlor. Instead, he went out the front door and around the house to make sure the chickens had enough water in their low metal trough. He pulled the few weeds from among the corn and bean plants, appreciating how well Laurie kept up the garden. When he finally heard music wafting through the parlor window, he went back inside to join the others.

"In Dublin's fair city where girls are so pretty…" Laurie played the Irish ballad and sang the tragic story of fishmonger Molly Malone.

Tolley had often heard Mabel Eberly sing the ballad but never so sweetly. Laurie had an uncommonly pretty voice. In a city like Boston, she would receive many invitations to give recitals and concerts. As he watched her get lost in the music, the delicate timbre of her voice caused his own heart to swell with emotion. Apparently Mrs. Runyan felt the same, for she sniffed and dabbed at her eyes with an embroidered white handkerchief. When Laurie finished the song, Tolley and Mr. Parsley clapped their hands. Mrs. Runyan applauded enthusiastically, bouncing in her chair as she clapped.

"Thank you." Laurie gave them all a gracious smile and went on to play two more pieces.

His request for the impromptu recital had been a good idea. However, if he expected the older boarders' music appreciation to carry over to approval in other areas, he found himself mistaken within seconds of Laurie's final song.

"I must say, Miss Eberly." Mr. Parsley stood and straightened his jacket. "You do have a prodigious talent. However, I caution you to avoid developing the character flaws afflicting many entertainers."

"Why—" Tolley's hands bunched into fists, and he took a step toward the little man.

Laurie stepped between them. "Why, thank you, sir. With all of the temptations this world offers, we younger folks can't have too many warnings."

"Humph." The man marched from the room and climbed the front stairs.

"You'd do well," Mrs. Runyan said, "to keep company with Anna Means or Mrs. Wakefield. They will provide the proper moral examples for you." Nose thrust into the air, she traipsed out of the room after the watchmaker.

Tolley felt as if the top of his head might explode. He turned to Laurie, who stared up at him, her eyes rimmed with red. "They aren't worth the grief they're giving you."

"Why don't you retire, too?" Her voice wavered as she spoke. "I have things to do."

Tolley longed to tug her into his arms and comfort her, but he didn't dare. "Very well. I wish…"

"Good night, Tolley." She spun around and marched toward the kitchen, her posture stiff.

He lay awake wondering what he could have done to help her. The unwelcome idea of washing dishes came to mind, but he quickly dismissed it. First of all, it was women's work. Second, and most important, he still couldn't be in the kitchen alone with Laurie, especially with the others in the house. Even if he did help out, she'd probably stick around to make sure he did it right. He could tell his quietness had hurt her this evening, yet he certainly couldn't tell her about her pa's harsh words. He just couldn't win.

Teardrops splashed into the dishpan as Laurie washed the supper dishes. She was so tired. Beyond tired. Again the question came to mind: How had dear Mrs. Foster managed all these years? Mr. Parsley and Mrs. Runyan added insult to injury. How awful of them to ruin a perfectly good evening with their baseless accusations and suggestions. Befriend Anna Means? Why, the girl was barely sixteen. As for Rosamond, she was already a friend, a very busy friend whose father lay seriously ill. Laurie wouldn't think of requiring anything of her, no matter how much she longed for help. Nor would she consider going home. Mrs. Foster needed the meager income from her boarders, her eggs sales and her piano students, and no one could help her but Laurie.

As for Tolley, she couldn't imagine what got into him this evening. First his coolness toward her, then his bright idea that she should give a concert. She didn't mind playing. In fact, she loved "Molly Malone." Growing up, she'd often sung it with Ma and her sisters to make their chores seem to pass more quickly. She supposed Tolley had meant to help. She released a mirthless laugh. If he really wanted to help her, he'd be with her right now drying these dishes.

She washed the last pot and poured the dishpan and rinse pan down the drain that emptied into the garden, then went to the back door, planning to step outside and gaze up at the stars. Standing here in the dark and looking at the splendors of the night sky always gave her a sense of peace and wellbeing, even made her feel closer to God, no matter how tired she felt.

Running footfalls and a moving shadow on her right shattered all feelings of peace. As the shadow disappeared around to the north side of the house, she gasped and withdrew back inside, locking the door behind her. Who was out there? She stared through the window into the dim moonlight. The gate to the chicken pen appeared to be open, and perhaps the henhouse door, as well. The hens would be sleeping now, but they'd surely wander away if they found the gate open in the morning.

That wasn't going to happen. Mrs. Foster needed those hens, needed their eggs. Laurie locked the front door, something folks didn't do around here because they trusted their neighbors, unlike the people in Denver. She made quick work of drying and putting away the last of the pans before tiptoeing upstairs and checking on Mrs. Foster. The dear lady lay fast asleep, so Laurie quietly retreated to her own bedroom. There she took her Colt .45 from its holster and made her way down to the backyard in the dark.

A soft evening breeze stirred the air, and she inhaled deeply to check for unusual smells, such as human sweat or even cologne. Nothing caught her notice. She closed the henhouse door and secured the latch on the chicken pen gate. It wasn't broken, so somebody had opened it.

She turned back to the house in time to see a large, dark shape moving toward her, silhouetted by the dim lantern light shining through the kitchen window. A violent shiver swept through her body. With great difficulty, she pulled up her gun and aimed with a shaky hand. "Wh-who's there?"

## Chapter Seven

"Laurie?"

"Tolley!" She sank to her knees, barely able to contain her relief. She felt him kneel beside her and grip her shoulders.

"What are you doing out here?"

When she could find her voice, she told him about seeing the open henhouse door and chicken gate.

"I came out a while ago to check their water, but I made sure the latches were secure." He chuckled as he helped her stand. "It only takes one time of letting chickens out to never do it again. They're awful hard to catch."

"That's for sure. But that's not all. Somebody was out here. I saw a shadow move around to the north side of the house, heard heavy running feet."

Tolley stiffened. "Let's get you back inside. Then I'll have a look-see."

Laurie and her sisters knew how to protect themselves, but it felt surprisingly good to turn the situation over to him. "All right. Get your gun. And be careful."

"Yes, ma'am." He held her arm as they walked back to the house.

They entered the kitchen to find Mr. Parsley in his dressing gown, arms crossed. "What is the meaning of this late-night tryst?"

Standing at his elbow, Mrs. Runyan mirrored his posture. "Miss Eberly, I am ashamed of you." She glared at Tolley. "As for you, young man, I've heard about your reputation. I am not in the least surprised at your—"

"Oh, hush!" Laurie stamped her foot for emphasis. "We had a prowler. Mr. Northam found me in danger and kept the man from creeping into the house." Not quite what happened but enough to stop their foolishness.

Again performing their imitation of a Greek chorus, the two boarders gasped in unison.

"A prowler!" Mrs. Runyan's voice rose to a shriek.

"Shush!" Laurie hissed out the word. "You'll waken Mrs. Foster. Now go back to bed. Mr. Northam will go outside and make sure the man's gone."

"Yes, ma'am, Miss Eberly. I'll get my gun and check the yard." Tolley edged past her, carefully avoiding touching her. Only five minutes ago, his grip had felt so reassuring. Now he was doing his best to protect her, not from a prowler, but from wagging tongues.

Mrs. Runyan tugged her dressing gown closer to her round form. "I do not care for your tone of voice, missy."

"Watch how you speak to me, young lady," Mr. Parsley added.

For Mrs. Foster's sake, Laurie swallowed a cross sigh along with a large measure of her pride. "Please forgive me, both of you. I saw the chicken pen open and knew you'd want your fresh eggs in the morning, so I went out to close it so the chickens wouldn't run off and lay their eggs who knows where. Seeing that prowler distressed me terribly, causing me to forget myself. I will not speak so rudely again."

"See that you don't." Mrs. Runyan turned and pushed through the door.

Mr. Parsley apparently couldn't think of a rejoinder to outdo the lady's comment, so he resorted to his usual "humph" as he followed her out of the kitchen.

Laurie sagged into a chair beside the table and lay across the flat surface. Seeing the leftover applesauce cake, she pulled the plate toward her and removed the glass cover. She didn't bother to fetch a fork, but used the triangular silver server to eat bite after bite. Funny how sweets could soothe a body's ravaged emotions. Funny how she'd much rather have Tolley's reassuring brotherly arms enfold her instead.

In keeping with the methodology learned at Harvard, Tolley formulated a schedule to accomplish all of his goals. After exercising Thor and taking care of the chickens, he spent his mornings in his law office and his afternoons working on the bathroom. However, at first light today, he added inspecting the grounds around the house. A good thing he hadn't found the time to trim Mrs. Foster's lawn. Large footprints pressed down the long grass in several places, and now a dewy film clearly marked the depths of the dented spots. Tolley couldn't see anything remarkable about the prints. Maybe he should have Sheriff Lawson check them. With his tracking experience, he'd notice anything significant.

At breakfast, Tolley told the others of his plan to report the incident to Lawson today. Annoyed with the boarders' behavior last night, he didn't care what they thought, but he spoke to the whole table so Laurie would be reassured.

"You should have gone to his house right away and reported the prowler." Mrs. Runyan poured a long stream of cream into her coffee and stirred up a whirlpool in her cup, her spoon clinking loudly against the china. "He could have caught the man."

"If you had any sense, you'd have done so." Mr. Parsley broke custom and agreed with the milliner for once.

"Tolley... Mr. Northam thought it more important not to leave us unprotected." Laurie spoke in her sweetest voice, causing Tolley to come near to choking on his jam-covered biscuit. Where was the spitfire who'd rebuked these two last night? "Didn't you, Mr. Northam?" She tilted her head and glared at him, commanding him to agree.

He smothered a teasing grin. Mustn't tease her anymore. "Yes, ma'am. I feared the varmint might come back while I was gone. I wanted to be sure you all were safe." He set his napkin beside his plate. "Now, if you'll excuse me, I'll go see the sheriff right now." He didn't dare to look at Laurie for fear he'd start laughing. Didn't these older adults hear themselves? Hear how foolish they sounded?

After breakfast, egg basket in hand, he strode up the dusty road toward Main Street. Behind him a horse approached, and Doc Henshaw drew up beside him.

"Was out at Four Stones. Thought you'd want to know there's some change in the Colonel's condition."

Tolley's pulse began to race. "Is he awake?" If he were dead, Doc wouldn't beat about the bush in telling him.

"He's still not fully conscious, but he's able to take some broth. It's a good sign."

"Thanks, Doc." How long would it be before his family let him see for himself how the Colonel fared? Even so, he felt encouraged. If all went as planned, he'd have plenty of good deeds to present to his father when they finally had a conversation.

With Doc's good news, the day seemed a bit brighter. Tolley hastened his pace toward Main Street. This time when he turned the corner, he gazed with pride at his sign swinging gently in the morning breeze. A woman stood at the front door, and Tolley's heart kicked up. His first client? As he drew near, he recognized Effie Bean.

"Good morning, Mrs. Bean." Tolley unlocked the door and ushered her in. "How are you today? What can I do for you?"

"Morning, Mr. Northam." Effie spoke in a monotone, and her face appeared expressionless. "Don't need anything from you. Homer says you need somebody to clean your office. I can do it for twenty-five cents a week."

"How thoughtful of Homer to notice." Tolley studied the tiny woman. She and Homer both appeared to be in their midthirties. Effie wore her hair in a severe bun, and under her eyes were dark circles. Her well-worn brown dress hung on her slender shoulders as if it belonged on someone taller and rounder. If Tolley remembered correctly, the couple had three children, perhaps more. Maybe Homer's income wasn't enough to support them all. "But twenty-five cents—"

"Make it fifteen." Effie's voice wavered.

"No, you misunderstand me. I'll gladly pay you a dollar a week."

Her eyes widened, and a tiny smile formed on her thin lips. "That's an awful lot for just cleaning, Mr. Northam. I don't want to take charity."

"You won't." Tolley shook his head. "If I can leave it to you without having to think about it, it'll be worth it."

She stared at him for a moment, and her formerly bland expression brightened. "I can do that." She looked around. "You have cleaning supplies?"

"By the back door. If you need anything else, buy it at the mercantile and put it on my tab." He remembered the eggs he carried. "While you're at it, please take these to Mrs. Winsted." He set the basket on the small reception desk.

"I can do that," she repeated as she started toward the hallway. Her answer to any challenge? If so, he liked it.

"Mrs. Bean, I'm going over to the sheriff's. If anyone comes in—"

She stopped. Her posture straightened. Her eyes grew bright. "Shall I send them over or have them wait here?"

Tolley considered her for a moment. Could she do more than cleaning, such as being his receptionist every day? She'd look more presentable if she wore her Sunday dress. Would she even want to leave her home and children and be employed all day? He didn't want to make an impulsive decision only to regret it later, so he'd delay asking her.

"Please ask them to wait."

"I can do that."

Tolley grinned to himself. Having a receptionist would surely cause others to see him as a professional man, a lawyer who could be trusted to handle their legal affairs. If he got home before the other boarders, he'd ask Laurie for her opinion on the matter.

Home? Ask Laurie? What strange thoughts. Yet they seemed natural to him.

Laurie handed the last breakfast plate to her sister Grace to dry. "Thanks for your help. It gets pretty hectic around here." She dumped the water down the drain and turned the dishpan upside down in the sink, then dried her hands.

"Glad to." Grace swiped the tea towel over the dish, set it in the cupboard and laid out the towel to dry on the back of a chair. "Micah's busy working on his Wednesday-night message and sermon for next Sunday. He concentrates best when I'm not buzzing around him like a honeybee." She grinned. "In fact, when he started calling me honeybee, I realized he was saying—in the nicest way, of course—I was keeping him from work."

"How funny." Laurie laughed as she pictured her minister brother-in-law trying to figure out how to tell Grace to leave him to his work without hurting her feelings. "You sure have a sweet husband." She set a hand on Grace's rounded belly. To her delight, she felt the baby moving. "Your little one is kicking."

"Yep." Grace laughed. "First time it happened, it scared me to pieces. Ma told me it was Micah Junior, wiggling around inside me. I told her it was *Grace* Junior." She gave Laurie a sly look. "Our doctor brother-in-law's going to be pretty busy delivering babies in the coming months."

"Who else is expecting?"

"Pshaw." Grace waved away her remark. "Everybody who has eyes can see Rosamond Wakefield is one of 'em. There's Electra Means." Her giggle sounded much more girlish than her former hearty guffaws. "Guess who else."

"I can't." Laurie shook her head. Then a memory surfaced, and she squealed. "Maisie? I thought she had a special glow about her." Their oldest sister had waited a long time for Johnny to come along. Now here came a little brother or sister to join him.

"She sure does." Grace chuckled.

Laurie sat at the table to shell the peas she'd harvested from the garden earlier, with Grace pitching in to help. Laurie enjoyed her companionship. She hadn't mentioned the prowler to Mrs. Foster, but Grace listened with interest and concern, saying she and Micah would keep an eye out for any strangers in the neighborhood. And of course they'd pray for everyone's safety.

Laurie would miss her family when she returned to Denver. Even more, her three older sisters' happy marriages generated a longing, even an ache in her heart. Would she be able to find a good man among the Denver elite? Many of the gentlemen she'd met were either wealthy snobs, social climbers interested only in her money or nominal church members who didn't seem to truly know the Lord. And none of them set her heart to racing or even caused a ripple of tender emotion. Although a few attempted to call her by fond names similar to "honeybee," she hadn't welcomed such endearments.

Sitting here with Grace in the midmorning peacefulness, a pie in the oven and a chicken stewing on the stovetop for supper, she caught a glimpse of her three married sisters' lives. They were content. More than content. Truly happy. Why did Laurie feel so strongly she wanted to teach at the conservatory and give concerts to those wealthy people? How could she weigh the contentment her sisters and mother enjoyed against the satisfaction of seeing her students excel and the joy of hearing audiences applaud her piano performances? Home and family meant so much to her. Yet if she never performed, had all her years of music studies been in vain?

"How are you getting along with Tolley?" Grace emptied her bowl of peas into Laurie's larger one. "Other than chasing off prowlers, is he helping out with chores?"

Laurie shrugged. "As much as one can expect from—" She started to say *a spoiled boy*, which she and her sisters had jokingly called him over the years. But somehow a man who'd use his own money to install a bathroom for an elderly widow could no longer be called spoiled. "From a man trying to set up a new law practice."

"I suppose so." Grace grabbed another handful of peas and began to shell them. "Micah and I are real concerned about his family situation." She frowned briefly. "We understand he wasn't allowed to see the Colonel. Pa and Micah both have visited him several times. I wonder why Tolley isn't allowed to. You know what's going on?"

Laurie shook her head. "No. I only know it hurt him deeply. But I think he's dealing with it pretty well." In truth, she hurt for him, even though he didn't seem to feel sorry for himself. Tolley's sudden formality did bother her, but Grace didn't need to know about it. How else could he protect Laurie from the two grouchy boarders and their rude, unreasonable suggestions of impropriety? For Mrs. Foster's sake, she'd try to step back from their lifelong friendship.

Leaving Mrs. Bean to clean his office, Tolley walked next door to the newly remodeled two-story jailhouse, with an apartment for the deputy on the second floor. The first-floor office boasted a large front room, separated from the cells by a wall. Beyond the door, a man hollered, his words indistinguishable. The calm, steady speech of Sheriff Lawson answered, but his words were also muffled.

Curiosity drew Tolley to the closed door the moment the sheriff opened it. Jumping back, Tolley barely missed a broken nose, or least a bloody one.

Lawson blinked in surprise as he came through and closed the door again. "Morning, Tolley. Can I do something for you?"

Feeling foolish, Tolley return a crooked grin. "Morning, Sheriff. Sounds like an angry prisoner in there."

Lawson exhaled a blast of air. "Angry probably comes about halfway to describing him."

"What's he in for?" With no alcohol permitted in

Esperanza's limits, Tolley assumed the man was a drunk who'd broken town law.

"You don't know?" The sheriff rubbed a hand against his chest in a seemingly unconscious gesture. "That's right. You were out of town last December when the Hardison gang came to town. Jud Purvis is in there, the last one around. Hardison and Smith are dead, and two of 'em got away. I doubt they'll be back."

Tolley's legal training brought out his curiosity. "What are the charges against Purvis?"

Again the sheriff's hand went to his chest. "He gunned me down."

Tolley drew in a sharp breath and took a step back. "Thank the Lord you're all right." He studied the man. "You *are* all right, aren't you?"

Lawson clicked his tongue and rubbed his chest again. "Don't tell my wife this, but the truth is I've seen better days. I'm sticking around town only until that varmint has his trial."

"When's that?" Tolley could probably learn some important skills from watching the man's lawyer present his case.

"Sometime in July. The circuit judge had several trials before his, so we have to wait our turn." The sheriff sat at his desk and invited Tolley to sit opposite him. "Haven't got a lawyer for this polecat." He waggled his bushy, graying eyebrows. "You want the job?"

Tolley snorted. "No, thank you, sir. I appreciate your trying to help me start my law practice, but representing a man in a clear case of attempted murder—of a lawman, no less—isn't the way I want to be known."

Lawson shrugged. "Purvis claims he's innocent. To tell the truth, I didn't see him shoot. My posse and I had ridden out in the hills to hunt the gang. We were ambushed. Deputy Grace and the reverend were too busy saving my life to track him down until several days later, what with the snow and all."

A myriad of thoughts churned around in Tolley's mind. Maybe he could work with the sheriff on this after all. "Has anyone taken Purvis's statement about what happened?"

"Nope. Nobody wants anything to do with him after all the grief that whole gang caused for folks around here."

"I can see why." Tolley had his own history with the gang. After his brother Rand killed Hardison's cousin over a card game in a Del Norte saloon, Hardison came to town to seek revenge and rob the bank. Tolley, Rand and three of the Eberly girls put a stop to the robbery, earning the outlaw's hatred and promises of revenge. But Purvis hadn't been a part of that, so surely he didn't have call to harm anyone around here.

Tolley could foresee some long, boring days ahead if he didn't find some work to do while the plumbers installed the pipes for Mrs. Foster's bathroom. "I don't suppose writing down Purvis's version of the incident would hurt my reputation, such as it is." He recalled his law lessons at Harvard. "Tell me why you think Purvis shot you."

"He and his gang had it in for me. When I was sheriff of a town in Kansas, I arrested him, his twin brother, Jed, and a fella named Heep Skinner for a bank robbery where they shot a teller. They weren't hanged because the man didn't die, but they were sent to prison. To a man, they vowed revenge against me and everyone who put them there." Lawson took a long, slow breath.

"When the Colonel hired me as sheriff of Esperanza, I figured it'd be a sleepy little town where I could end my sheriffing days in peace." He chuckled without mirth. "Turned out Purvis's and Hardison's gangs were in cahoots. They all escaped prison and joined forces to get revenge on both me and this town."

Frowning, the sheriff brushed a hand down his face. "I should've asked about your pa. How is he?"

Tolley shrugged. "Doc says he's starting to take broth, but he's not fully awake yet." Good thing he'd seen Doc before coming here so he'd have an answer for anyone asking.

Lawson grunted. "He's a good man. My wife and I pray for him every day."

Tolley forced a smile. "Thanks. Me, too."

The sheriff tilted his head and questioned him with one raised eyebrow. Tolley sighed. He didn't want the whole town to know his business, but also didn't want the sheriff to have expectations Tolley might not be able to live up to in regard to his family. And if they planned to work closely together on legal matters, the sheriff should know the truth.

"I'm sure you remember when the Colonel sent me back east."

The sheriff nodded.

"I don't think anyone ever saw him as angry as he was with me for, well, for all the mischief I'd caused." Unwanted emotion rose up to choke Tolley. He leaned back in his chair and forced himself to swallow. "Mother and my brothers agree it's best for me to stay away until my father recovers." *If* he recovered. "I think they're afraid seeing me might set him back."

Lawson regarded him for a long time. Then he shook his head. "I don't know what to say, son."

Before self-pity could weigh him down, Tolley sat up. "I didn't come over here to grumble about family matters. You know I'm boarding at Mrs. Foster's. Last night we had a prowler, and I wanted to report it."

"Prowler?" The sheriff pulled out an official-looking form and took his pen in hand. "What happened? Did you get a good look at him?"

"He went in the henhouse and left the door and pen gate open. I didn't see him, but Laurie did." The memory of her collapsing in fear caused a knot in his chest. If the man had harmed her, Tolley would've chased him to the moon and back to make him pay for it. "It was too dark to see which way he went, or I'd have followed him."

After writing on his form, Lawson stared out the window, a thoughtful expression on his well-lined face. "Maybe some youngster stole eggs or a chicken for food. We've got some poor folks around here and plenty of strangers passing through. If they're hungry enough, some parents won't think twice about having their youngsters steal food. I suppose they figure a child won't get punished like an adult would."

"No doubt about that. But this morning I found some mighty big footprints in the grass, too big for a child."

"Huh." The sheriff wrote the rest of the details as Tolley recited them. "I'll go take a look, and we'll keep an eye out for anyone who's suspicious looking. Probably best to tell folks to start locking their doors at night." He clicked his tongue again. "What a shame this fine town has to lose its innocence. Sad to say, that's the way things are all over the Wild West."

"Yessir, I suppose so." Tolley stood and donned his hat. "I'll get back to you about taking Purvis's statement."

He took his leave of the sheriff and returned to his office. The furniture was dusted and oiled and the floors swept and mopped. The windows sparkled in the sunshine. At the back door, Mrs. Bean swept out the last of the sandy soil. Other than needing more furnishings, the office looked professional.

After thanking her for a job well-done, Tolley said, "Anybody come by?"

"No, sir." She brushed a handkerchief across her face. "Weekdays are pretty quiet in town."

"True." They were also the days when people took care of banking and legal matters. Yet he couldn't expect people to know about his law practice this soon.

His earlier idea returned. "Mrs. Bean, what would you think of working for me every day?" The woman obviously took pride in her work, so surely she could manage greeting people.

"I can do that. I'll come in every morning and give the place a once-over. You know how bad the dust is here in the Valley."

"No, I mean would you like to be my receptionist? Work morning and afternoon, with an hour off for dinner. I'll pay you—" He quickly calculated a fair-sounding wage. The cowboys at Four Stones Ranch earned twenty dollars a month, plus meals and lodging. She wouldn't need the latter two. "How does five dollars a week sound?"

Her jaw dropped open, and her brown eyes widened. "Why, I don't know what to say." She smiled broadly, then stared down at her dusty dress and sobered. "No offense, Mr. Northam, but you don't know anything about me. Why do you think I could do the job?"

He appreciated her honesty. "You tell me. Did you ever have a job other than taking care of your family?"

"Yessir. My father owns a store back in Philadelphia, so I worked for him from the time I could stack tins and fold fabric. When Homer came to work as a clerk for Father, I took over the bookkeeping."

"Sounds good to me." Tolley noticed her proper grammar, another asset. "If you want the job, it's yours."

"Let me speak to Homer about it, and I'll let you know."

"You do that." Satisfied with his morning, Tolley headed back home. He couldn't wait to tell Laurie his news.

Once again, he realized how well "Laurie" and "home" went together. If George knew how honorable his intentions were, maybe he wouldn't disapprove of him. Tolley cared for Laurie in a brotherly way as he did for Rosamond, so he could only offer her a marriage of convenience. Should he propose? Or would that ruin everything? Only one way to find out.

## Chapter Eight

"You don't have a thing to worry about, Pa." Laurie had been up to her elbows in deboning a stewed chicken when her father arrived at the boardinghouse. If she hoped to get all of her work done this morning, she couldn't sit down to visit with him. "Tolley is a perfect gentleman. You know as well as I do he's always acted like a brother to us girls." She returned the chicken bones to the pot along with fresh water to make additional broth and then stoked the fire to bring it all to a boil.

"Brother?" Pa sat at the kitchen table eating a slice of the leftover applesauce cake. "I recall you were mighty fond of him when you were a slip of a girl."

"That's true." She smiled at the memory of sighing over his good looks with her friends. She also remembered some of his mean tricks. Long before he put a burr under Gypsy's saddle, he'd put nettles in the schoolteacher's coat. And he'd teased Grace for being so tall until Laurie threatened to call him Bartholomew in front of the other children. She and Grace never told their parents about it because they'd managed the situation on their own. "But I've grown far beyond child-hood infatuations."

"Have you?" He studied her sternly, then returned her smile. "You can't blame me for worrying. He got into a heap of trouble as a boy, even if he did treat you girls all right. If he met the wrong people in Boston, he could've changed."

"If he did, it was for the better." She divided the cooked meat into two portions, one for soup and one for pot pie so one chicken would last for two suppers. "Look at the way he's using his time and money to install a bathroom for Mrs. Foster. Isn't that generous?"

"Never said he wasn't generous. The Colonel and Charlotte reared 'em all that way, same as your ma and me reared you girls." Pa drained his cup of coffee and held the cup out to Laurie. "Good coffee, daughter."

Her heart warmed. This was just like being at home, which she dearly missed in her quieter moments. "Thanks. I learned from the best." And had learned from her earlier mistakes.

"I guess only time will tell about Tolley." She recalled the way he'd withdrawn from her yesterday. "Say, did you talk to him?"

Instead of answering, Pa shoved a large bite of cake into his mouth.

"Did you?"

He shrugged and pointed to his full cheeks.

She shook her head. "That's answer enough for me." What a rascal. Still, she appreciated his protectiveness. If she could find a man in Denver with the same godly character and sense of humor, she'd marry him quick.

"Sure smells good in here." Tolley poked his head in through the hall doorway. As his gaze fell on Pa, he drew back in surprise. "Why, howdy, George. Good to see you."

If Laurie had doubts that Pa had spoken to him, the hesitation in Tolley's demeanor dispelled them. "Come on in. You may as well finish up this cake." She served out the last piece and poured coffee for him.

"I don't want to interrupt anything." He gave Pa an awkward grin. Actually, more of a grimace.

"I'll be leaving soon." Pa's eyes narrowed. "What have you been up to? Other than running off prowlers, that is."

Shrugging, Tolley sat at the table and accepted the cake and coffee. "Thanks, Laurie." He regarded Pa with a guarded look. "You don't need to worry about the prowler. I'll be keeping watch here and making nighttime rounds. I told the sheriff about it. He's coming over later." He ate a bite of cake. "Mmm-mmm, Laurie, this is even better today."

Laurie recognized his slightly furtive expression. The poor dear couldn't think of what to say to Pa. Like the Colonel, Pa could be intimidating when he wanted to be.

Instead of addressing Pa, however, Tolley spoke to her. "I got my shingle up and my law office opened. Even hired Effie Bean to be my receptionist, if Homer gives his approval." He turned to Pa. "If you have any legal matters that need tending, I'd be proud to handle them for you."

His cake all gone, Pa set his fork on his plate with a clatter. "Never needed a lawyer. Don't expect to need one now." He stood and carried his plate and cup to the sink. "Daughter, you remember what we talked about." He stalked out of the room and left the house.

Hurting for her friend, Laurie sat in the vacated chair. "I'm sure he didn't mean to be rude, Tolley."

"No, of course not." Tolley stood, leaving his cake and coffee unfinished. "Excuse me."

He walked from the kitchen, his shoulders slumped, and Laurie's heart broke for him. What would it take for Pa, and many others in this town, to see how hard he was trying to prove he'd changed? Would they even give him a chance?

After getting his business satchel and a box of books from his room, Tolley strode up the street toward his office, his temper vying with his wounded sense of worth. George Eberly didn't trust him, not only with living in the same boardinghouse as Laurie, but with his legal affairs. With him setting the example, would Tolley ever be able to get any clients?

He'd show George. He'd show all of them. Jud Purvis needed a lawyer, and Tolley needed a client. A perfect match, in his book. If the sheriff didn't object, what could anyone else say? After all, Lawson was the victim, and he wasn't certain Purvis shot him. With the right evidence...or lack thereof, Tolley could get him off. Not from prison, because he deserved it for his part in the gang's robberies, but at least from hanging.

The two bites he'd consumed of Laurie's cake whetted his appetite. After dropping off his books and satchel at his office, he headed over to Williams's Café for a quick lunch. While he ate Miss Pam's tasty beans and ham and corn bread, he mulled over his human assets.

In spite of George's dislike, the sheriff approved of him, as did Mrs. Foster, shopkeeper Mrs. Winsted, banker Nolan Means and Tolley's hotelier brother-in-law, Garrick Wakefield—all important citizens of Esperanza. Best of all, Laurie remained his friend. Her encouragement meant the world to him. If he offered her a marriage of convenience and she accepted, they could be happy together and maybe in time even fall in love. Without question, the Colonel would approve, and being a devoted father, George would eventually come around. He'd see Tolley had changed, had grown up. When he saw Tolley taking good care of Laurie, his opinion would surely improve. It would work. Tolley would make sure it did.

First things first. He'd meet Purvis and take his statement and then go home and propose to Laurie before the other boarders came home. Then they wouldn't catch him alone with Laurie and misunderstand a perfectly respectable situation.

Gobbling down the last of his dinner, he paid his bill and headed back to his office. After placing his law books and dictionary on the shelves in his office and sundry office supplies in his desk drawers, he took a white legal pad and pencil and headed next door.

"Afternoon, Sheriff." Tolley removed his hat and hung it on a peg by the door. "If you don't mind, I'd like to talk to Purvis."

Lawson gave him one of his long looks, the kind that would probably intimidate a troublemaker and make him think twice about breaking the law. Instinctively, Tolley swallowed hard. Not long ago, he'd been a troublemaker.

After an uncomfortable silence, the sheriff said, "You sure you want to do this?"

"Yessir." Now that he finally had a plan, Tolley wasn't about to change his mind.

"All right." Lawson stood and grabbed a ring of keys from a peg behind his desk. "Let's go." He led the way through the door and into the large room containing three cells, each connected to the next one by a single wall of heavy iron bars. "Purvis, you got company."

The jail's sole prisoner half reclined on a cot in the middle cell. When the sheriff spoke, the scowl on the man's face wavered slightly, then hardened again. "Yeah? Who's the dandy?"

Tolley had never been called a dandy, an insult for any cattle rancher or hard-riding cowboy. Somehow he managed to grin. "Howdy, Purvis. I'm Bartholomew Northam, attorney-at-law. Mind if I join you?"

This brought the outlaw to his feet, and he gripped two of his cell bars. "So you got me a lawyer, eh? It's about time. Come on in, Northam. Make yourself comfortable."

Lawson opened the cell next to Purvis's. "Sit in here to do your writing. I'd put you in there with him, 'cept I don't trust him." He waved Tolley into the small chamber. "I'll leave you to it." He exited the jail area, closing the door behind him.

"Northam, eh? You part of that rich ranching family south of town?" Purvis grinned as he studied Tolley up and down, probably taking his measure and figuring out how to manipulate him. Before Tolley could respond, he plopped himself back down on his canvas cot. "You're a mite young to be a lawyer, ain't ya? Why don't you go home to Mama and send in a real man?"

Sitting on the cot, Tolley chuckled. He'd been harassed by his older brothers and countless cowboys over the years, excellent training for dealing with this man's insults. Instead of responding in kind, he looked around the room. "How're they treating you?"

With open windows on either end—neither within reach of a man in a cell—it smelled surprisingly fresh rather than stuffy. Purvis didn't reek of sweat, so Lawson must provide an occasional bath for the prisoner. Tolley viewed the man's few belongings. A couple of books. A Bible in pristine condition, probably donated by Reverend Thomas but clearly never opened. A harmonica on the shelf. A tin pitcher filled with water. A tin cup. Some clothes piled on the floor, a pair of boots lying haphazard beside them. He wore no belt or neckerchief, but his dust-free brown trousers, spotless tan shirt, clean-shaven cheeks and well-trimmed mustache proved Lawson a thoughtful jailer. More than the outlaw deserved from the man he might have tried to kill.

"You get enough food? An occasional change of clothes?"

Purvis perked up at Tolley's continued questions. "Ain't et no steak since they locked me up, but the sheriff's old lady cooks pretty good. Mostly. Don't care for those greens she's always sendin' over." He kicked the pile of clothes with his sock-covered foot. "This here's my laundry. You want to take it to her?"

Tolley shook his head. He wasn't about to become this man's errand boy. "I'm sure the sheriff has it all worked out. How about you and I get busy?" He wrote "Jud Purvis" on the top of the page. "Sheriff Lawson has informed me that you are charged with attempted murder of a law enforcement officer. What can you tell me about the situation?"

Purvis gave him a sly look. "What've you heard?"

Tolley set down his pencil and sighed, as his law professors had taught him. "That's not the way it works, Jud. You don't mind if I call you Jud, do you? You need to tell me your version of the events that brought you to this jail cell."

The man's eyes shifted and narrowed as if he'd been caught off guard. "Sure, you can call me Jud." He swiped a hand over his mouth. "Listen, I didn't try to kill nobody. Never stole nothing, neither. I was just the lookout for Hardison's gang." His voice took on a slight whine. "Hardly knew the man. Was just trying to survive until I could get an honest job. You know anybody who needs a ranch hand?"

"So when you were sentenced to prison in Kansas for bank robbery, you were *just* the lookout for the actual robbers? You didn't shoot the teller, as the banker claimed?"

Purvis's face hardened again. "Lies. All lies."

"You didn't threaten Abel Lawson when he arrested you in Kansas? Didn't break out of prison and help Dathan Hardison and Deke Smith escape from Canon City Penitentiary? Didn't try to make good on your threats against Lawson?"

Purvis slumped back on his cot and stared at the ceiling. "If I hadn't gone along with the other men, they'd've killed me."

"Your twin brother, Jed, would've killed you?"

Purvis shot to his feet and grabbed the bars, his eyes blazing. "Listen, you punk, yer just tryin' to git me to say something you can use against me."

Tolley hadn't expected the outburst, but he managed to hide his startled reaction. "Mr. Purvis, I'm trying to get to the truth so I can build your defense. If you truly were dragged into the gang, truly only the lookout, then we need to prove it. I understand how stronger gang leaders can manipulate their weaker followers. Did your brother and the other men influence you? Threaten you?" He stood and moved close to the bars, staring hard into the shorter man's eyes. "I'm trying to keep you from hanging."

Purvis seemed to wilt before his eyes. "Why? What do you get out of it? I got no money. Can't pay you."

"We'll worry about that later. Tell me your version of the day last December when Sheriff Lawson was gunned down while his posse searched for Hardison and the rest of you. The circuit judge won't arrive until mid-July. We have a month to prepare your case. If you don't want me to represent you, simply say so." Tolley moved toward the open cell door.

"No. Wait." Purvis reached a hand through the bars, palm up in a pleading gesture. "I'll tell you everything."

Tolley sat back on the canvas cot and prepared to write. Over the next hour, Purvis unfolded a story, some of it obviously untrue, of his forced involvement in Hardison's gang. When he finished, Tolley thanked the sheriff and returned to his office to make further notes. By four o'clock, he had all he needed to build a case for reasonable doubt.

Then it hit him. He'd forgotten his plan to propose to Laurie today. He wanted to get the matter settled, and if he hurried, he might have enough time to secure her agreement to their marriage before the other boarders arrived at Mrs. Foster's house.

With Mrs. Foster watching from the settee, Laurie listened to a very tentative Anna Means stumble through her scales. After several minutes, Laurie set the girl's open piano book on the music rest. Again, Anna faltered through her lesson.

"How often and how long did you practice this week?" Laurie spoke gently, hoping to encourage Anna. She remembered the girl's perpetual resistance to these lessons, but her brother and guardian, Nolan Means, insisted the young lady must develop the skill.

Anna sighed, and her shoulders drooped. "Once or twice for maybe ten minutes each." She glanced behind her to Mrs. Foster. "You both know I'd prefer to be out riding or seated on our front balcony painting the mountain views. Even Elly supports my wish to quit these lessons." Since Nolan married Elly last December, the woman had provided some much-needed feminine influence over Anna.

"I'd think five years is long enough to know whether this is what you want to do." Laurie glanced at Mrs. Foster. "What do you think?" The suspension of lessons would reduce the lady's income.

"I've hinted that Anna's talents don't lie in this direction." She grimaced and gripped her splinted broken arm. "Perhaps it's time to tell Nolan right out."

"Would you?" Anna twirled around on the stool to face Mrs. Foster. "I'll leave my music here for another student." She hurried over to kiss the older woman's wrinkled cheek. "Thank you!" She gathered her reticule and dashed from the house.

Laurie laughed as she joined Mrs. Foster on the settee. "Isn't it funny how I've worked so hard to shed my tomboy ways, and she's so eager to embrace them?"

Mrs. Foster chuckled. "Indeed, that's—"

"Laurie?" Tolley barged into the house with the

same energy with which Anna departed. Appearing in the hallway outside the open pocket doors, he skidded to an abrupt halt. "Mrs. Foster!" Disappointment flitted across his face, but he quickly covered it with a genuine smile. "How good to see you up and about."

She laughed softly. "Up but not about too much." She patted Laurie's hand. "Thank you for bringing me downstairs, but I think I've done enough for one day."

"Of course. Tolley, would you help me?"

Between the two of them, they escorted Mrs. Foster back up to her room and settled her comfortably in bed. As they exited her bedroom, Tolley checked his pocket watch and then gripped Laurie's hand.

"Will you go down to the parlor with me for a few minutes?" Smiling broadly, he seemed nearly breathless with excitement.

"All right. I'm expecting another piano student soon."

"Ah." He sighed. "That's all right. This will only take a minute."

When they reached the parlor, he directed her to the settee and sat beside her. He gazed into her eyes with an odd intensity. Was this the same man who'd avoided being alone with her for the past few days?

"What is it, Tolley? Did something wonderful happen at your office today?"

He grinned. "Not particularly, but I'm hoping something wonderful will happen right now."

"What might that be?" Perhaps he was going to offer some help around the house.

"Laurie, will you—"

"Hello, Miss Laurie." Seven-year-old Molly Starling

appeared in the hall. None of the students ever knocked on the door. "I'm ready for my lesson."

Tolley sagged against the settee back and groaned softly.

Laurie sent him a scolding glare before hurrying over to greet the child with a brief hug. "Come right in, Molly. We can get started as soon as I put my chicken pie in the oven. You go ahead and get your fingers warmed up."

She walked through the adjoining dining room and the swinging kitchen door. Before the door could close behind her, Tolley grabbed it and followed her.

She stoked the fire and added a medium-sized log. "Would you fetch me the chicken pie from the icebox?"

"Sure." He retrieved the unbaked pie she'd assembled earlier and handed it to her. "Laurie, I have to ask you an important question."

"Miss Laurie?" Molly entered the kitchen, music in hand. "May I try this book that was sitting on the piano?"

"Yes, indeed. I think you're ready for the next level." She glanced at the book. "Try the first song."

"Yes, ma'am." Molly waited while Laurie shoved the pie tin into the oven.

Tolley's posture slumped. "I'll talk to you later, Laurie."

Oh, dear. He'd been so happy when he came home. What did he want to ask her? While her curiosity was piqued, the matter would simply have to wait until later.

# Chapter Nine

Molly was the kind of student every teacher dreamed of. She practiced her lessons and played with enthusiasm, making the most of her God-given talent. After an excellent lesson, Laurie served her milk and cookies at the dining room table just as her brother Adam arrived to help Tolley work on the bathroom. Before he went upstairs, he took Laurie aside and told her this would be his sister's last lesson.

"She needs to be learning to sew so she can help Ma with her dressmaking business." The deep sorrow in Adam's eyes revealed a broken heart over this change.

Laurie touched his arm. "Adam, you can't do this. Molly has real talent. She needs to develop it."

"Yes, ma'am, it'd be real nice if she could." He shook his head. "But with the new baby, Pa still sick and Jack too young to work, she has to help Ma and me support the family. We can't be spending food and rent money on piano lessons."

Laurie thought of Tolley's insistence upon paying for Mrs. Foster's bathroom. She could do no less for her most talented pupil.

"This is too important for Molly's future, Adam, so I won't charge you for her lessons. It's a rare thing to teach such a gifted student. Please don't deny me that privilege." She wouldn't think about what would happen with Molly's lessons after she left in the fall. Could Mrs. Foster continue providing them for free when she had so little money herself?

Adam stuck his hands in his pockets and stared at the floor. "I don't think so, Miss Laurie. The folks of Esperanza have done a lot for us these past two years. Ma says it's time for us to stand on our own."

"I'll speak to your mother." Laurie lifted the young man's chin and stared into his dark brown eyes. "In the meantime, I forbid you to let your pride prevent your sister from developing her prodigious talent."

Adam stepped back, one hand over his heart. "Ma'am, I don't mean to be proud—"

"No, of course not." Laurie's eyes burned. For Molly's sake, she must win this disagreement. "And I don't mean to be hard on you. Please help me convince your mother this is the best course. Molly can continue to practice on the piano in the church fellowship hall." An idea came to mind. "If it'll make you feel better, she can help me with the dusting." She waved a hand toward the parlor. "I could also use her help in the kitchen. That would be worth more to me than your paying for her lessons. What do you think?"

Adam's eyes lit up. "Trading work for lessons? Yes, ma'am. Ma would like that just fine. Thank you." He grabbed Laurie's hand and pumped it. "When would you like for her to start?"

Laurie thought for a moment. "How about right away? She can dust the parlor and dining room." That would be enough for today. She would figure out more small tasks for Molly later.

Adam glanced toward the hallway. "I guess I'd better get upstairs and help Tolley. The bathroom won't get itself built." He took the front stairway three steps at a time.

Laurie's heart soared with joy. "Thank You, Lord," she whispered.

Tolley lay on his bed wondering why he hadn't been able to propose. Old Reverend Harris would probably say the Lord had intervened, maybe to slow Tolley down. In spite of her talk of returning to Denver, he figured Laurie really wanted to get married like her three older sisters, who'd all lassoed husbands. By offering a marriage of convenience, he'd be making it easy for her. He could see in her eyes that she liked him. Maybe to make sure about how deep her feelings went, he should consider courting her, but he needed a plan for how to go about it.

He should bring her flowers, but Esperanza didn't have a florist like the ones in Boston. Occasionally folks brought in their garden flowers for Mrs. Winsted to sell. And of course Mother grew roses at the ranch, far out of his reach. Maybe he could bring Laurie candy from the mercantile. For now, he'd have to come up with some other reason for trying to talk to her earlier.

A soft knock on his door interrupted his musings, and he felt a little kick in his chest. "Come in."

To his disappointment, Adam Starling opened the door.

"Afternoon, Tolley. I know it's late to get started,

but are we working on the bathroom today?" The boy's well-tanned face lit up with eagerness.

How could he forget? "We are indeed. The plumber will be here around five o'clock to tell us how to prepare for him to install the pipes." He clapped Adam on the shoulder. "Looks like we'll both be learning about plumbing."

"Yessir. It'll be a good skill to have. I expect more people out here will want indoor plumbing soon."

"Yep." He'd enjoyed such conveniences in Boston, but not enough to keep him away from his Colorado home. "Folks moving out West will want what they had back in the city."

Bud Cummings arrived a half hour later to evaluate the small bedroom they would transform into a bathroom. "Shouldn't be too hard. These are good drawings, Mr. Northam. You mind if I make a few changes?"

"Not at all. I was just guessing." In the past he would've basked in the man's praise, but he'd learned not to be so full of himself.

"Vent pipe there." Cummings pointed to the ceiling and then looked out the window. "Leach field out there, well away from the artesian water supply. The men are ready to dig when we give them the word." He went on to discuss the timeline for various phases of the work.

With all in agreement about the details, Cummings and Adam left. Tolley returned to his room to ponder the expenses. When he first came up with the idea for the bathroom, he'd only thought about buying the fixtures and doing the work himself. With Garrick providing those, Tolley would be able to pay the experienced workmen and buy various supplies, including a stronger hydraulic pump than the one in Mrs. Foster's kitchen. If careful, he should be able to afford everything.

Good thing he'd saved his allowance while in Boston instead of spending it on gambling and carousing with his fellow students. The one time he'd gone drinking down on the waterfront, he'd been pulled from the gutter by Reverend Harris and brought back to health at the man's Grace Seaman's Mission. The experience changed his life forever. From then on, he'd spent his free time under the good reverend's godly influence.

Why couldn't the people of Esperanza give him a chance to prove himself? Hadn't he been a part of the posse that stopped Hardison and Smith's bank robbery three years ago? Two years ago, hadn't he organized the building of the high school for Rosamond? Hadn't he helped put out the fire at the hotel? Instead, they'd remember his accidentally burning down George's haystack, his mischief at school, his cheating in the Independence Day horse race, his temper tantrum over the shooting match Garrick won. The shameful memories brought an ache to his chest. The Lord might have forgiven him, but Tolley doubted the people of Esperanza would ever be so generous.

At supper that evening, Laurie had never seen Tolley so glum and his posture so stiff. While he kept his eyes on his plate and ate slowly, the other two boarders focused all of their conversation on the smallness of the chicken pie slices, the thinness of the gravy, the thickness of the crust, the softness of the peas. When she could speak without interrupting them, Laurie inserted some cheery tidbits of news into the mix.

"Mrs. Foster enjoyed a short trip downstairs today." She smiled at Mrs. Runyan and Mr. Parsley. "She wishes you all well and hopes to be back in the kitchen by September." Laurie fervently hoped the same thing.

"Won't be soon enough for me." Mrs. Runyan, in spite of her complaints, held out her plate for a second piece of pie.

Mr. Parsley echoed a similar sentiment and presented his plate to be refilled.

As the two gobbled down their seconds, Laurie managed to catch Tolley's gaze and wrinkled her nose at him, as she used to when they were children. After staring at her for a moment, questioning her with one raised eyebrow, he seemed to understand her attempt to cheer him. He responded with a sweet grin and a wink. She couldn't catch the giggle trying to escape. It came out as more of a snicker, which brought glares from the two older boarders.

"Something amusing, Miss Eberly?" Mr. Parsley sniffed with disdain. "It is rude to laugh without sharing the cause of your mirth with the rest of us."

For one reckless moment, she wanted to shout that she and her childhood friend had just enjoyed a happy moment in the face of these boarders' grumpiness. Good sense prevailed, however. "Please accept my apology. I'm simply happy."

"Humph. Seems you've little reason to be." Mrs. Runyan must think everyone should be as unhappy as she was.

Laurie wouldn't dignify her words with a response.

Tolley kept to his plan for tending to all of his responsibilities. Early each morning, he rode Thor for an hour, though both he and his stallion wanted to run longer. Then, after taking care of the chickens and eating breakfast, he spent the rest of the morning in his office. Effie Bean had secured Homer's permission to work, but she didn't have much to do. In spite of his own discouragement, Tolley kept up a good front, telling Effie business would pick up soon. In the meantime, she kept the office spotless, and she'd changed her older dress for a dark blue one, as befitting a lawyer's receptionist, and softened her severe hairstyle.

At the boardinghouse, he remained vigilant in case the prowler returned. He considered asking Nate for one of the herding dogs to help him keep watch but consulted Laurie first.

"What do you think? I'm sure at least one of them is housebroken."

On her way upstairs with a pitcher of water, she appeared harried. "I don't think so. Mrs. Runyan has voiced her dislike for animals in the house."

"Would that include cats?" Tolley grinned at her.

She gave him a wilting frown. "Pepper stays. He can be our watch cat." She proceeded up the staircase.

Tolley shook his head. Watch cat. Whoever heard of such a thing? Other than chasing mice, cats were useless critters.

By week's end, the plumbers made significant headway on installing the inside pipes, and other workers had dug the leaching field. Each day when Doc came to check on Mrs. Foster, he brought a report about the Colonel. Seemed the old man responded to Mother's constant care. He'd wakened but still couldn't speak.

While the news encouraged Tolley, he still felt the sting of rejection. How he longed to go out to the ranch and sit down with his family for Sunday dinner. As much as it would hurt his pride, he made up his mind to ask permission of whichever brother came to church on Sunday. Turned out almost the entire clan except Mother showed up. Before the service, he met up with them in the churchyard.

"Hey, Tolley!" Nate shook his hand and clapped him on the shoulder. "I saw your shingle. Congratulations on setting up your office."

Before Tolley could suggest his oldest brother should bring him some legal business, Nate's seven-year-old daughter flung her arms around Tolley's waist.

"Uncle Tolley, when are you going to teach me to ride? You promised." She challenged him with round blue eyes.

"I don't know when, sprout." Tolley resisted the urge to tousle her neatly braided hair. Instead, he lifted her up on his hip. How could he keep his promise if he couldn't even go out to the ranch? "Let's ask your dad." He looked at Nate.

"How about this afternoon?" Nate glanced down at his wife, Susanna. "You don't mind if he gives her a riding lesson, do you?"

"Well." She drawled out the word with her Southern inflection and stared up at Tolley, worry creasing her smooth forehead. "I don't know. Which horse were you going to use?"

Tolley thought for a moment. Other than Thor, he didn't know the Four Stones horses anymore. "What do you think, Nate?"

"Gypsy's a good, steady mount." Nate's expression held no accusation. "I trust her with my daughter."

Had Nate forgotten how Tolley had put a burr under

the mare's saddle for the race two years ago? Or had he chosen Gypsy to show he had put the past behind him?

"Gypsy it is, then." Tolley hugged his niece while she hugged his neck. Her innocent acceptance of him felt mighty good. "I'll come out after dinner."

"Nonsense." Susanna smacked his arm. "You'll come out for dinner, too."

A lump formed in Tolley's throat. Was his exile about to end? "Sure. I'll let Laurie know so she won't set a place for me."

Excited about seeing Mother, seeing home, Tolley couldn't concentrate on the sermon. Something about God's grace, Reverend Thomas's favorite topic. Reverend Harris's, too. While in Boston, Tolley tried to grasp the idea that the Lord forgave him, but when the Christian people he knew here in Esperanza held his past against him, it made it hard to believe. Even now, as he sat in the pew, several folks gave him sidelong glances without greeting him. He tried to give each a smile and friendly nod, but often they frowned and turned away before he could. Or so it seemed.

Finally, the service ended with the popular hymn "Amazing Grace." As the congregation filed out of their pews or clustered with friends to visit, Tolley made his way to the front. After Laurie played the final chord of her exit hymn, she gathered her music and gave him an expectant smile. His heart jumped. My, what a pretty lady. A bit prickly sometimes, but overall real sweet. He remembered his plan to start courting her today, but first things first.

"Just wanted to let you know I'm going out to the ranch for dinner, so don't—"

"Oh, Tolley." She grasped his hand, and her eyes

reddened. "I'm so glad. I'll be praying for a wonder-ful visit. Give my best to your folks."

Her rush of emotion caught him off guard, and he cleared his throat. "Thanks."

Yet as he rode Thor southward toward his fami-ly's ranch, he pondered her remarks and the emotions they'd caused. She truly did care for him, which bode well for his courting her.

The fine weather also seemed to bode well for a good visit with his family. The sun shone brightly, and the brilliant blue summer sky boasted a few puffy white clouds. Blue-gray cranes stuck their long beaks into the roadside stream fishing for frogs, red-winged blackbirds chased insects that flitted over the marshy landscape and an occasional rabbit scampered about on drier ground seeking edible vegetation for its Sun-day dinner. In the distance off to the right, Tolley saw the upper level of George Eberly's red barn and the brown roof of his house. Less than a mile down the road on the left, the front gate to Four Stones Ranch came into view.

As he turned down Four Stones Lane, a war erupted inside him. How he loved this beautiful piece of land where his family had settled after the War. Although just five years old, he'd helped to build every struc-ture, including the white two-story house now gleam-ing in the sunlight. He longed to be out here working the ranch alongside his brothers instead of setting up a useless law office where no one would seek his services and he had only one outlaw client to defend.

Four Stones Ranch was his very life, yet against that love and conviction came the assault of his all-too-familiar shame from being rejected by his father.

Would he be fully welcomed back into the family only if the Colonel died, an idea he abhorred? If so, maybe he should continue to stay away. Should turn Thor around and head back to town.

Too bad he hadn't thought of it sooner, for as soon as he reached the kitchen yard, Lizzie and her brother, four-year-old Natty, ran from the house to greet him. Too late to escape.

"Uncle Tolley!" Lizzie barely gave him a chance to dismount and tie Thor's reins to the hitching post before she sprang into his arms, Natty right behind her.

"Unka Dolly," Natty cried. Tolley would have to work with the boy on pronouncing his name.

"Hey there, partners." He shook away his self-pity, tucked a child under each arm and jogged toward the back door. "I'm starving. Let's go eat."

Both children squealed with delight. They were met in the mudroom by Rand's eldest, three-year-old Randy, who jumped up and down in borrowed excitement, although he hadn't seen Tolley since his first year of life.

Tolley knelt and gathered all three children in his arms. "What a fine bunch of cowboys—" he looked at Lizzie "—and a pretty little cowgirl." How blessed his brothers were to have these precious children. One day, he'd like a half dozen of his own.

"Tolley." Mother stood in the kitchen doorway, arms extended. Behind her, Rosamond, Susanna and Marybeth waved and continued their dinner preparations.

"Hello, Mother." He disengaged from the children and stood to embrace her.

She rested her head on his chest and held him tightly.

She'd lost weight, and dark half-moons under her eyes revealed her weariness.

"How are you?" He held her back and brushed a hand over her cheek.

"As well as can be expected." She glanced at her grandchildren. "You three run along. I need to speak to your uncle." She returned her gaze to Tolley. "How are you? I understand you've already set up your law office."

"Yep." He shrugged, unwilling to talk about it when a more important question needed to be answered. "How's the Colonel? Doc said he woke up, so I'd like to see him."

She emitted a long sigh. "Only somewhat awake. He doesn't seem truly aware of anything. He—" her voice broke, and she cleared her throat "—he does seem to enjoy it when I read the Bible to him."

"Sounds promising." Tolley hugged her close and kissed the top of her head.

"Come sit with me in the ballroom while the girls fix dinner." She led him through the back hallway to the large room the Colonel built seven years ago so Mother could entertain as she had in their large home back East.

They sat on a green brocade settee and clasped hands.

"Son, this is going to sound harsh, but I don't think you should see your father yet." She stared away toward the large window on the eastern side of the room. "Doc has urged us not to trouble him with anything that might upset him and cause a relapse." Tears formed in her eyes. "I haven't said this to anyone else, and I won't. It breaks my heart to tell you because I'd never want to hurt you, my dear son. But I must think of my husband. I didn't tell him about your letter saying you were coming home because I didn't want him to wire you not to come. So I told him the night before you were to arrive that you were on your way. That's the night his stroke happened."

A giant weight seemed to drop on his chest, and Tolley suddenly couldn't breathe. So *he* had caused the Colonel's stroke. Mother didn't notice his distress, for she went on.

"Mind you, when I told him, he didn't say anything. Nothing at all. He clammed up and went to the barn to do his evening chores. You know how he is when he has to think over a matter. Later Seamus came to the house and said your father had collapsed. We brought him up to the house and sent for Doc. You know the rest."

Tolley couldn't bear the news, nor could he bear to hurt Mother. Nonetheless, he'd clearly made a mistake in coming back to Esperanza. "Um, I'm—I'm gonna leave now." He kissed her cheek and then hurried from the room before he broke down. He rushed past his sister and sisters-in-law, who bustled about the kitchen, and dashed out the door.

Before he could mount Thor, Lizzie tore out of the house, her sweet pink face covered with tears.

"Uncle Tolley, you can't leave. You promised…"

Her plaintive cry wrenched his heart, and he somehow managed to subdue his anguish.

"That's right, I did." He reached out to take her hand. "So let's get started." He'd give her a quick lesson before dinner. Then he could send her into the house and slip away unnoticed.

Together they crossed the barnyard and entered the

barn. If Gypsy held any resentment toward Tolley, she didn't let on.

Lizzie took her lessons in stride. Standing on an overturned bucket, she brushed Gypsy and helped Tolley put on her blanket and saddle. He taught her how to sit, how to hold the reins, how to use her knees to give directions, how to take care of the animal after the ride. The plucky little gal listened carefully to everything he said, and her eyes sparkled with happiness the entire time. She showed all the grit and natural ability with horses every Northam possessed.

They were emerging from the barn when Susanna came out to announce dinner.

"Oh, my." She looked at her daughter with mild vexation. "You'll have to clean up before you can eat. You, too, Tolley."

"Sure. I'll be—" No, he wouldn't be "right behind" them. Once Susanna and Lizzie entered the back door, he mounted Thor and headed back to town. He had no idea how he'd keep his promise to Lizzie about further riding lessons, but he wouldn't come back to Four Stones again, not with the Colonel's illness being his fault.

He should've stayed in Boston. Should've sought a position in a law firm there. If not for his commitments to finish Mrs. Foster's bathroom and defend Jud Purvis, he'd slip out of town today and never look back.

# Chapter Ten

As Laurie finished the dinner dishes, she heard the front door open and close. The boarders and Mrs. Foster were taking their Sunday-afternoon naps, and surely Tolley wouldn't be home yet. She opened the hall door in time to see him trudging up the stairs, shoulders slumped.

"Tolley?" She entered the hall. No matter what the other two boarders might say if they saw them talking, she'd find out what happened to him.

He stopped his ascent but didn't look her way. "You need something?"

Any other time, his sullen tone would've annoyed her. He seemed eager to go to his room, so she needed to think fast. "Yes. Can you come help me?" She gave him her sweetest smile, although she had no idea what she'd ask him to do for her.

He followed her into the parlor.

"Sit." She pointed to the settee. Might as well get straight to the point.

He stuck his hands into his pockets and rolled his head with annoyance. "Just let me go."

"No. Sit. Talk."

He dropped his muscular body onto the settee. "What do you want me to say?"

She sat beside him and touched his arm. "What happened at the ranch?"

His stomach growled loudly, and he gave her a sheepish grin. "For one thing, I didn't get dinner."

"Easily remedied. Go sit at the dining room table. I'll give you something to eat."

She made sure he obeyed, however reluctantly, and then hurried out to the kitchen, returning in less than five minutes with a plateful of leftover roast beef and vegetables. She sat adjacent to him, gratified to watch him devour the food. Ma always said the way to a man's heart was through his stomach... Wait. She didn't want his heart, just wanted to be his good friend.

When he'd eaten half of his dinner, she repeated her question. "So, what happened?"

He shrugged. "It's best for me not to go out there."

"Are you sure? I mean, Doc says the Colonel appeared to be waking up and—"

"Leave it alone, Laurie." His sorrowful tone and the sadness in his eyes broke her heart.

"Your brothers and Rosamond are very happy you're back home. I've seen it these past two Sundays." When he stared down at his plate, she kicked his foot under the table. "You'd be surprised by what I can see while seated at the organ."

When he didn't respond, didn't even smile, she decided on another approach. "Of course, Micah sees a lot from the pulpit, too, and he has the best insights of anybody in town. Maybe he could...help you." She dearly wanted to be the one to help him, but if she couldn't, her minister brother-in-law was her second choice.

Now he gave her a sad little grin. "You know, you're right. I'll go over there now and see if he's busy." He stood and tossed his napkin on the table. "Thanks, Laurie. You're a real pal."

Pal? Not the way to address a girl he planned to start courting, even if it was for a marriage of convenience. He couldn't think about it too much right now because of the grief weighing on his heart. But he did appreciate her attempts to cheer him up.

For now, he wished he'd visited Reverend Thomas on a neighborly basis before today. He couldn't remember ever having a single serious conversation with the man. Seemed sort of disrespectful to approach him about his pathetic life without first establishing a friendship. But if he didn't get this weight off his chest, he'd suffocate.

Grace answered his knock on the parsonage door. "Hey, Tolley. Come on in. Good to see you. Have a seat." She waved him into the parlor. "What brings you out on a Sunday afternoon when most everybody else is home taking a Sunday nap?"

Laurie's next-older sister seemed a whole heap happier these days. Growing up, she'd often hung her head because, being so tall, she'd been teased by the fellas at school, including him. Shame filled him over that cruel behavior, but Grace seemed to have forgotten all about it, if her friendly greeting was any indication. Besides, Reverend Thomas didn't mind how tall she was. The preacher's love for his bride always radiated from his gray eyes.

"Afternoon, Grace." Tolley sat in the chair she'd indicated, and she sat on the settee next to it. "Is the reverend here?"

She touched his arm. "Is everything all right? Is the Colonel—"

Tolley wrestled his emotions again. "He's doing better." No need to say he didn't know firsthand. "Doesn't anybody come around for a visit unless there's a problem?"

His grin felt a little stiff, but she didn't seem to notice. Instead, she laughed.

"I'll call Micah. He's working on his hobby, but he never minds having a visitor." She rose and left the room.

In less than a minute, the minister entered the room, hand extended. "Afternoon, Tolley. It's good to see you."

Tolley stood and shook his hand, and they went through the usual friendly banter. Then Reverend Thomas studied Tolley with an insightful gaze reminiscent of Reverend Harris's. "What can I do for you?"

Sudden emotion closed Tolley's throat. He coughed into his fist. "Well…" No other words would come.

"Tell you what." The minister gripped his shoulder. "Let's go over to my office. Grace, would you please bring us coffee and some of that wonderful lemon pie?"

They walked across the parsonage's backyard and through the church's back door to the minister's office. Instead of sitting at his large oak desk, the pastor sat in a chair beside Tolley. The simple gesture made talking to him much easier than expected. While he'd never been one to confide in anyone, his two-year friendship with Reverend Harris taught him the right confidant could help a man solve his problems or at least help him find a measure of peace.

Grace brought the refreshments and set them on the desk. She gave the preacher a kiss on the cheek, waved to Tolley and left them alone. As good as the lemon pie looked, Tolley couldn't eat a bite after Laurie's delicious roast beef dinner. Those Eberly girls sure could cook. He did take a sip of the coffee the minister poured for him.

"Reverend, I need you to pray for me. With me, I mean." He didn't need to start at the beginning of his sad story because the reverend knew about most of it. Instead, he spoke of his father's constant disapproval through the years, how Tolley finally tried to straighten out his life while in Boston only to return home and find the Colonel struck down. Repeating what Mother had said proved hardest, that news of Tolley's imminent homecoming caused the stroke. While his heart wanted to cry out in anguish, he ended his tale on a whispered question. "Am I so evil, so unacceptable, that my return nearly killed my father?"

Through it all, Reverend Thomas's kindly, interested expression never wavered, never showed a whit of accusation. When Tolley finished, they sat in silence for several minutes.

"I think many of us have problems of one kind or another with our fathers. I confess I did." The reverend punctuated his words with a mirthless chuckle. "Yours seems a bit more complicated than most."

"You had problems with your father?" Tolley couldn't imagine this agreeable, godly man having difficulties with anyone.

"I did. He wanted me to go into politics...his brand

of politics. I wanted to preach the gospel and minister to people seeking the Lord. The only way to keep
peace between us was for me to put some physical
distance between us. That's why I came out here. I
learned an important lesson from it. We can't change
other people. We can only change ourselves, and then
only with God's help."

Not the answer Tolley hoped for. "I have changed,
and I've tried to stay close to the Lord so He can guide
me. But is it wrong for me to still want the Colonel's approval? I mean, I did what he wanted. I went to college,
earned good grades, became a lawyer." He wouldn't
mention his plan to marry Laurie for further approval.
"What more can I do?"

Reverend Thomas sat quiet for a moment. "It's not
about *doing*. God's love for and acceptance of us aren't
conditional. They're freely given. We don't have to do
anything to earn them." He turned to Tolley, his tone
conversational. "So what we *do* isn't as important as
what we *are*. God wants to us to be Christlike, but
that's His work, not ours. Our work, for lack of a better word, is to seek His face through the scriptures and
prayer, learn who He is, what his attributes are and then
ask Him to fill us with His character."

Tolley fought the urge to say, *Yes, but I'm already
doing that.* He wasn't really. Hadn't been since he arrived home and found out about the Colonel's stroke.

They bowed their heads and, as each prayed for
the situation, the weight on Tolley's chest lifted, and
a small measure of joy and peace entered his heart.

On his way back to the boardinghouse, he rumi-
nated on the minister's soothing ways. He'd spoken
to Tolley as if they were friends, equal in every way.

Tolley came away from the meeting feeling well liked, well respected.

Yet in the back of his mind, he couldn't help but wish for, pray for the day when his father would like him and respect him as an equal in that same way.

Tolley poked his head through the kitchen door and smiled. "I'm back."

Her hands floury with biscuit dough, Laurie returned a smile. "Hey, there." From the spark in his eyes, she could tell Micah had encouraged him, as she knew he would. The people of Esperanza were blessed to have her brother-in-law for their minister. Although she'd prayed their meeting would go well, she wouldn't intrude by asking Tolley about it.

"Say—" he entered the kitchen and helped himself to a cookie from the platter on the table "—would you like to go out for a buggy ride?"

"I really shouldn't." Even on a Sunday afternoon, she had plenty of work to do. She brushed a stray strand of hair from her forehead with the back of her hand. "Don't eat any more of those cookies. They're for tonight's dessert."

"Come with me, Laurie. It's a beautiful day." He gave her that devastating smile she would miss when she returned to Denver, and her silly heart did a little skip.

"Well…" She rolled out the dough and cut it with an upside-down glass, placing the round shapes on a cookie sheet. "These have to bake first."

"Great. I'll go over to the livery stable and fetch the buggy. Be back in twenty minutes."

"But—" Although on Sunday evening everyone

made their own sandwiches of leftover roast beef and cold biscuits, she still felt responsible for managing the meal so everyone got a fair share. Still, she hadn't been away from the boardinghouse except for church for over a week, so maybe a buggy ride would do her good.

While the biscuits baked, she checked on Mrs. Foster, who appeared especially glad to see her.

"My dear," the lady said, "do you suppose you could help me get dressed and take me down to the front porch? I'd love some fresh air on this fine summer day."

The request sent a tiny thread of disappointment through her. Taking care of Mrs. Foster right now meant she must forgo her own outing with Tolley. She quickly dismissed the idea as selfish. "Of course. Now that you're getting better, I should've asked if you wanted a change of scenery. I'll be right back after I take the biscuits from the oven."

She moved the cookie sheet from the oven to the pie safe to cool and returned upstairs.

"Let's get you dressed." She selected Mrs. Foster's Sunday-go-to-meeting gown from the mahogany wardrobe and helped her put on all the necessary underpinnings. "Let me fix your hair." The task accomplished, she helped the widow from her room and down the front stairs.

As she'd expected, Tolley had returned with the buggy and waited on the front porch. When they emerged, disappointment crossed his face but quickly disappeared.

"Say, would you two lovely ladies do me the honor of accompanying me on a buggy ride?" To his credit, he didn't miss a beat in expanding his original invitation.

"A buggy ride?" Mrs. Foster's voice held a child-like wonder. "It's been so long since I took a Sunday afternoon drive." Tears formed in her eyes, and she gave Tolley an adoring smile. "Not since Major Foster passed away."

Tolley returned a crooked grin, as he did when deeply moved. Laurie felt the same way. The major, one of the three founders of Esperanza, along with her pa and the Colonel, died six years ago. Why hadn't anyone, herself included, thought to give his widow an outing?

"I'll get our bonnets." Laurie dashed back into the house and fetched bonnets, parasols and gloves, returning as Tolley lifted Mrs. Foster into the buggy.

The delight on the widow's face banished Laurie's disappointment that she and Tolley wouldn't be alone. She traded a look with him. From the twinkle in his eyes, she could see he felt the same way.

Two people fit in the padded leather driver's bench and one person in the small front-facing jump seat behind it. Tolley helped Laurie into the back and took his place beside Mrs. Foster. Then they were off, headed toward Main Street.

"Look at those mountains." Mrs. Foster gazed off toward the distant Sangre de Cristo Range in the east. "Here it is June, and Mount Blanca still has snow on its summit." She ducked out from under the buggy's canopy and stared upward. "Look at that blue sky. Major Foster used to say the San Luis Valley has the bluest sky in the world."

"I agree." Tolley glanced over his shoulder and winked at Laurie. "What do you think, Laurie? Is our San Luis Valley sky bluer than Denver's?"

Her heart skipped a beat…again. Why were his

winks and smiles causing such foolish reactions? "Definitely bluer than Denver's." Hardly a reason to stay here.

As they drove west out of town, Mrs. Foster continued to remark about the scenery, the cattle in the field, the San Juan Mountains ahead of them, the rapid summer flow of the Rio Grande, the flight of birds overhead. The dear lady seemed to be making up for her usual quietness.

Tolley stoked her commentary with questions about the major and the early days of the community, clearly interested in her perspective. Laurie watched in wonder from the jump seat. My, how he'd changed from a self-centered boy to a generous, kindhearted man. If she didn't have an important career waiting for her in Denver, she could easily see falling in love with him.

No, she mustn't think that. Marrying Tolley would mean abandoning all of her long-held dreams. She couldn't. They meant far too much to her. She loved her home, but like her second-oldest sister, Beryl, who'd married an Englishman and now lived across the ocean, Laurie wanted something beyond the quaint and quiet ways of people in the San Luis Valley.

Late in the afternoon and a few miles down the road, Mrs. Foster confessed to weariness, so Tolley turned the horse back toward town. Soon they drove past the church, and the lady eyed the building longingly.

"How I miss hearing Reverend Thomas's fine sermons. I'm so grateful for his daily visits."

"We miss hearing you play the organ," Laurie said. "But here you are, out for a buggy ride. No doubt you'll be ready to attend services next Sunday."

Laurie understood how Mrs. Foster felt about the

church. She would miss her home congregation when she returned to Denver. The church she'd attended there had a more formal atmosphere, and many congregants seemed more concerned about fashion than faith. More concerned that no one usurped their pew. The pastor spoke from an elevated pulpit, appropriate for the way he spoke down to his congregation as though he loved to impart his superior wisdom to them. Very different from Micah's friendly sermon delivery. Yet Laurie had enjoyed singing in the choir and playing piano for a children's Sunday school class. If she weren't leaving in September, she might consider organizing a choir right here. For a small town, Esperanza boasted many fine singers.

Oh, bother. Why couldn't she stop thinking of the good things about her hometown? How foolish it would be to turn down the position at the conservatory when she'd worked so hard to earn it. She must return to Denver, and that was that. She must not let family and church hold her here, no matter how much she loved them.

Even more important, she must reject Tolley's winsome ways, a little hard to do when he kept doing such generous things for others and smiling at her so charmingly. To defend herself from those appealing smiles, maybe she should step back from their friendship. Seeing Micah had helped Tolley overcome whatever bothered him, maybe she could begin to look out for herself. She wouldn't turn a cold shoulder to him, but she could make herself a little bit less likeable.

And she knew exactly how to do it.

## Chapter Eleven

Tolley appreciated Laurie's fine job of tending the house and cooking and teaching piano lessons. Those jobs should have kept her too busy to poke her nose into his construction of the bathroom. But all that week, to his annoyance, she still managed to inspect the room several times a day and make comments and suggestions, usually contrary to his decisions. She particularly bossed Adam, who always took her orders with good humor.

Viewing the pipes sticking up from the floor where the plumbers installed them, she said, "I thought I told you to put the bathtub over there." She glared at Adam, who wiped dust from a section of the freshly sanded floor in preparation for laying tiles, and pointed to the spot nearer the stove. "Now Mrs. Foster will have to carry the hot water across the room."

"Yes, ma'am." Adam gave her an apologetic smile. "I'm sorry."

"But surely you can change it."

"As you can see, the pipes are already in." Tolley tried to keep the irritation from his voice. "Can't change them now."

"Oh, you!" She posted her fists at her waist, looking mighty pretty in spite of her protest. "You did that on purpose."

Was she trying to start an argument? She'd been a mite grumpy since their buggy ride last Sunday, though Tolley couldn't imagine why. He couldn't seem to do anything right, so he'd postponed thoughts of courting her. She'd even stopped trading companionable looks with him over the supper table when the other boarders made their annoying complaints.

"The plumbers did it this way," he said, "because it means only one drain pipe is needed for all three fixtures. And being deeper inside the house, it means they won't freeze in winter."

"Oh." She blinked those big blue eyes at him.

Something inside his chest kicked like an unbroken colt. Sure, she was being awful prickly, but she could also be real sweet when she wanted to be.

Laurie looked around, apparently trying to find something else to complain about. "I do wish we could have a gas heater attached to the tub. Some Denver hotels have them."

"Maybe one day," Adam said, "if Esperanza brings in gas for the whole town."

"Or electricity." Tolley had read about electrical plants being built in some cities.

"Now what about the windows?" Laurie continued her perusal of the room. "Do you plan to seal them up or leave them so they can be opened for airing?"

Tolley glanced at Adam, who appeared to be stifling a grin.

"We're leaving them…for now." Tolley counted out the tiles for the first row under the north window. "When winter comes, we can seal out the cold same as we do in any other room."

"Oh," she repeated as she dropped her hands from her waist. "Very well." She spun on her heel and marched out of the room.

Adam chuckled. "Glad that's over."

"Whew." Tolley also laughed, then felt a tad bit disloyal. "She's not so bad, just opinionated. You seem to get along with her."

"A handyman shouldn't argue with a customer." He shrugged. "Besides, if I see a plan won't work, I do it the right way and folks are usually pleased."

Tolley grunted his agreement. Adam's easygoing acceptance of Laurie's bossiness helped him feel better about it. Adam probably put up with a great deal of nonsense from folks, but his attitude was always cheerful.

"How's your law business going?" Adam spread a patch of glue, then reached for a small, six-sided white tile and placed it snugly in the corner, adding tiny wooden pegs as spacers around it.

Tolley counted out more tiles. "I have one client, Jud Purvis." Several people had already made known their disapproval when Tolley met them on the street, but Adam merely nodded as he worked.

He was glad to work with someone who didn't condemn him. Maybe he should pay a visit to the Starling family to see if they needed anything. He didn't have much available money, what with paying Adam and the plumbers. But he might be able to help in some other way.

"How's your pa doing?" Adam paused in his work. "I meant to ask first thing today."

As always, Tolley repeated what Doc told him that morning. "Still taking only broth. Still not able to talk." Doc also said the Colonel had begun to focus his eyes on Mother's movements around the room, but Tolley's throat closed on the words.

"Sorry to hear it." Adam shook his head. "I have a lot of respect for the Colonel."

Tolley could only nod. Everyone respected the Colonel. If he were looking in from the outside, he would, too. But he had a hard time thinking well of a father who rejected his son, a man who became sick when he learned that son planned to return home after being away for two years. Tolley considered it the ultimate rejection. Perhaps even hatred.

He shook off the thoughts. After his talk with Reverend Thomas, he'd promised himself he wouldn't dwell on the Colonel's rejection, a difficult promise to keep. Maybe he should turn his attention to helping out Adam's family.

"How's your father?" Tolley set some tiles on the floor beside Adam.

"He has his good days and bad days." Adam shifted his shoulder, maybe to hide his face…and emotions. After a few minutes, he coughed softly. "Sort of sad how we both have pas who are laid up."

"Uh-huh." Tolley grunted. "I'll pray for your father."

Adam shot him a sad smile. "I'll pray for yours."

What an odd thing to bond over, yet Tolley felt closer to Adam right now than he did to his own brothers.

On Friday afternoon, after another day with no new clients at the law office, he joined Adam in laying the flooring. The process was slow because the tiles were barely an inch across, like tiny mosaic pieces. Adam clearly knew how to do it, so Tolley did the legwork, handing him tiles and spacer pegs, making sure the glue didn't dry out, fetching lemonade and cookies from Laurie when they needed a break.

"I told my pa about that fella Purvis." Adam stopped working and looked at Tolley. "We don't generally bring up bad news to Pa, but he always asks me about my day. I told him you were representing the prisoner accused of shooting the sheriff. When I mentioned Purvis, Pa just about jumped out of bed."

A sick feeling crept into Tolley's belly. "Doesn't sound good. Is he all right?"

"Yeah." Adam went back to work, apparently finished with the topic.

"Does he know the man?"

"Pa said when the gang beat him and stole the railroad payroll, one of the men said something like, 'Be sure he's dead, Purvis.'" Adam shrugged. "I suppose a lot of people could have that name."

"I suppose." Tolley shook off the dread trying to take hold of him. He'd need to talk with Bob Starling about this matter. "Say, I'd better head over to the bank before it closes. I'll bring your pay over after supper."

Instead of withdrawing the cash before he came home for lunch, he'd waited until midafternoon so he'd have an excuse for visiting the Starling home in the evening. While he took Adam's weekly pay to him, he'd see if he could do anything for the family.

After supper, he walked the three blocks to the small house the Starlings rented. As he drew close, he could hear the laughter of children and the happy squeal of a baby. He paused at the front door, enjoying the pleasant family sounds. A deep longing welled up inside of him. Would he ever know such happiness? Finally, he knocked. Instead of the merry noise ceasing, it crescendoed, accompanied by the percussive sound of running feet.

The door opened with a bang, and Molly and her little brother, Jack, greeted him, each grabbing a hand and dragging him into the living room. "Comp'ny, comp'ny," they cried gleefully.

"Do come in, Mr. Northam." Mrs. Starling sat in an overstuffed chair, her baby daughter on her lap. "Adam, fetch some coffee for Mr. Northam."

"Please don't trouble yourselves." Tolley waved Adam back to his chair beside his mother.

"Have a seat." Adam picked up the book he'd set down. It appeared to be a volume of Mother Goose stories. "Just reading to these little pests."

Molly and Jack giggled in protest.

"Don't let me stop you." Tolley sat and gathered his young escorts onto his lap. My, it felt good when they leaned trustingly into his embrace. What a truly happy home. He swallowed down the bothersome emotions rising in his chest and throat. Once upon a time, his own family enjoyed such laughter and love. Had he caused the end of their happiness?

Without a hint of self-consciousness, Adam finished the last few pages of "Jack the Giant Killer," making vocal sounds for everything from rolling wagons to honking geese to a giant ogress, while the little ones giggled. Mrs. Starling then read a Psalm from her Bible, and they all shared a bedtime prayer.

While Adam and his mother put the children to bed,

Tolley waited in the parlor, envisioning such a scene for Laurie and him. Laurie had a way with children, so he knew she'd be a good mother. Would he be a good father? Would a man who'd been rejected by his own father even know how to be a good father himself?

Adam returned, his face expectant. "I'm grateful to you for hiring me, Tolley. It's enjoyable work, and we sure can use the pay."

"Don't know what I'd do without you. You do most of the work." Rising from the chair, Tolley fished the folded bills from his pocket and handed them to Adam. "Do you think your pa is up to talking to me this evening?"

"Is something wrong?" Mrs. Starling entered the room, her face now lined with worry.

"No, ma'am." Tolley gave her an easy grin. "I want to ask him about Jud Purvis."

While Adam slipped out of the room, her expression tightened. "Adam already spoke to him. If it turns out he's the same man who tried to murder my husband, Bob will leave his sickbed to testify against him."

"Hmm." Tolley tried to appear calm, but his insides churned.

Adam returned and beckoned to Tolley. "My pa will see you."

Mrs. Starling gave him a reluctant nod, and Tolley followed Adam into the dimly lit back room where Bob Starling lay on an iron-frame bed. The man had a feeble handshake, but he made the effort, which caused an ache deep inside Tolley. If only he could touch his own father's hand that way.

"My family never tells me anything." Chuckling weakly, Bob gazed at Adam with unfettered love.

How Tolley longed for such a look from the Colonel. The Starlings didn't own much, but he'd trade his financial security for the same kind of love so evident between this father and son.

"We do, too." Adam sat on the edge of the bed and nudged Bob's shoulder. "I told you they caught the man who shot the sheriff."

"You didn't tell me his name." Bob coughed, a harsh sound from deep inside that brought a frown to Adam's face. When he could talk again, he spoke to Tolley. "When they attacked me, I only heard his last name. First name might not be Jud."

While his insides continued to tumble around, Tolley pasted on his lawyer face. "Maybe this will help." He pulled a wanted poster from inside his jacket and handed it to Bob.

He studied the page and then let out a long sigh. "That's him, all right. A man doesn't forget the face of the person who's tried to kill him."

"Very well." Tolley took the poster in hand. "Thank you."

"You still gonna defend him?" Adam's eyes held no accusation, only sadness.

Although he wanted to say no, Tolley recalled his training. He mustn't make promises when he might be forced to change his mind later. "Remains to be seen."

He took his leave of the Starlings and headed home. Tomorrow he'd confront Purvis with the news he had a witness to a past attempted murder. With a history of violent attacks with deadly intent, he'd have a hard time proving he didn't shoot Sheriff Lawson, the man he'd threatened to kill for putting him in prison. At the least, he was an accomplice of whoever did the deed.

The next morning after breakfast, he went to the kitchen to fetch the full egg basket he'd collected earlier. "Laurie, these eggs aren't wiped. Mrs. Winsted has a hard time selling them when they're covered with—"

"Well, then—" standing at the sink and up to her elbows in suds, she withdrew one soapy hand, snatched up a tea towel and threw it at him "—you clean them."

Tired of her crossness and dreading his necessary talk with Purvis, he tossed it right back. "Look, I don't mind gathering the eggs and feeding the chickens, but this is women's work."

She jammed her wet fists to her waist in her feisty way and scowled at him. "Don't be ridiculous. We both must do anything and everything necessary to help Mrs. Foster." She tossed the towel back to him. "As you can see, I'm busy. You do it."

Tolley stared at her for only a few seconds before taking on the task of gently cleaning the sticky straw and other debris from the fragile eggs. Jumping frogs' legs, this woman could be irritating. If he wasn't careful, she'd have him cooking meals and cleaning house.

After delivering the eggs to Mrs. Winsted, he stomped across the street to the sheriff's office, dodging wagons and pedestrians in town for their weekly shopping. He wasn't in the best mood for confronting his client with his new and damaging information, so he paused at the door to calm himself. Inside, he found the inner door open and Deputy Justice Gareau seated outside the cell playing checkers with the prisoner through the bars.

Gareau jumped three of Purvis's checkers and reached the opposite side of the board. "Crown me."

Purvis briefly scowled. Catching sight of Tolley

through the open door, he jumped to his feet, knocking over the board and scattering checkers—a clever ploy by a man clearly in danger of losing the game. "Northam! You gonna get me outta here?"

Ignoring him, Tolley said, "Morning, Deputy." He removed his hat and left it on a peg before entering the cell area.

"Morning, Tolley." Gareau retrieved the checkers within his reach and put them in a small cotton bag. "Hand me those," he ordered Purvis, pointing to the game pieces on the cell floor. The outlaw scowled again but obeyed. "What can I do for you?" Gareau reached out to Tolley, and they shook hands.

Laurie had told him that Justice, a former Texas Ranger, had been hired by banker Nolan Means as a bodyguard last year when Hardison's gang terrorized the town. After Hardison was shot and his partner died, Nolan no longer needed a bodyguard. Then Grace married the reverend, and Justice took Grace's place as the town deputy. A tall, broad-shouldered man of somewhere between twenty-five and thirty years, with dark blond hair and piercing gray eyes, the deputy exuded an air of uprightness and authority.

Tolley gave the man an easy smile. "If you don't mind, I'd like to speak to my client."

"Sure thing." Justice gathered the checkerboard and checkers. "I'll be right outside the door if you need anything." He gave Purvis a dark, meaningful look.

Purvis stiffened, but Tolley could see he understood Justice wouldn't allow any guff.

Once the door closed between the rooms, Tolley sat in the chair the deputy vacated. "Sit down, Purvis."

Perhaps still under the lawman's influence, the outlaw did as he was told. "What've you got for me?" He crossed his arms over his chest.

"I won't waste time. There's a man in town who says you and your gang robbed and beat him and left him for dead."

A sly look briefly crossed Purvis's face, quickly replaced by a fabricated confusion. "Can't imagine who that could be. I ain't never left nobody for dead."

Clever man. From his present demeanor, one would think him the very image of innocence.

"He got a good look at you, Purvis, so when I showed him this—" he retrieved the wanted poster from his jacket's inside pocket and unfolded it "—he said you're the man."

"Oh, no. Not again." Purvis put his face in his hands and said a curse word. He looked up at Tolley and lifted his hands in a gesture of appeal. "You know I've got a twin brother, don't you? He's caused me trouble since we was tadpoles. If that man saw this face, it was Jed's, not mine."

Schooling his features into a bland expression, Tolley continued to study Purvis. He hadn't considered the possibility the other brother had beaten Bob Starling. Then again, maybe brotherly love went only so far when it came to being hanged. Jud might gladly give up Jed to save his own neck. Tolley didn't know how far he'd be willing to go for his own brothers, but he'd never once in his life tried to shift the blame for his mischief onto either Nate or Rand.

"So what did Jed steal from this man?" Purvis sounded concerned. "Money? Gold? A woman?"

Bile rose up in Tolley's throat over Purvis's attempt to rile him. He'd keep his answer short and true. "Railroad payroll. Over three years ago down near Antonito."

"Nope." Purvis clicked his tongue and shook his head. "Couldn't be me. I never stole no train payroll. Besides, three years ago, I was in prison in Kansas. You can check the facts, and you'll find I ain't lyin'."

"I will." Tolley couldn't bear to breathe the same air as Purvis, but on the slim possibility the outlaw had told the truth, he had the obligation to prove it. He stood and headed toward the door.

"Wait." Purvis's voice sounded plaintive, and he reached a hand through the bars in supplication. "Can't you get me out of here until the trial? I'm going crazy in here with nothing to do."

Tolley pointed to the unopened Bible on his shelf. "There's the Good Book. Read it. It'll do you some good." As he opened the door and left the cell area, Purvis's muttered curses followed him.

Laurie needed Tolley's help too much to continue her campaign to distance herself from him. She had the responsibility of arranging the entertainment for the Independence Day celebration, and she needed him to do some heavy lifting, such as moving the piano from the church's reception hall to the bandstand in the park.

Why lie to herself? In truth, she couldn't bear to see the sadness filling Tolley's eyes when he thought no one was looking. After promising to be his friend, she'd grown fearful of becoming more. To protect her own interests, her own future, she'd selfishly chosen a ruse more characteristic of one of her Denver society friends than the good people of Esperanza, where she'd grown up. How could she change course? An idea immediately came to mind.

On Sunday morning before breakfast, she tapped on his bedroom door. When he answered, his surprise was evident in his crooked grin and doubtful expression. Already dressed for church, he stepped into the hallway and closed the door behind him.

"Morning, Laurie. What can I do for you?"

How like the new Tolley, eager to help whenever, wherever needed. At his beguiling smile, Laurie's heart did a familiar little hop, and she almost forgot her own question. Somehow she shook off her flurry of emotions.

"Mrs. Foster would like to attend church this morning. Since I go over early, do you think you could accompany her?"

Tolley brightened. "Sure thing. I'll be happy to."

"Thank you." She patted his arm, feeling the strength beneath his jacket sleeve. "I'll get her ready right after breakfast."

Later, as people began to arrive at church, Laurie sat at the organ playing a quiet hymn to set a worshipful tone for the service. In the corner of her eye, she saw the two of them enter and choose a pew several rows from the front. Mrs. Foster's beaming smile revealed her delight to be there, especially when other congregants clustered around to welcome her.

Laurie noticed some of them brushed right past Tolley, ignoring him completely. At least his brothers and sister greeted him. Hurting for him, Laurie deliberately hit a wrong note and succeeded in catching his attention so she could give him a sweet smile. He gave her that crooked smile, clearly confused by her change.

To confirm her kind intentions, over dinner after church she made faces at him, not caring whether Mrs. Runyan or Mr. Parsley saw her. Mrs. Foster joined them at the table, and she didn't seem to mind those mischievous silent exchanges. At first, Tolley didn't seem to know how to react. Finally, he waggled his dark eyebrows and crossed his eyes, and she knew he forgave her and all would be right between them.

"I must say—" Mrs. Runyan paused between bites "—this roast is quite tender. Mrs. Foster, I am so pleased to see you are back in the kitchen."

Mrs. Foster sent Laurie a questioning look. "Why, no, Mrs. Runyan. Our Laurie prepared dinner. Didn't she do a fine job?"

Mrs. Runyan stared at each of them for a moment. "The meat could use a bit more seasoning, but I didn't want to mention it."

"The dinner rolls," Mr. Parsley chimed in, "didn't rise properly before they were baked."

"The dinner rolls—" Tolley leaned toward the smaller man, his dark eyebrows bent in a menacing frown "—are perfect. Laurie, please pass me another one."

"I agree," Mrs. Foster said. "Everything's perfect, Laurie. You've prepared a wonderful dinner."

Very little was said for the rest of the meal.

After the effort of attending church and eating in the dining room, Mrs. Foster wasn't up to a buggy ride. Laurie helped her upstairs for her afternoon nap, hoping Tolley would ask her out alone. She wanted to discuss next Saturday's Independence Day celebration with him. When she found him in the parlor rereading last week's *Esperanza Journal* for about the tenth time, it seemed likely he'd suggest the ride.

She sat at the piano and softly played "My Country, 'Tis of Thee," one of several songs she'd practiced for the celebration. To her frustration, Tolley didn't say anything, so she'd have to take the initiative.

"I suppose you remember the Independence Day doings next Saturday," she said over her shoulder.

He didn't answer right away. At last he said, "Uhhuh," without a hint of enthusiasm for the event he'd always loved to participate in.

She spun around on the piano stool. "Are you going to enter the horse race? I know you've taken Thor out every day, so I'd expect he's eager to run."

"Nope." Tolley buried his face in the newspaper as though searching for gold.

"But you always…"

She let her words trail off. How could she have forgotten? At the celebration two years ago, he'd cheated to win the race, and everyone in town knew it. Some of them still spoke of his dirty tricks. This morning she'd wanted to shout to the people at church, *Don't you see how he's changed?* Now she moved to the settee and plunked herself down beside him.

"Do you mind helping me with the preparations?"

He gave her a furtive glance, still pretending to read that old newspaper. "Sure. Whatever you need."

"Good. I'll make a list." She gently lowered the paper. "Right now what I need is some fresh air. How about taking me for a buggy ride?" If need be, she'd fetch the buggy herself. People of Esperanza should see at least one upstanding citizen of the town would proudly call Tolley her friend.

He sat back to give her a puzzled look. "Just the two of us?"

"Sure. Why not? That's what we planned last Sunday before Mrs. Foster joined us."

There went that adorable crooked smile again. There went her heart, skipping up and down. He folded the paper and set it on the coffee table. "I'll fetch the buggy."

His jaunty gait as he left the house pleased Laurie more than she'd expected.

His heart lighter than it had been in many days, Tolley jogged to the livery stable. Maybe he could ask Laurie if he could court her since she seemed over whatever had bothered her. He found Adam brushing down one of the horses for rent. The young man greeted him with a friendly wave. "Need the buggy today, Tolley?"

"Yep. I'll hitch it up." As he approached the tack hanging on the wall, Thor nickered to him from a back stall.

"I'll do it. You visit Thor." Adam cast an admiring glance at the stallion.

"You've already had your outing, old boy." Tolley grabbed a carrot from Adam's basket and fed it to Thor.

He'd sure like to enter the race on Saturday, but after the last time, that door was closed forever. A shame, too, because Thor deserved to run against the other horses. He eyed Adam.

"Say, what would you think of riding Thor for me in next Saturday's race?"

Adam's face brightened. "You mean it? Don't you want to ride him?"

Tolley thought fast. "Sure do, but I want him to win even more. I've grown a few inches and put on more than a few pounds in the past two years. He doesn't seem to mind it when I ride him, but you'd be the better jockey for the race." He rubbed Thor between the ears, and the stallion leaned into his hand.

Adam continued his work of hitching up the buggy horse, but Tolley could see his wide grin. "I'd be proud to ride him for you. We can split the prize if he wins."

"Nonsense." Tolley nudged Adam's shoulder. "*When* you two win, you'll keep the winnings." A ten-dollar gold piece, if that was still the prize, could help the Starling family.

"Hello in the stable." A man's tenor voice resonated from outside. Bank teller Reuben Brandt stuck his head through the wide doorway. "Adam, do you have a buggy I can rent this afternoon?" Brandt caught sight of Tolley and blanched. "Never mind." He turned to go.

"Hold on, Brandt." Tolley couldn't let this pass. Why would a man whose job Tolley helped to save back when he, Laurie, Grace and Rand stopped the bank robbery not want to be near him? "You can have the buggy."

Brandt stopped, looking doubtful.

"But, Tolley—" Adam quit tacking up the buggy horse.

Tolley waved away any objections. "We'll take a walk instead." He strode toward Brandt, who stood against the wall as if Tolley had a contagious disease. Tolley turned back to Adam. "We're all set on what we talked about."

"Yessir." Adam, who couldn't afford to alienate anyone, gave his attention to Brandt. "Mr. Brandt, it'll be ready for you in five minutes."

"You're a good boy, Adam." Brandt cast another disparaging look at Tolley.

As Tolley strode away, a familiar ache erupted in his chest. Once again he'd received a townsperson's contempt, and he couldn't blame anyone but himself. He didn't mind knowing Adam earned everyone's affection because of his hard work and honesty. He liked the boy himself. But it was galling to miss out on that same approval, which should be his as a scion of one of the town's founding families.

Maybe he shouldn't take Laurie for an outing after all. He wouldn't want anyone to think less of her because of him. Yet when he arrived at the boarding-house and saw her standing on the porch all decked out in her pretty blue dress and matching bonnet, he couldn't resist.

"Someone else needed the last buggy." He hopped up the steps and held out his arm. "If you don't mind walking, I'll be proud to escort you."

"And I'll be proud to walk beside you." She grasped his arm with her gloved hand.

After Brandt's rejection, nothing could have repaired his damaged feelings like her sweet, open-hearted acceptance. Yes, indeed, this was the day to ask if he could court her.

## Chapter Twelve

"Oh, Tolley." Laurie gazed up at him as they stood inside the newly repainted bandstand in the park. His shy, vulnerable expression offset his tall, strong physical presence. Her heart had been doing somersaults since she'd put her hand on his arm on the porch as they began their walk. "I'm truly fond of you. Always was."

The hope blossoming in his bright green eyes required her to continue quickly before he misunderstood. "But I'm returning to Denver in the fall. The conservatory has offered me a position teaching piano. I also have students from the most prominent families waiting for me to instruct them. I'll even give recitals and concerts. It's something I've wanted for years. It's what I've worked so hard to achieve. So you see, it wouldn't make sense for us to start courting."

His postured slumped, and he nodded, looking as though he'd expected her to turn him down. "I understand."

"Besides—" she patted his strong forearm, which felt like a steel girder "—we've always just been friends, more like sister and brother. Don't you want to be in love with the girl you court?"

There went that crooked smile again. "My mother always said she and the Colonel started out as friends when they began courting."

"Oh, Tolley." At least he didn't pretend to love her romantically, as one Denver beau had done. "I do care for you, but I've always wanted to see places outside of the San Luis Valley. It's a wonderful place to come home to, but there's a much bigger world out there. Didn't you ever feel that way when you were in Boston?"

He shrugged. "Nope. I couldn't wait to get home. I don't even care about being a lawyer. It's what the Colonel wanted…wants." He coughed as though clearing away strong emotions. "*I* always wanted to work on the ranch."

"Well." She sighed long and deep. "You can see we're at cross purposes. If we married, friends or not, one of us would have to give up lifelong dreams. I don't believe that's the way to happiness in marriage."

"I suppose." He gazed west toward the San Juan Mountains, his eyes unfocused. "We have opera houses right near here where folks go for entertainment like piano concerts. One up in Creede, the San Juan in Alamosa and the Del Norte Opera House over in Del Norte. Maybe we could get Rosamond and Garrick to put a stage in the hotel dining room. Then people like Jenny Lind and Lilly Langtry might come here on a tour if they were invited to perform in at least three or four places."

Laurie held on to a giggle trying to escape. "Miss Lind hasn't toured in years, and Miss Langtry…well,

I'm not sure many people in Esperanza would approve of her, um, social life."

Tolley sighed with exasperation. "You know what I mean. It doesn't have to be those entertainers." He grinned down at her and waggled those dark eyebrows. "I know of a talented concert pianist who might consider performing at the hotel."

She shook her head. "I'm afraid I've given away too many free concerts in my hometown. People won't want to pay to hear me."

"Aha." He drew back a few feet as though viewing her for the first time. "Now I see. You aren't talking about artistic expression." The grinning smirk on his face was almost as adorable as his winsome smile. "You want to become a rich and famous pianist."

"Oh, you." She playfully smacked his arm and almost hurt her hand doing so. What a good ending to a difficult conversation. "Now I have to make the biscuits for our Sunday night sandwiches."

He offered his arm again, the perfect gentleman, and they walked down the bandstand's four steps. "Now that you mention food, I've been thinking about the meals you're fixing."

"Is something wrong?" She wouldn't let his complaints annoy her. He'd been wonderfully supportive in front of the other boarders at dinner today.

"Nope. Everything's fine. But it seems like you fix a lot of expensive food for those grumpy boarders. I mean, meat at every supper? My mother didn't even do that."

"Mine didn't, either." She looked up at him, and when he gazed down at her with those bright green eyes, her heart did another silly tumble. *Bother.* What was wrong with her? "But both Mrs. Runyan and Mr. Parsley say it's part of their rent and board payments."

"You've collected rent?"

"Yes, of course. Every Friday evening."

"Kept the books?"

"Ye-es. What are you suggesting?"

He scrunched up his forehead thoughtfully. "Would you mind if I looked at the books?"

A streak of annoyance shot through her, but only briefly. Maybe he'd see something she'd missed. "Of course not. Mrs. Foster trusts you as much as I do."

Her words seemed to surprise him. "Wow. I guess she does." A pleased smile crossed his face. "I guess she does."

Laurie could only wonder why that surprised him.

He'd done it again. Proved his own selfishness. Why did he assume Laurie wanted the same things her sisters did, marriage and a passel of children? He knew about the teaching position in Denver, but he hadn't known she'd always dreamed of securing it. Nor did he know about her dream of playing the piano professionally. No, the only dreams he'd ever thought about were his own. At least Laurie would achieve hers, while he'd likely never find his place again at Four Stones Ranch. And once she returned to Denver, he'd be more alone than ever.

She didn't appear to hold his courtship suggestion against him. All week, she chatted with him as she had before. Never once did she comment on the work in the bathroom except maybe to poke her head in the door, look around and give him a nod and a smile. Mrs. Foster also gave her stamp of approval on the progress.

If he didn't have the Independence Day preparation to do, he and Adam could finish tiling the bathroom by Saturday and the plumbers could install the fixtures on the following Monday.

On Friday, with Adam's help, he moved the piano to the bandstand and built a few of the temporary booths needed for various vendors who'd come from all over the San Luis Valley to sell their wares. In spite of himself, he felt a growing excitement about the coming celebration, even though he planned to keep a low profile once people began to arrive. He wouldn't even attend the horse race to watch Adam and Thor compete because folks might suspect him of doing harm to Adam's competitors.

How did a man live down what he'd done, not only putting the burr under Gypsy's saddle but striking out at Garrick with his crop while they were racing along the back streets? Garrick still bore a slight scar on his cheek from the injury. If he'd hit Garrick's eye, he could have blinded him. Later, everyone saw Tolley trip Garrick with a lariat while the Englishman danced with Rosamond, knocking him out for several minutes. When Garrick awoke, he'd marched over to Tolley and struck him. When Tolley returned the blow, Garrick knocked him down again, to the applause of bystanders. Even back then, a stranger to the town received more approval than Tolley. They all seemed to think he had it coming. That night the Colonel ordered him out of town. And he had only himself to blame. But after two years, wasn't there anything he could do to live it down?

Independence Day arrived, and hundreds of people poured into town. To stir up excitement early in the day and to wear out the active little ones, the committee always started with the children's three-legged race. Tolley's oldest brother, Nate, brought his family, and both Lizzie and Natty participated with friends. Neither won in their age group, but from their giggles and hopping around, neither seemed to mind. Lizzie did remind Tolley they were due for another riding lesson. Unable to speak, he answered her with a hug.

Next came the formal opening of the celebration, with Mayor Edgar Jones's brief introduction and Reverend Thomas's invocation. Then came the reading of the Declaration of Independence by various and varied members of the community, everyone from Mrs. Winsted to former slave Bert to laundry owner Mr. Chen to rancher Rafael Trujillo. After the reading, Laurie accompanied the children, who sang "America," with Molly Starling singing a solo on the first verse. My, the little girl had a pretty voice, almost as pretty as Laurie's. When the song ended, the crowd burst into boisterous applause. All around him, Tolley heard generous praise whispered for Adam's little sister.

One woman said, "How we love that sweet little girl."

Another said, "We're so blessed when our little songbird sings for us."

The mayor quieted the throng and made a few more remarks, at last announcing the celebration open.

Tolley wandered among the booths, idly viewing the various items for sale. He bought a shirt from Mrs. Starling and paid her extra so Adam would deliver it to the boardinghouse. Next he paused at Bert's table. The blacksmith, who'd originally followed the Colonel out to Colorado and who'd worked at Four Stones

Ranch for years, now owned his own blacksmith business next door to the livery stable. He took care of any
ironwork folks needed and also made spurs and silver
items. When Tolley was a child, Bert taught him a few
things about metalwork, enough for him to appreciate
that it wasn't easy.

"Howdy, Tolley." The blacksmith reached out a
large, callused black hand.

Tolley gladly shook it, appreciating the man's
friendly acceptance. Perhaps, like him, Bert endured
cold shoulders from some people in town. "Howdy,
Bert. You sure do have some fine things for sale." He
picked up a long silver filigree necklace with a turquoise jewel at its center. Would Laurie like it? An
impulse seized him. "I'll take this."

"Yessir." Bert named the price and, while Tolley
counted out the money, placed the necklace in a small
satin-lined box. "Thank you, sir."

"Thank you." Tolley stuck it in his pocket. Now,
when should he give it to Laurie? And what excuse
would he offer for giving such an expensive present
to a gal he wasn't courting?

"Time for the single ladies' egg race!" Mrs. Winsted called from the bandstand.

An idea entered Tolley's mind. Two years ago,
Laurie won second place in the contest for unmarried
young women. If she entered this time, he'd give her the
necklace as a prize whether or not she won. He strode
across the park to the grassy area where lines for the
race course were chalked. Seeing some disapproving
looks, he stood at the back of the crowd. Tall enough
to see over most heads, he did his best to ignore the
all-too-familiar hurt.

Laurie stood in line with the other young ladies. Unexpected emotion rose up in his throat, and Tolley swallowed hard. She was by far the prettiest one there, and he loved seeing the competitive glint in her eyes. How well he knew that feeling. How sad he couldn't allow himself to enter any of the events.

Each girl held a wooden spoon with an uncooked egg in its bowl. Deputy Gareau, clearly enjoying the festivities, made sure every entrant's foot was behind the line before he shot his Colt Peacemaker into the air. At the gun's loud report, the girls scurried across the grass, some losing their eggs right away. Shattered shells and gooey yolks slid down their skirts. Only Laurie, her sister Georgia, Anna Means, and two girls Tolley didn't know managed to make it to the finish line without dropping theirs, with Laurie stepping over the chalk finish line a half second before Georgia. Cheers and congratulations went up from the onlookers.

Laurie carried her egg back to the judges. They cracked it into a bowl, proving it to be raw, and proclaimed her the winner. More cheers and applause erupted. Across the lawn, Tolley caught her eye, and she beckoned to him with one slender index finger.

Then he remembered. The winner of the race won a blue ribbon and a china bowl, but she also got a kiss from the gentleman of her choice. Was she summoning him for that purpose? He quickly closed the distance between them, elbowing his way through several cowboys vying for her attention with "Kiss *me*, Miss Laurie," or "You're the prize I'd like to win." Tolley had never thought about other possible suitors. A gal as pretty and sweet as Laurie could have her pick of men.

"Yes, ma'am? You summoned me?" He gave her a teasing grin.

"I did." She glanced around at the expectant crowd and whispered, "You're the only one I trust not to misunderstand this." She stood on tiptoes, wrapped her arms around his neck and planted a quick kiss on his lips.

In fact, too quick for Tolley. Without thinking, he wrapped his own arms around her waist and pulled her close, kissing her soft, rosy-pink lips and holding on to her for all he was worth. He'd never really kissed a girl, had no idea how powerfully the gesture would affect him. His knees went weak. His mind went numb. He could only feel something wonderful surging through his chest. Best of all, Laurie didn't pull away but seemed to enjoy the kiss every bit as much as he did.

At last they separated. Well, their lips separated. Then they stood staring at each other while hoots and hollers from the cowboys made their way into Tolley's consciousness, along with some less-than-kind remarks from some of the older ladies. Laurie looked a bit dazed, exactly the way Tolley felt.

"Um, thanks?" she murmured.

"No. Thank *you*." What else could he say? How could he react so strongly to a girl he cared for only as a friend? How could a girl who'd rejected his courtship kiss him with such obvious feeling? With very little experience with women, he had no idea how to figure it out.

Laurie had no idea what just happened. She recalled thinking she could kiss Tolley without him misunderstanding her intentions, but she seemed to be the one who hadn't understood what it would mean to her to kiss him. Never in her life had she ever felt so connected to another person, so at one with him. Why? They were just friends.

"Laurie!" Pa's sharp voice and firm hand on her upper arm yanked her out of her kiss-induced stupor. "What do you think you're doing? And you!" He moved Laurie to his side and faced Tolley with an angry expression such as she'd never seen on her good-natured father. "I told you to stay away from my daughter. What's the idea of making a public spectacle of her?"

"But—"

"Pa!" Laurie couldn't bear the stricken look on Tolley's face. "I kissed him. You know, part of the egg race?"

"What?" Pa frowned down at her.

Before she could explain, Tolley said, "Never mind, Laurie."

He strode away, his shoulders slumped. Across the yard, two men accosted him briefly. She couldn't hear what they said, but his shoulders dropped even lower as he walked toward the edge of the park grounds, probably heading back to the boardinghouse. Tears scalded Laurie's eyes as she turned on Pa.

"Now see what you've done?"

"Me? I'm trying to salvage your reputation."

"George, that's nonsense, and you know it." Ma appeared at Pa's side, a stern look on her usually smiling face. "Tolley's still trying to find himself. We gotta give the boy a chance."

"He can find himself someplace else as far as I'm concerned."

"George!" Ma repeated.

He muttered a response.

Laurie didn't try to make out his words. She marched away to help with the cakewalk. Maybe Tolley would come back later. She'd save some dinner for him. Or maybe take it to the boardinghouse. She'd promised to bring Mrs. Foster over for a spell, so she'd have an excuse for carrying a plate to Tolley.

The last event before dinner was the horse race. When Laurie saw Thor lined up with the rest of them, her heart skipped. It skipped again when she saw Adam atop the stallion. But he wouldn't ride the animal if Tolley hadn't given permission. Surely they would win. How she'd love to carry news of Thor's win to Tolley along with his dinner. A new excitement filled her as she joined the onlookers lining the boardwalks of Main Street.

Sheriff Lawson described the course, a mile run through the streets of town and circling back to the starting point. He warned riders against cheating because there were watchers along the way. That was how everyone knew Tolley struck Garrick two years ago. Laurie sighed. She mustn't dwell on the past. As Tolley's friend, she must be the first one to forget his past mistakes and wrongdoings and urge others to do the same.

After Fred Brody took a photograph of the riders for the *Esperanza Journal*, the sheriff fired his gun, and the horses took off heading west, crowding each other for the inside position as they rounded the corner onto Foster Street. Hooves pounded on the dry road, throwing up dust as the horses followed red flags marking the course, while onlookers cheered for their favorites.

Soon the sounds of galloping horses resonated from several blocks to the south, and then to the east. In less than five minutes, Thor emerged from Kirkland on the east end of town, far ahead of the pack of quarter horses doing their best to catch him. No one was surprised when Tolley's Thoroughbred thundered across the finish line under the Independence Day banner.

While the noisy cheering continued and many people filled the streets to congratulate Adam, Laurie wiped tears from her cheeks. She hurried back to the park where the churchwomen waited to serve dinner from long tables laden with their best cooking. Filling a plate with cold chicken, Ma's potato salad, baked beans and several other tasty-looking dishes, she covered it all with a napkin and headed toward the boardinghouse. Before she could reach the edge of the park, Pa accosted her.

"Where do you think you're going?" He crossed his arms over his chest and glared at her.

"To see Mrs. Foster." Not a lie. "She wanted to come over for a while."

He studied the plate, suspicion filling his expression. Then he waved her away. "Don't take too long."

"Yessir." She hurried away before he could say more.

Tolley had a lot of experience in sulking. He'd spent a good deal of his youth doing it whenever he got into trouble. But was it sulking to lie on his bed and ruminate on the unbearable mess his life had become?

He wasn't even sure of the names of the two men who'd stopped him as he left the park. They were local ranchers with small spreads, but they spoke as though they were important pillars of the community. Both proclaimed they'd volunteer for the jury when Purvis's trial came up. Both also promised to vote for hanging, no matter what evidence Tolley produced. They almost made it sound like Tolley was guilty for defending the outlaw. If other people in town felt the same way, no wonder they were standoffish.

Feeling sorry for himself wouldn't help. He sat up on the side of the bed. Sounds from beyond his closed door drew him into the hallway.

To his surprise, Laurie approached with a covered plate. "You forgot to eat before you left." Her sweet smile dispelled the ache in his chest.

"Wow, thanks, Laurie." He took the plate and peeked under the checkered napkin. "I suppose I should eat this in the dining room."

"If you like." She giggled, suddenly shy. "I would've left it down there, but I didn't want anyone else—" she tilted her head toward Mrs. Runyan's door "—to think it was meant for them." Her cheeks grew pink. "That wasn't kind. Forget I said it."

He gave a mirthless laugh. "I make too many mistakes to judge you." Heading toward the stairway, he added, "Are you coming?"

"I can't. I promised Mrs. Foster I'd take her over to enjoy the festivities." She took a step toward him, clapping her hands together. "Thor and Adam won the horse race."

Tolley emitted a whoop, almost tipping his plate in his excitement. "That's wonderful!" He slid the cold chicken back to safety and then licked his fingers. "Mmm. Makes me hungry."

While he ate in the dining room, Laurie prepared

Mrs. Foster for the afternoon. With Laurie's help and using her late husband's cane, the older lady made her way toward the park four blocks away. As Tolley watched them leave, he stamped out the depression again trying to claim him. Instead, he remembered the kiss he'd shared with Laurie. They avoided the subject when she came home, but very soon they'd discuss it. He'd make sure of it. In the meantime, he could privately bask in borrowed glory, knowing he'd helped Adam win the horse race. The blue ribbon would give Adam bragging rights, though Adam never bragged. More important, that ten-dollar gold coin would help the Starling family. Pride over the event would cause Tolley trouble, but he'd permit himself the satisfaction of a deed well-done by suggesting Adam should ride.

In the evening, when music from the bandstand wafted on the breeze to the boardinghouse, he had another sad moment. He'd sure like to dance with Laurie. Would some of those cowboys who'd lined up after the egg race in hopes of a kiss hold her in their arms for a waltz or swing her around in the Virginia reel? He'd ask her when she came home. That'd give him a good opening for talking about their kiss.

Later, seated in a rocking chair on the front porch, he watched the colorful fireworks exploding over the distant park. Before the fiery display ended, Laurie walked out of the darkness toward the house. She'd brought Mrs. Foster home hours ago, along with supper for Tolley, and returned to the festivities. Now she bounded up the steps like the cowgirl she used to be.

"Hey, Tolley." Even in the dim lamplight shining through the parlor window, he could see her sweet smile and maybe a hint of weariness after a long day.

She dropped into the rocking chair beside him. "Nice fireworks, don't you think?"

The perfect opening. "I liked the fireworks this morning a whole lot better." He waggled his eyebrows, which usually brought a laugh or at least a smile.

Instead, she dropped her jaw and stared at him for a moment. "Don't bring that up. Pa was unfair to blame you." She closed her eyes and shook her head.

"I prefer to think about the first part. You know, the part where you kissed me, and then I kissed you, and then we both kissed each other." When she slid him a shy look, he took the encouragement to go on. "Seems like two people who share a kiss like that are a bit more than friends and might ought to consider courting. What do you think?" He shouldn't have said that. Now if she rejected him, after a day filled with rejections, it would be unbearable.

A warm expression blossomed over her face like one of Mother's blooming roses. "Oh, Tolley…"

"What's going on here?" Mrs. Runyan marched up the steps, Mr. Parsley right behind her, both looking loaded for bear. "What are you two doing?" She stood over Laurie and wagged a finger in her face. "I saw your father scolding you, young lady. And here you are keeping company with this…this *person* against his explicit orders."

"Shameful, shameful." Mr. Parsley, never one to be outdone, fisted his hands at his waist. "Explain yourselves, or I shall report what I've seen to Mr. Eberly."

Poor, sweet Laurie looked about to cry. Tolley ground his teeth and prayed for patience. He rose to his six-foot-three-inch height and mirrored Mr. Parsley's threatening pose. To offset the effect, or perhaps balance it, he smiled like Reverend Thomas, all free and easy. "Exactly what did you see, Mr. Parsley?"

"Why, why…" The little man dropped his fists and stepped back about three feet. "The two of you sitting here alone in the dark."

Laurie snickered. As they were wont to do, the two boarders glared at her and gasped in unison. Before Tolley could stop himself, he burst into laughter, further outraging his elders. Both sputtered out further indignation.

"Come on, Laurie." He grasped her hand. "Let's finish our conversation in the parlor. Tell me all about the dance. Did you have a good time?"

"Tolley! Laurie!" Mrs. Starling ran toward the house, her face stricken. "Have you seen Molly?"

# Chapter Thirteen

Laurie opened her arms to the distraught mother and held her tight. "No, ma'am. I haven't seen Molly since the opening ceremonies this morning." She questioned Tolley with a glance.

"No, I haven't seen her since then, either." He looked at the boarders. "Did you see her?"

"Humph. Seems a mighty poor mother who can't keep track of her own children." Mr. Parsley moved toward the front door.

Mrs. Runyan opened her mouth, but Laurie could stand no more.

"Hush, you horrid people! Mrs. Starling is an excellent mother."

Mr. Parsley started to reply, but Tolley cut him off. "Either come help us find the child or shut your mouth and get out of my sight."

As the two boarders silently slunk into the house, Tolley turned to Mrs. Starling. "Where's Adam?"

Mrs. Starling stood back from Laurie and wrung her hands. "He went looking for Molly before the fireworks started."

"Jack and the baby?" Tolley appeared ready to take charge. Laurie's heart swelled over his concern for the young Starling children.

"With their father. They were tired, so I took them home early." Mrs. Starling began to cry.

"Ma'am, could you start at the beginning?" Tolley was clearly trying to calm her. "It may help us find her."

Mrs. Starling sniffed back her tears. "Molly wanted to stay with Adam for the fireworks. When I went back to the park to join them, Adam realized she was gone." She hiccoughed on a sob. "He said she'd chased a puppy, but he didn't expect her to leave the park. When we couldn't find her, he went off in the same direction just as the fireworks began."

"We'll find her." Laurie hugged her again. "You come inside and sit in the parlor to catch your breath while I check on Mrs. Foster. Then we'll join the others."

"Molly probably got tired and fell asleep someplace." Tolley gently touched Mrs. Starling's shoulder. His tender concern moved Laurie. "I'll get a lantern and join the searchers."

Even though Mrs. Starling wanted to return to the park, Laurie persuaded her to wait for her. She went upstairs to tell Mrs. Foster about Molly and to settle her for the night. She found the older woman in the doorway of her bedroom, her steel-gray hair hanging loose, and her dressing gown clutched around her.

"Who was that man?" Concern and a hint of confusion filled the lady's expression. At least it seemed so to Laurie in the shadowed hallway.

"Which man, dear?" Laurie guided her back to the

bedchamber. "Tolley was home most of the day. Mr. Parsley just returned." She could hear the watchmaker fussing about in his room.

"I'm not in my dotage, child." Mrs. Foster permitted Laurie to prepare her for bed. "About ten minutes ago, I saw a man, a rather shabby cowboy, I think, going down the back staircase. He saw me and ducked his head. It was dark, so I couldn't make out his features, but he was of medium height."

*The prowler! Inside the house!* An icy chill swept down Laurie's back. "Can you settle yourself in bed?"

"Yes, of course."

"Good. Lock your door, and don't open it for anyone but me."

"Bring a lamp when you come." Determination filled Mrs. Foster's face. "I'll load my derringer and put it on the side table. Wouldn't want to shoot you by mistake."

"Yes, of course." Making one's identity known quickly was the rule for everyone in the West.

Laurie hurried to her room, fetched her own Colt .45 and loaded the chamber. She met Tolley in the upper hallway. "I can't go with you. The prowler was here."

"I know." The tightness of his voice drew her attention to his stricken face and then the paper in his hand. "Someone slipped this under my door. Molly and Adam have been kidnapped."

Laurie inhaled a sharp breath. She took the note in hand and tilted it toward his lantern.

We got the brats. If you want them alive, bring Purvis to the hills above Cat Creek tomorrow morning. Come alone. No law, or they die. Bring five hundred in gold.

Laurie's knees threatened to buckle, but she refused to succumb to the weakness. "What can we do?"

He shook his head, looking lost for a moment. Then determination came over him. "I can't exactly get Purvis out of jail by myself." He took note of the gun in Laurie's hand. "You take care of things here. I'll go see the sheriff." After placing a quick kiss on her lips, he turned toward his room.

"Tolley." She gripped his arm, wishing she had time to return his kiss. "Be careful."

He brushed a hand across her cheek. "I will."

They parted ways, Tolley to gather his hat and gun, Laurie to go downstairs and give Mrs. Starling the bad news.

*Lord, help me say the right thing to her. Please help us all. Please keep the Starling children safe. Please bring Tolley back safely.*

Tolley ran the four blocks to the sheriff's office, where he found Justice Gareau on duty. Huffing to catch his breath, he poured out the story to the deputy and handed him the note.

Gareau's face turned to granite. He opened the door to the cell area. Tolley peered past him to see Purvis lying on his cot, apparently asleep. Gareau closed the door.

"Go get the sheriff," the deputy said. "He's still at the park leading the search for the girl. Don't say anything to anyone else. When he gets back here, we'll make a plan."

Tolley shook his head. "The note says no law. I only showed it to you so I could get Purvis out of jail."

Gareau glowered at him. "That's not the way it works. Go get the sheriff. And while you're at it, figure out how to get five hundred dollars in gold."

His mind numb except for desperate prayers, Tolley bowed to the man's experience. He dashed to the park, beyond which lantern light winked among the trees and houses as townspeople continued their quest. To his credit, banker Nolan Means walked with the other searchers. Nate had also stayed in town, sending Susanna and the children home. Tolley prayed the outlaws hadn't found his sister-in-law and her children alone on the road toward Cat Creek.

His heart cold with fear for Molly and Adam, he reported his news to Sheriff Lawson. The lawman's entire demeanor changed from concerned to a brick wall, like Justice's. He sent a man to call in the searchers. So much for not telling anyone else. Tolley couldn't fault him. It wouldn't be fair not to tell people they could go home.

Once the crowd gathered, Lawson said, "We know where Molly is. You're free to go. Thanks for your help."

Very clever. He hadn't mentioned the outlaws at all. Tolley was learning new things by the minute.

The sheriff called aside several men, including Nate and Nolan. Now Tolley began to worry.

"Sir, the note said—"

"Son, you let me handle this."

Tolley exhaled sharply. Maybe he should've taken care of the matter alone. Except he had no way to get five hundred dollars either in gold or in cash.

"Men, we have a situation." The sheriff told the five men about the kidnapping.

Nate stepped over to Tolley. "You all right, little brother?"

"Not sure. I'm afraid of the way the sheriff's handling this."

Nate nudged his arm. "God hasn't given us a spirit of fear, Tolley. Lawson always seeks the Lord's guidance, and neither he nor the Lord has ever let us down."

After the sheriff finished his report, Nolan stepped forward. "I'll get the money from the bank right now."

The sheriff waved away his offer. "That's mighty generous, son, but I think a bag of rocks'll do fine. We aren't gonna fund a getaway for these varmints."

Nolan laughed. "Actually, I have some fool's gold collected from hapless miners who thought they'd struck it rich. I'll put it in a bag."

Lawson snorted out a laugh. "Good idea. All right, men, follow me." He waved his arm again, this time like he was leading a cavalry charge.

The "troops" fell in behind him and made their way to the sheriff's office. First, he closed the door between the office and the jail cells so Purvis couldn't hear them, then deputized the lot of them, including Tolley. As he quietly unfolded his plan to rescue the young Starlings, Tolley's mind eased considerably. He'd trust in the Lord first and then in the two experienced lawmen.

"Now go on home and get some sleep. Be back here at four a.m., and we'll go get those young'uns."

After parting from his brother and the other men, Tolley couldn't imagine how he'd sleep, so he went to the parsonage to tell Reverend Thomas and Grace what had happened and ask for their prayers. Then he returned to the boardinghouse. Laurie had walked Mrs. Starling home and then returned, as well. He wished he could tell her the plan for the rescue. But the fewer people who knew about it, the better. Only problem, he didn't count on her wiles.

"I have some chocolate cake left over from last night. Come out to the kitchen and eat a bite before you go to bed."

"Well…"

She snagged his arm and dragged him through the dining room and the swinging door to the kitchen. "Sit. Talk." Seemed like she'd done this to him before.

He snorted out a laugh. "You sure are bossy." Even so, he accepted the cake and glass of milk, feeling very much like a boy back home in his mother's kitchen.

Laurie sat beside him, arms crossed on the table. "So, what's the plan?"

She loved Molly and had a right to know. Between bites of the mouth-watering cake, he explained the sheriff's plan. A glint of determination filled her eyes.

"I'm going with the posse."

"No, you're not."

"We'll see." She stood and snatched up his plate and carried it to the sink. "Don't bother to gather the eggs tomorrow morning. I'll take care of that for you."

He studied her in the dim light of the kitchen. She was planning something, and it wasn't Sunday dinner for the boarders. But weariness overcame him, so he didn't confront her.

"Thanks. We all need to work together on this."

"Right." She gave him a too-sweet smile. "We sure do."

After making certain the front and back doors were secure, Tolley climbed the stairs to his room while worry teased at the back of his mind. He didn't need Laurie to interfere in the rescue. But he was far too tired to figure out a way to stop her.

Laurie could hardly sleep for the anxiety tumbling around inside of her alongside a sense of purpose she'd never felt even in her most ambitious moments regarding her music career. She had so much to do in preparation. Molly was too dear for her to sit and wait for someone else to save her. All of those men might scare the excitable child more than calm her.

*Lord, help us to save this precious child and her brother.*

Hours before first light, she hurried to the kitchen to do morning chores, prepare a buffet breakfast and put the usual Sunday roast in the oven. Because Mrs. Foster assured her she could come downstairs for meals from now on, Laurie left a note under her door saying she'd be away for the morning. She also said not to worry about "that other matter," knowing Mrs. Foster would understand she was referring to the prowler. No need to say anything about the kidnappers.

The landlady would need to check the stove fire before going to church, something she could do without hurting her injured arm. Everything else should run smoothly. This morning's church service might have to go on without an organist, but somehow the congregation must manage. Maybe either Susanna or Marybeth Northam, both fine pianists, would step up. Unless Nate and Rand wouldn't let them leave home knowing the kidnappers were not far from Four Stones Ranch.

Shortly before four, Tolley came downstairs. Eyeing her suspiciously, he helped himself to the buffet breakfast and sat at the dining room table. "You're up early."

"I wanted to be sure you ate before you left."

"Thanks." He acknowledged her with a dip of his head. "Did you practice the hymns for this morning's church service?"

"Of course." Silly man. He was testing her. She poured him a cup of coffee, hoping he wouldn't notice the riding boots on her feet or the trouser hems peeking out from beneath her skirt. To her relief, he appeared too focused on the job ahead to notice in the dimly lit room.

After he left, she allowed enough time for him to get to the livery stable, saddle his horse and join the posse at the sheriff's office. She hurried to the livery to fetch Little Bit and rode south ahead of the men, passing her family's spread and Four Stones Ranch. Before reaching Cat Creek, she took a detour, crossing the creek nearer the hills she knew so well. Surprised, and yet not, she found Nate and Rand Northam lying in wait on a ridge some thirty yards away from the outlaws' campsite. Seemed Tolley hadn't told her everything about the sheriff's plans.

"What are you doing here, Laurie?" Rand whispered as he gave her a big-brother frown.

"Go back to town." Nate mirrored his brother's expression. "We don't need to look out for you while we're doing this."

"Look out for me?" She kept her voice low. "You forget I was right in the thick of it when we took down Hardison and Smith during the bank robbery four years ago."

The brothers traded a look and rolled their eyes.

"Don't do anything foolish." Nate gave his attention to the campsite.

Laurie peered down, too, and her heart lurched at what she saw. One outlaw stood watch—not too well, obviously, since he hadn't heard this little rescue group—while the other one slept comfortably in a bedroll. Molly lay sleeping on the ground with nothing to protect her from the night's cool air but her brother's arm wrapped around her. Laurie's temper flared at their cruelty. She didn't worry much about Adam. He was a hardy young man. But poor little Molly, still dressed in her blue skirt, thin white shirtwaist and red kerchief she'd worn to sing yesterday morning, must be chilled to the bone by now. Laurie longed to dash to the site and rescue the precious little girl right away, but that would be foolish.

"There's only two. Why can't we pick them off now?"

"And risk hitting Molly or Adam?" Nate glanced at her handgun. "A pistol's fine for closer shooting, but not so good at this distance."

As if she didn't know that. Why hadn't she brought her rifle? Easy answer. Because she planned to join Tolley when he made the prisoner exchange so she could take care of Molly. She could hide her Colt under her jacket, but not a rifle.

"There." Rand pointed toward the trail from Cat Creek.

Tolley rode Thor toward the campsite, with Purvis beside him on another horse. Laurie's heart lodged in her throat, and tears stung her eyes. Sitting tall in the saddle, Tolley looked so brave, so competent. If only Pa could see him now, he'd be proud to know him. She'd never admired him more than she did in this moment.

Soft sounds behind them caused all three to turn. Rifles in hand, Sheriff Lawson and Deputy Gareau hustled toward them on foot, keeping low to the ground. They must have left their horses down the other side of the hill with the brothers' and Laurie's. Without a word, they slid into place beside Laurie.

The sheriff tipped his hat to her and whispered, "Tolley said you'd be here."

She suppressed a nervous giggle. Tolley knew her better than she'd thought.

"Since you insist on helping out," Lawson said, "here's what I want you to do."

As he and Purvis approached the campsite, Tolley had a hard time keeping his eyes forward when he desperately wanted to look up toward the ridge where his brothers were supposed to be. No doubt Laurie had gone to the familiar overlook, and by now, the sheriff and deputy should be there, too. It'd been tricky to convince Purvis only Tolley accompanied him, but the two lawmen and two other deputies left town not far behind. Tolley did his best to keep Purvis engaged in conversation, appealing to him to mend his ways, turn over a new leaf, get religion and every other cliché Tolley could think of so Purvis wouldn't notice they were being followed by four men on horseback. Purvis's only responses were some interesting words Tolley had never heard before, even among the sailors on the Boston waterfront. His ploy must have worked, though, because Purvis had eyes only for the bag of fool's gold hanging from Thor's saddle. His mind dull from seven months in jail, he truly thought those pale yellow rocks were gold nuggets.

As they drew closer to the outlaws' camp, Purvis called out to his twin. "Jed! I'm here. We got the gold." He cackled with laughter like a madman.

Yep. He'd been in jail so long he'd lost his mind.

One man stood guard with a Winchester, and the other one began to stir from his bedroll. Tolley saw Adam sit up and gather Molly into his arms. Neither had a blanket or any other covering, which nearly sent Tolley's temper over the edge. Men as cruel as that would stop at nothing to achieve their ends, not even harming a small child. How Tolley wished he had his gun, but Purvis had made sure he hadn't brought one. But the outlaw had been so eager to get out of jail, he hadn't checked his own gun, which the sheriff had jammed before returning it to him.

They entered the camp, and now two firearms were trained on Tolley. Before he could dismount, Molly emitted a piercing cry and began to weep hysterically.

"Shh, shh." Adam held her close, but she refused to be comforted.

"Make her shut up, or I'll do it for you." Heep Skinner, the third outlaw, pointed his handgun at the child.

His face pale and solemn, Adam moved his sister behind him, which only made her cry harder.

Tolley didn't try to give them any reassurance. Instead, he addressed the outlaws. "Now, now, no need for shooting." He slipped out of the saddle and fussed with the rope around the canvas bag of fool's gold. "Uh-oh. Got a knot here." Where was Laurie? He didn't dare look back toward the trail.

Purvis dismounted and greeted his brother, who held one hand over his ear closest to Molly's wails.

"Hey, wait up." Laurie rode up, waving a hand in the air.

Tolley heaved a quiet sigh of relief.

"What's this?" Jed Purvis hollered over Molly's ruckus as he pointed his gun at Laurie.

"Aw, don't shoot nobody." Jud set a hand on Jed's gun and lowered it. "Leastways not yet. Besides, we might find a use for that pretty little gal."

Fighting nausea at his evil suggestion, Tolley nodded to Laurie before going into his planned tirade. "I told you to stay in town. What's the matter with you?"

"And I told you—" she jumped from the saddle and marched to him, using Thor to shield her actions "—I was coming for Molly." Throwing one arm around his neck, she slipped a gun into his jacket pocket, but the handle stuck out.

"Hey, what's going on over there?" Heep Skinner peered around Thor, looking meaner than a rattlesnake.

"Lovers' quarrel." Tolley shrugged his entire torso, causing the gun to slip from sight. Or so he hoped.

"I'm taking Molly." Laurie held out her arms to the little girl, who clung to Adam instead. Laurie's courage didn't surprise Tolley, but his admiration for her soared.

"Look, Purvis, let Adam and Molly go." Tolley lifted a hand in appeal. "I'll be your hostage, even help you find the trail through the hills to New Mexico Territory."

"I ain't lettin' 'em go." Jud scowled. "Leastways not till we're clean through *New* Mexico and all the way south of the border to *old* Mexico. What if we get caught afore we cross the border? I ain't riskin' their pa tellin' lies on me in court."

Jed nudged his twin. "Let the brat go. I ain't gonna listen to that caterwauling all the way to Mexico."

Adam knelt and gripped Molly's arms. "Go with Miss Laurie, you hear?"

"Nooo!" Molly flung her arms around his neck.

He peeled her off and gave her a gentle shake. "You mind me right now."

She gulped back her tears and gave Laurie a solemn glance. "Yes, Adam." Sniffing loudly, and much in need of a handkerchief, she made her way to Laurie, stumbling over rocks as she went.

Tolley pulled his bandanna from his pocket and held it out to her. "Here you go, sprout." As she took it, he eyed Laurie and tilted his head toward town. "Go. Now."

Without a word, she mounted her horse and snatched Molly up in front of her. At her command, the mare spun around and took off at a gallop.

"Hiya!" Tolley slapped Thor's haunch. The stallion remembered his training and sped after Laurie. "Adam, down!" As the younger man obeyed, Tolley also flattened himself on the ground, pulling the gun from his pocket just as warning shots rang out from below the ridge. Dust rocketed into the air, and the coffeepot that was on the fire flew across the ground.

Their diversion with Laurie and Molly worked, giving the posse time to get close enough to end this situation. The confused outlaws couldn't seem to figure out which way to shoot. Jud aimed at Tolley, but his gun wouldn't fire. Jed and Heep got off a few shots, but the bullets found no targets. The posse was on them before they could gather their wits, if they ever had any. In two short minutes, the three men were kneeling on the ground, hands behind their heads, with five guns trained on them and five good men daring them to give them an excuse to shoot.

After clapping handcuffs around their wrists, Sheriff Lawson sent up an ear-piercing whistle. The two other deputies rode around from the other side of the ridge, bringing the posse's horses. Tolley and Adam saddled the outlaws' horses and soon the group rode back to town. Laurie awaited them across Cat Creek, where Molly insisted upon riding with Adam while the outlaw twins were forced to share a mount.

They arrived in Esperanza just as the church's new bell began to ring, calling them all to worship.

After Laurie made sure the Starlings were reunited, she rode over to the church. If she hurried, she could still play the opening hymn despite her slightly disheveled appearance. Inside, the two older Northam brothers had already begun to address the congregation about the events of the morning. Once they sat down, Micah stood on the podium to offer a prayer of thanksgiving, after which he added his own commentary.

"Sheriff Lawson has the three men locked up, and their trial will take place a week from tomorrow, Lord willing and the judge finishes his current trial in time. Let us continue to pray this is the last of the Hardison-Purvis gang. They've given Esperanza entirely too much trouble."

A hearty round of amens filled the room.

Micah nodded to Laurie, signaling she could begin the opening hymn. Tired and shaky, she still managed without too many mistakes. As she held the chord at the end of each verse, she glanced out across the room, wondering where Tolley was. This would be a good time for him to make an appearance so everyone would know he was the main hero in the outlaws' capture and saving the Starling children. He'd been utterly selfless, risking his life, even offering himself in their place. If the people of this town didn't appreciate how such courage made up for all of his past mistakes, then they weren't worthy of him.

As the hymn ended, the church doors opened, and Tolley entered, Mrs. Foster on his arm. Laurie's eyes stung. Even after his trying morning, he'd thought of his dear landlady, who never liked to miss church services. Forget about how the people of Esperanza regarded him. In that moment, Laurie didn't think *friend* was a strong enough word to describe her feelings for that brave, selfless man.

## Chapter Fourteen

With the church being almost full, Tolley had to find a pew near the back where he and Mrs. Foster could sit together. She was still a bit shaky, so he wanted to stay close by her. A few people nodded silent greetings to his companion. One or two appeared to include him in their smiles, but he wouldn't count on it meaning anything. Across the aisle, Nate and Rand acknowledged him with brotherly grins they hadn't sent his way in a long time. Or so it seemed. While their acceptance made him feel pretty good, Laurie's smile, clearly aimed at him as she stepped down from the organ bench, sent warmth and joy surging through his chest.

Reverend Thomas preached a sermon on making the most of the talents the Lord gave a person, which set Tolley to thinking about his future. Although he had a pretty good head for the law, he still preferred working on the ranch. Besides, nobody in town wanted his legal services. On the other hand, unless the Colonel woke up and let him go back to Four Stones, ranching wasn't in his future, either. His only certainty was Laurie's friendship.

After the sermon, the minister made some announcements, ending with one that perked up Tolley's ears. "The first crop of berries in Raspberry Gulch should be ripe in about two weeks. Grace and I want to invite all of the young unmarried adults to camp out with us on Greenie Mountain so we can bring back enough berries for anyone who wants them. We'll have a ladies' tent and a gentlemen's tent for sleeping, and we'll be along as chaperones, so you can be sure propriety will be observed."

He went on to describe his plans for the event, but Tolley's mind cut away in a new direction. What would happen if he skipped courtship and straight-out proposed marriage to Laurie? If, as he suspected, her feelings for him had grown to at least a little more than friendship through their shared adventure in rescuing Molly, maybe she would be willing to marry him. His own feelings for her had deepened considerably after her display of courage. His relief that she'd come through the situation safely was palpable. If he chose a nice location for the proposal, say Raspberry Gulch during the raspberry picking, she might be more receptive to the idea of living in the San Luis Valley instead of Denver. He couldn't keep from grinning at the idea.

The minister dismissed the congregation, and everyone got up to leave.

"Good work, Northam." Mayor Jones clapped Tolley on the shoulder. "You men did a good job bringing in those outlaws."

Before Tolley could answer, the mayor stepped over to Nate and Rand to say the same thing. Several others commented on the rescue, but the two men whose approval meant the most hadn't come to church today. The Colonel, of course. And George Eberly.

Dinner at the boardinghouse included the usual roast beef, a tender and probably expensive cut. Tolley had forgotten to check Mrs. Foster's books to see how the boarders' rent, including his own, could manage such fine fare every day. Before he could ask Laurie about it, she excused herself to take a basket of food to the Starlings. Mrs. Runyan and Mr. Parsley fussed about her leaving right after she served them dessert, forsaking her post as hostess. Seemed to him those two people had to work pretty hard to find things to complain about. Seemed to him they wanted more than they were paying for, but he must be sure before saying anything. Otherwise, they might abandon Mrs. Foster for some other abode and leave her struggling to make ends meet.

Laurie returned late in the afternoon and sat at the piano, idly playing a soft tune Tolley didn't recognize.

"Something troubling you?" He sat in the chair beside the piano where Laurie usually sat when giving lessons.

Her eyes got all red and watery. Maybe he shouldn't have asked.

"Mr. Starling had a setback, probably because of the kidnapping." She wiped away a tear rolling down her cheek. "He promised to hang on until the trial, but I think he's resigned to letting go after that."

The lump in Tolley's chest lodged there for the rest of the day. The sheriff had enough evidence against Purvis to send him to the gallows, but Bob Starling's testimony would clinch it. As for defending the outlaws, Tolley wouldn't do it, especially not after they threatened to shoot sweet little Molly because she cried.

On Monday morning, he visited the Starlings to see if Adam felt like working on the bathroom floor.

"Sure thing." Adam spoke in his usual cheerful manner, but dark circles under his eyes bespoke worry and sleepless nights. "I'll be over right after dinner, if it's all right with you. I'm working in the livery stable this morning."

"Sure thing." Tolley echoed Adam's words, adding a tight smile.

How did this young man manage? Considering all he and his family suffered, seemed he should have a sour disposition, yet he didn't. Tolley remembered his own lifelong bitterness before Reverend Harris took him under his wing. Why had he been bitter? Because of a father whose approval he could never win? If memory served him, Nate struggled with that, too. Only Rand and Rosamond escaped the Colonel's constant criticism. Yet Tolley always had plenty to eat. Always had money in his pocket and in the bank because the Colonel shared the ranch profits with his children, the "four" in Four Stones Ranch. With so many blessings, how could he have felt sorry for himself?

He stopped by his office to ask Effie Bean whether anyone had sought his services. No one had, but the entire office gleamed, and Effie had gone a long way toward completing matching wool sweaters for her two children. Tolley stepped back outside to go next door and deliver some bad news to Purvis and his gang. As he walked under his shingle, he wondered if he might as well take it down before it, or he, became a laughingstock to the town.

"Morning, Sheriff, Deputy." Like Adam, both men bore the signs of lost sleep. After a brief exchange of pleasantries, he said, "How are the prisoners?" The inside door stood wide-open, probably so the lawmen could hear any escape plans the outlaws might devise.

"Sufficiently uncomfortable to suit me." Lawson sat at his desk, the usual pile of wanted posters in front of him.

Seated across the room whittling on a wooden spoon, Justice Gareau snorted out a laugh.

"Then I'll be happy to add to their discomfort." Tolley grinned, daring to feel a bit of camaraderie with the two lawmen after yesterday's rescue. "I've decided not to defend Purvis. Either one. Or that Skinner fella."

"You got a reason?"

"Because I know they're guilty, and I won't pretend otherwise just to keep them from hanging."

Justice nodded his approval.

"I suppose I'll have to get 'em a lawyer from Alamosa." The sheriff scratched his chin. "You want to tell 'em, or shall I?"

"I will." Tolley would gladly let the lawman do it, but since he'd offered to represent Jud Purvis, he should be the one to *un*represent him.

Justice gave him another approving nod, as did the sheriff.

When Tolley entered the cell area, all three prisoners stood and gripped the bars of their cells. Viewing the twins side by side, he could see their remarkable resemblance, right down to their dark eyes and wiry brown mustaches. Too bad they were equally evil on the inside, too.

"Howdy, Northam. Boys, this here's my lawyer."

Jud's sniveling, ingratiating demeanor sickened Tolley. He acted as though yesterday's confrontation hadn't even happened. Did he truly believe Tolley would defend him now? "If you ask real nice, he might just—"

"No, I'm not your lawyer."

"What?" Jud's jaw dropped, and his face took on a wounded look. "Why, you promised—"

"Purvis, do you really think I'd try to keep you from hanging when you kidnapped a child and threatened to harm her? When you pointed a gun at me and pulled the trigger?" Tolley felt his old anger rising up. Before he said something he'd regret, he turned to go. "I'm done here, Sheriff."

A string of curses followed him out the door. The last thing Tolley heard was Sheriff Lawson warning the outlaws not to use that kind of language in his jailhouse or they'd live to regret it.

"All finished?" On Friday evening, Laurie stood in the hallway outside the closed bathroom door. Beside her, Mrs. Foster beamed with anticipation.

"All finished." Tolley, along with Adam, grinned broadly as they prepared to show off the results of their labors.

Even Mrs. Runyan and Mr. Parsley awaited the grand opening in the hallway. Although both tried to appear indifferent, the flicker of interest in their eyes gave them away.

"Ta-da!" Tolley opened the door with a flourish and then bowed to Mrs. Foster. "My lady, your days of carrying water upstairs are over." He stepped back to grant her admittance.

"Oh, my." Mrs. Foster stood at the doorway, hands

clasped over her chest. "How very grand." Her eyes bright with happy tears, she looked around the room.

Laurie peeked over Mrs. Foster's shoulder. "It's beautiful. You've done a wonderful job, both of you."

Although she'd seen most of the construction, Tolley had kept her out for the past two days while the plumbers installed the fixtures. Now, seeing the completed room, she found it truly spectacular. Everything gleamed with newness. The white mosaic tiles on the floor, the white porcelain tub with bear-claw feet, the white pedestaled sink, even the flushing water closet, with its porcelain bowl and oak seat and water tank.

"Mr. Starling." Tolley bowed to Adam. "Would you be so kind as to demonstrate the facilities?"

"Why, Mr. Northam." Adam bowed back. "I do believe the honor should go to you."

The two were as comical as a vaudeville act. While Laurie and Mrs. Foster laughed at their performance, Tolley demonstrated how the water flowed into and out of each fixture.

"Unfortunately, there remains the problem of heating the bathwater. Until Esperanza brings the proposed gas lighting and heat to its citizens, we'll still have to boil the water here." He waved a hand over the small woodstove and the box of wood beside it.

"Humph." Mr. Parsley crossed his arms over his chest. "Surely you don't expect me to heat my own bathwater?"

"Humph." Mrs. Runyan stuck her head into the room. "I still say bathing in a tub is indecent."

"Well, then." Laurie had heard enough. "You certainly aren't required to use these modern conveniences. I'll deliver your pitcher of hot water each morning as usual so you can bathe the old-fashioned way." She tempered her sarcasm with as sweet a tone as she could muster.

"Humph," Mrs. Runyan repeated before turning to march back to her room.

Even Mrs. Foster couldn't keep from snickering at the silly woman's attitude.

"My dears." The lady's gaze took in Tolley, Adam and Laurie. "How can I ever thank you? Imagine, a boardinghouse with a full bathroom for my boarders."

"And for you." Laurie gave Mrs. Foster a hug as she sighed with satisfaction. "It's amazing what can be accomplished with a little imagination." She glanced at the men. "And a lot of hard work."

"Humph." Mr. Parsley pulled out his watch and snapped it open. "Miss Eberly, it is five minutes past seven. Where is my supper?"

"Coming right up." Laurie caught Tolley's attention and rolled her eyes before descending the back staircase. Adam went home for supper, but at least two people would appreciate her cooking tonight. Dear Mrs. Foster never complained about anything. And Tolley, like Pa did for Ma, always complimented whatever she prepared.

In fact, this past week, Tolley complimented how she looked each morning, her patience with her piano students, the meals she prepared. A girl could get used to such remarks. She could get used to just about everything regarding Tolley. With every passing day, Denver dreams were fading, replaced by his handsome face and kind deeds. Would she be satisfied to stay in Esperanza to see what became of their friendship? Or would she always regret giving up the opportunity of a lifetime?

* * *

The following Monday, Judge Enos Hartley arrived in Esperanza to conduct the trial. Sheriff Lawson sent Deputy Gareau over to Alamosa to enlist the services of Ed Busey for the defense. With Busey's reputation for clever maneuvering, Tolley wanted to observe how he tried to save the outlaws' necks. Men crowded into the front room of the jailhouse, with others standing in the cell room and outside the building's open front door. Nate and Rand arrived early so they could get good seats in the first row beside Tolley.

With his steel-gray hair, matching mustache and muttonchop sideburns, Judge Hartley possessed the imposing presence of a man who wouldn't shrink from sending a guilty man to the gallows. He sat at the sheriff's desk and drew a gavel from his pocket. With Lawson's assistance, and due to the tight quarters, he selected only six men for the jury, who sat between the desk and the front window.

Tolley watched to see who'd volunteered for the duty. The men who'd accosted him in the park on Independence Day had said they'd vote guilty no matter what evidence the lawyer presented. They weren't chosen. Tolley didn't know whether to be pleased or disappointed. It was a solemn matter to send a man to his grave, and every man deserved a fair trial, even polecats like these.

Tolley and Adam had offered to carry Bob Starling to the trial, but Bob insisted upon walking. The moment he entered the room, the entire audience gasped. Gaunt and gray, he seemed like a walking skeleton, like the men in photographs who'd emerged from the notorious Andersonville Prison at the end of the War.

Tolley had seen the man in his bed, so he wasn't surprised, but Judge Hartley appeared stunned.

The trial opened. Sheriff Lawson testified first, describing the gang's threats when he put them in prison in Kansas. Reverend Thomas and Grace testified about their encounter with Purvis, Hardison and Smith. A representative of the Denver and Rio Grande Railroad testified about the gang being suspected of the payroll robbery during which Bob Starling was beaten. As an aside, he said there'd be a reward to anyone who found the stolen payroll. That brought on a flurry of chatter from the onlookers, and the judge banged his gavel to restore order.

Last, Bob Starling testified. Ed Busey said there was no way Bob could be certain which Purvis beat him or even if one of them had. Both now claimed to have been in Kansas at the time of the robbery. With great effort and helped by his son, Bob walked to the cells and studied each man. At his sign, Adam held out two of Mrs. Starling's apple tarts, one to each twin. Jed reached through the bars with his right hand, Jud with his left.

"Thank you kindly." The brothers spoke in unison, a hint of mockery in their voices.

"That's him." Bob pointed to Jud. "The man who tried to kill me was left-handed."

"Now, Mr. Starling," Busey said, "do you expect us to believe that while you were beaten, you paused to notice which hand the man used?"

Tottering back to his chair beside the desk, Bob wheezed as he caught his breath. With a trembling hand, he pointed to the vicious scar running down the right side of his face. "Is this proof enough?"

The room erupted again, and the judge pounded his gavel. "Order. I will have order!" Once quiet returned, he said, "Busey, what do you say to that?"

"Hey!" Heep Skinner called out from his cell. "I want to talk. I ain't gonna git hung for what they did."

"You shut up," Jed called out. The twins reached through the bars, trying to grab Skinner.

"Go on, Mr. Skinner." The judge pointed at him with his gavel. "You can testify from there."

Tolley noticed that while the man kept order in his makeshift courtroom, he didn't adhere to as strict a format for the trial as judges in Boston did.

Deputy Gareau held the Bible while Skinner reached through the bars and put his hand on it, promising to tell the whole truth.

Judge Hartley nodded in his direction. "Go on, Skinner."

Tolley could see the outlaw hesitating and prayed he wouldn't change his mind. After a glance at the Purvis brothers, Skinner appeared to steel himself with a deep, shuddering breath.

"Last December, Jud Purvis shot Sheriff Lawson, intending to kill him. I saw him shoot with my own eyes. That's when Jed and I lit out. Shootin' a lawman ain't no small thing. I was done with this place." He swiped a hand over his mouth and stared at his former friends. "Will I get a lighter sentence if I tell it all?"

"We'll treat you fair and legal," the judge responded.

"What if I tell you where the rest of the payroll is?"

That stirred up the room again. Once the judge regained control, he said, "We'll see."

"Awright. I'll do it."

Tolley noticed Fred Brody taking notes about the

trial. When Skinner began talking, he turned over a new page and tapped his pencil against his tongue, then began to write rapidly to keep pace with the man's testimony. Even though Tolley was watching the trial, he looked forward to reading Brody's report in the *Esperanza Journal*. Once the memories faded, the facts would be archived for future generations to read.

Skinner explained that the gang indeed robbed Bob Starling of the railroad payroll back in February of '81. They divided up part of the money, both cash and gold, and Hardison, being the leader, kept the rest. Then the gang split up. Skinner and the Purvis brothers went on to rob a bank in Kansas, and Lawson put them in prison for it. Hardison and Smith stayed in Colorado, where they hid the rest of the money.

"We heard tell they tried to rob your bank next door and was put in the Canon City Penitentiary. Me and the Purvis boys broke out, then come to Colorado and broke them out. I wanted to git the money and hightail it down to Mexico, but Jud Purvis said he'd kill Sheriff Lawson first. Hardison said he had a beef with some people here in Esperanza, and he'd get his revenge afore he went anywhere. Me? I didn't want no part of it, but the only way I could git my share of the railroad gold was to stick around. I never shot nobody."

Even though the Purvis brothers continued to scowl at Skinner, they didn't contradict anything he said.

Satisfied with the man's testimony, the judge instructed the jury in how to deliberate. Without even leaving the room, they put their heads together, consulted quietly and pronounced their verdict: guilty. Once the cheering crowd settled down, Judge Hartley delivered his sentence. The twins would be delivered to the Canon City Penitentiary for hanging. Skinner would serve a life sentence.

Skinner cursed and yelled at the judge. "I ain't gonna tell you where that payroll is. I'm gonna git outta prison on good behavior and come back and git it. It'll all be mine." He eyed his former cohorts. "Whatcha think of that?"

Once again, the twins attempted to lunge at him through the bars, to no avail, although their antics caused a good deal of laughter among the onlookers.

Judge Hartley ordered Sheriff Lawson to deputize ten men to accompany the three prisoners to Canon City Penitentiary. They had to leave early the next morning and ride hard to make it before nightfall. He then declared the trial over and dismissed the onlookers.

Giving his brothers a quick wave, Tolley made his way through the milling crowd and headed back home. He couldn't wait to tell Laurie what had happened. He also wanted to make sure she'd be going on Reverend Thomas's expedition next week. Only this morning, Effie Bean agreed to tend the boardinghouse for the three days they'd be gone, which should ease Laurie's concerns about leaving Mrs. Foster.

Now he needed to practice how to propose once they reached Raspberry Gulch. He had to say it the right way, or she'd turn him down. In fact, it might even ruin everything between them. After the way he'd begun to care for her beyond friendship, he'd be crushed if that happened.

"Molly, I think we should begin your voice lessons." Laurie knew it was a little soon, but if she taught the child carefully, she wouldn't harm her voice, and spending time with Molly could help the child recover from her trauma. "Would you like for me to teach you?"

Molly blinked her big brown eyes. As far as Laurie knew, she hadn't smiled since the kidnapping. Now a hint of a smile appeared on her lips. "Yes, Miss Laurie. I'll be happy to do more chores to pay for it."

"We'll see, sweetie. Maybe you could help me make cookies. We eat a lot of cookies around here."

Her words brought a long-overdue smile. "That would be fun." The smile quickly faded.

A sharp ache stung Laurie's heart. At not quite eight years old, Molly shouldn't have to worry about how to pay for her lessons. None of her Denver students ever thought about such things. Only one or two cared even about playing piano or singing. How could Laurie leave such an eager, talented student? The longer she spent with Molly, the more she became devoted to the child. She couldn't expect Mrs. Foster to give free lessons. Nor could Mrs. Foster teach Molly the advanced techniques Laurie had learned at the conservatory. The more she thought about it, the more she began to understand why her determination to return to the city had always been accompanied by doubts about it being the Lord's will for her. Did this mean He wanted her to stay here? For the first time in all her life, she sensed she could stay in the San Luis Valley forever and never regret it.

The front door opened, and Tolley appeared in the wide doorway into the parlor. He gave her the devastating smile that always thrummed on her heartstrings.

"Afternoon, ladies." His green eyes twinkled. "Want to hear some good news?"

"Sure do." Laurie gave Molly a hug while questioning him with her eyes. Perhaps his news wasn't appropriate for a child's ears. "Is it—?"

Tolley nodded his understanding, which only added to his appeal. "Let's just say the bad men are going away for a long, long time. In fact, they won't ever come back."

Laurie's eyes stung. She couldn't let herself think about what lay before those evil men. Maybe Micah could visit them before they left and share the Gospel with them. After all, their fellow gang member, Deke Smith, trusted the Lord before he died.

Molly gave Laurie a solemn look. "Will Adam be here soon, Miss Laurie? I want to go home."

"I don't know, honey." Laurie traded a look with Tolley. "I'd take you home, but I must fix supper. Would you mind if Mr. Tolley took you?"

Tolley gave Molly a gentle smile. "I'd be pleased and proud to walk you home, Miss Molly." He sketched a bow even his proper English brother-in-law would approve of.

Molly giggled, bringing more tears to Laurie's eyes. She didn't know Tolley managed children this well. It only added to his appeal.

"Well, then, off you go." Laurie closed the music book and handed it to Molly. "Don't forget to practice at the church every day."

Doubt crossed the child's face, but she said, "Yes, ma'am."

Laurie watched as Tolley walked up the street with the small child. What a sweet picture they made as he waved his hand toward the sky, the trees, the houses they passed, perhaps intent on distracting Molly from her fears. What a good father he'd make one day.

Something shifted deep inside Laurie's heart, a swell of emotions, a fierce affection for him that she could almost call love. If he asked to court her again, maybe she should say yes. After all, courtship wasn't engagement. It was a time when people discovered whether they were suited for marriage.

A horse and rider passed the two walkers, and Molly desperately clutched Tolley's hand with both of hers. How long until this sweet child, until all the people of Esperanza, could feel safe again in their law-abiding little town?

One thing Laurie knew for certain. When she was with Tolley, she felt entirely safe, more than she ever had in Denver, even among the elite families whose children she taught. Some in higher society could be such snobs, as though money made them better than other people or more loved by God. That wasn't the way her salt-of-the-earth parents raised her and her sisters. While some wealthy people gave to charitable causes or even raised money for the less fortunate, they always seemed to maintain a safe distance from the hard work. But giving hands-on help, such as Tolley's installing a bathroom for an elderly lady, showed true character. For Laurie, running Mrs. Foster's boarding-house had given her more satisfaction than she'd ever imagined possible. She now felt confident she could run her own household one day.

Would it be a fancy brick house in Denver or a wood-frame clapboard house in the San Luis Valley?

# Chapter Fifteen

After Saturday supper, Tolley added the columns of figures for a third time to be sure he hadn't made a mistake. "Just as I thought." He showed the ledger page to Laurie, who sat beside him at the dining room table with that silly cat curled up on her lap. "Mrs. Runyan and Mr. Parsley have taken advantage of Mrs. Foster for three years. She's not making a living from them at all. In fact, she's practically supporting them."

Setting the cat on the floor, Laurie leaned close to the page. Tolley could smell the sweet, heady scent of lilacs on her hair. For a moment, he forgot their purpose here and considered proposing right away.

"How horrid." She ran a long, slender finger down the page where the services and their costs were listed. "Doing their laundry, cleaning their rooms and, most of all, feeding them as if they were royalty. What an outrage."

Brought back to the moment by her vehemence, Tolley shook off his romantic dizziness. "Why didn't she notice? I mean, she kept these books up-to-date, so why wouldn't she see she spent more than she brought in?"

Laurie sat back and glared at him. "At the end of the day, I'm far too tired to think about balancing the books. Imagine how exhausted Mrs. Foster gets at her age."

"Hey, this isn't my fault." Why did she turn cranky when he was doing his best to help?

"I know." To his relief, her expression softened, and she touched his hand, sending a pleasant tickle up his arm. "I also noticed you're paying twice as much rent as they do, and you help me pay to send out the laundry. And of course installing the bathroom. Mrs. Runyan and Mr. Parsley don't contribute anything to the household except complaints."

"It's the least I could do." Mrs. Foster had given him a home when his own family cast him out. He'd do anything for her. "Besides, you've given up your whole summer to help her. You can't buy that time back."

"As you said, it's the least I could do for such a dear lady." Laurie copied his shrug. "So what are we going to do about it? I mean, isn't there something legal we can do?" Trust now emanating from her eyes, she batted her dark auburn lashes at him.

*Kiss her!* How he longed to surrender to temptation. But then he'd be tempted to propose, which would ruin his plans for making it a special event at the raspberry picking.

"Tolley?" She tilted her head in an appealing manner and gave him a sweet half smile. "Are you all right?"

"Um. Uh. Yes. I'm fine." He coughed softly. "I don't think we need to resort to legal methods. We can't exactly sue them for back rent when they've paid what Mrs. Foster asked." His mind back on track, he considered possibilities. "We can take either of two courses. One, we can raise the rent, provided Mrs. Foster agrees. Or, two, we can cut back on room cleaning and laundry service or at least the number of times prime beef and such things are served."

Laurie reached down to pet the cat, which had wedged itself between them as if it were their chaperone. "They'll raise the roof, of course."

He shrugged. "We can't let Mrs. Foster go on like this. Considering the way things are now, it'd be better for her if they left."

"I suppose." She wrinkled her forehead. "Let's ask Mrs. Foster if we can tell them she's raising the rent. They may throw a fit but, well, they can take it or leave it."

"Sounds like a good idea." Tolley gazed at her, his heart warming at their camaraderie. "You know what? We make a good team."

The cat began to purr as if it agreed.

Laurie gave him a smile he felt clear down to his toes. "Yes, we do." An expectant look in her eyes hinted at something, but he couldn't figure out what.

He closed the ledger and stood. "We'd better get a good night's sleep so we'll be ready for church tomorrow." As he left the room, he heard her muttering something he couldn't quite make out. Probably talking to the cat.

"How thoughtful of you." On Sunday afternoon, Mrs. Foster, looking better than she had since her accident, sat at the kitchen table while Laurie and Tolley showed her the pages of her ledger. "I suppose you're right to be concerned. However, when Mrs. Runyan first came to Esperanza to set up her millinery shop, she appeared quite destitute. I wanted to help her get started, so I only required twenty dollars a month for room and board. While she set up shop that first week, I agreed to do her laundry, but I didn't realize she'd expect me to continue doing it. Mr. Parsley arrived shortly after and of course, being a man, considered laundry to be women's work, so I agreed to do his, as well. I couldn't exactly charge him more than I charged her, but I never thought to consider my own costs."

Laurie gave Tolley a teasing smirk. Maybe he'd see how foolish his own thoughts were about "women's work." Instead, he questioned her with one raised eyebrow. She shrugged and spoke to Mrs. Foster. "Would you give Tolley and me permission to tell the boarders you're going to raise the room and board to thirty-five dollars a month, and that they must take their laundry to Mr. Chen?"

Mrs. Foster sighed. "Seems like a great deal of money, and I know they'll be unhappy about it. I dislike unpleasantness of any sort."

Reaching across the table, Tolley took Mrs. Foster's hand. "But you shouldn't support those two people. They make very good livings in their businesses."

"Are you certain?"

"Yes, ma'am." Tolley gave her a knowing wink. "I checked with Garrick. Travelers staying at the hotel often spend money on hats and watches in their shops. Local folks do, too, of course. And both of them eat expensive dinners in the hotel dining room every day. Why shouldn't you receive payment for the fine food you provide for them?"

"Well, then." She sighed again. "Let's pray about

the matter. When you come back from the raspberry picking, we'll talk more about it."

With that settled, Laurie busied herself preparing for the coming excursion. Grace had assigned her the task of baking bread, biscuits, cakes and cookies. She also packed enough eggs in a box of straw for two breakfasts for twenty people.

On Monday morning, she left Mrs. Foster and the boardinghouse in Effie Bean's capable hands. Micah and Grace arrived with a large box wagon and helped Laurie load the food and her own carpetbag filled with clothes and other necessities. Along with camping gear, others had packed empty buckets and boxes to fill with berries.

Laurie climbed up behind the driver's bench to join her sister Georgia, Effie's daughter May, and Anna Means in finding somewhat comfortable seating on the rolled canvas tents and blankets. Riding Thor, Tolley led the way out of town toward the northwest hills. He looked so strong and capable, and her heart performed tiny somersaults as she watched him. Behind them, other members of the party squeezed into a three-bench covered surrey, while five cowboys on horseback brought up the rear.

With the weather sunny and mild, everyone was in high spirits, singing jolly songs and laughing often. Wes, one of the Four Stones Ranch cowboys, taught them a new song, "My Darling Clementine." While the lyrics were sad, the melody lent itself to many boisterous hoots and howls. Laurie's favorite old song, "Jeanie with the Light Brown Hair," gave the travelers a chance to blend their voices in beautiful harmonies. What a fine choir they'd make for the church. A few of the best basses and tenors among the cowboys didn't attend services, so maybe an opportunity to sing would entice them to come.

Why was she thinking of starting a choir? Was the Lord revealing one more reason for her to stay in Esperanza?

When the sun reached its zenith, Micah ordered a stop for dinner. Sandwiches and potato salad served off the lowered back of the box wagon provided sufficient nourishment for the rest of the journey. By early evening, they reached Greenie Mountain and descended into Raspberry Gulch. Even with the sunlight fading over the mountain summits, Laurie could see the bright red raspberries sparkling like rubies on the fields of bushes.

While the men tended the horses, set up the two tents and laid out bedrolls, the ladies placed cast-iron Dutch ovens over the campfire to reheat stew they'd prepared the night before. With everything settled, Laurie waited at the back of the food line. She looked for Tolley but couldn't find him among those serving themselves. Maybe he was fetching water from the creek. Whatever way he occupied himself, he hadn't sought her out today. Had she done something to annoy him?

She sat on a log at the edge of the crowd and began to nibble at her supper. In spite of the jolly mood of the other campers, melancholy crept into her. She'd soon be leaving these dear people for good, exchanging wilderness adventures with friends for elegant dinner parties with members of Denver's elite society. Did she really want to do that?

On the other side of the fire, Grace and Micah

leaned their heads close together. Like Ma and Pa, they shared an intimate emotional bond only married couples could enjoy. Someday, maybe soon, Laurie wanted a marriage like that. Ever since last Saturday evening, when Tolley said the two of them made a good team, she'd thought he would ask to court her again. Instead, he'd walked out of the room. Maybe he'd never repeat his offer. Yet she could see how their mutual affection had deepened since that day, not to mention the wonderful feelings their Independence Day kiss had stirred within her heart. Couldn't he?

Later, as she curled up in her bedroll in the ladies' tent, Grace lay down beside her.

"Whooeee, what a day." Grace reached over and punched Laurie's shoulder. "You having fun?"

Instead of answering with a partial truth, Laurie said, "I'm more concerned about you and your baby. Are you sure you're all right?"

"We're doing fine." Grace snickered. "Don't think I didn't notice what you did there." She tugged her blanket up over her shoulders. "You and Tolley have a falling-out?"

"No." She'd answered too quickly. In the dim lantern light, she could see Grace's skeptical look. "In fact, the other day, we agreed…" She pulled up on one elbow and noticed two of the other single ladies watching her, at least one of whom had shown interest in Tolley. She didn't need them to gossip and misquote her words when Tolley heard them. "We agreed Mrs. Foster's new bathroom was a very worthwhile project. You should get Micah to install one in the parsonage. Sure would help once your baby comes." She lifted her chin toward the other women.

Grace nodded her understanding. "Good idea. Now baby and I need some sleep." She sat up. "Girls, I'm a light sleeper, so don't any of you get the idea to go out picking raspberries in the middle of the night."

They all giggled, including Laurie, knowing exactly what this minister's wife meant. No secretly meeting up with their beaux. Grace truly had found her place. Laurie wondered when she'd find her own place and whether it would be here among the warmhearted people of Esperanza or in the colder society of Denver.

Nervous excitement filled Tolley's chest as he sat on a log beside Reverend Thomas for the first watch of the night. Once he could hear all the other fellas snoring in the men's tent, he told the minister his plans.

"I got this at Mrs. Winsted's." He took the small box from his pocket and opened it. The diamond-and-ruby ring sparkled in the fading firelight. "Tomorrow I'm going to ask Laurie to marry me."

Reverend Thomas nodded as though he wasn't surprised. "So you already have George's permission to court her?"

"Um. Well…" He should've expected the question. This man had endured that very ordeal with George Eberly last Christmas so he could marry Grace. But what father would say no to a fine man of God like Reverend Thomas?

The minister shook his head. "You know it's always wise to get permission from the lady's father before you propose."

"I suppose so." How could Tolley tell him George warned him to stay away from Laurie? He closed the ring box and returned it to his pocket. "What would you think if I asked her, and if she says yes, I'll go to George? I mean, if she says no, I don't have to face him."

Reverend Thomas chuckled. "He scares you that much, huh?"

"No." Tolley shrugged. "Yes."

He laughed again. "I won't stop you, Tolley. But after our talk about your father, I hope you've thought this through. Are you proposing to Laurie to please the Colonel?"

"No." He didn't think that was still the reason, but the minister's question gave him pause.

"And you love her enough to spend your life taking care of her, even through the hard times?"

Tolley nodded, even though he hadn't thought much beyond marrying Laurie to the life they'd live together. He only knew he deeply valued her friendship and wanted it to go on forever.

They sat in silence for a while until Wes and Joe came out of the tent to take up the watch.

"No grizzlies?" Wes said, checking his Winchester for ammunition.

"Nope." The minister stood and stretched. "No mountain lions, either."

"We'd best build up the fire to keep 'em away." The two men added a chunk of a dead log to the flames, sending thousands of red sparks into the night air.

Before Tolley entered the tent, Reverend Thomas put a hand on his shoulder. "I won't say you can't propose to Laurie," he whispered. "In fact, I'd be proud to be your brother-in-law. But I still think you should get George's approval."

Tolley nodded, but he heard exactly what he wanted to hear. Reverend Micah Thomas would be proud to call him brother.

"Georgia, don't eat so many." All morning, Laurie managed to discipline herself to only an occasional bite of the sweet, juicy raspberries. "Leave some to make preserves."

"I know." Georgia laughed as she brushed away a stray drop of red juice from her chin. "This is my last one. I promise." She popped another berry into her mouth.

"Time to set up dinner, ladies." Grace made her way down the hillside through the tangle of bushes, agile in spite of her condition. "Don't know about you gals, but I'm hungry."

While the men continued their picking, the women carried their buckets to the campsite and stored them in the nearby stream. Using eggs, corn oil and vinegar, Grace whipped up some fresh mayonnaise for potato salad. Others sliced bread and ham for sandwiches. Still others kept close watch on the food to prevent bears…and hungry cowboys…from devouring everything in one meal.

Before she'd gone to sleep last night, Laurie had decided not to search for Tolley today. Yet this morning, her gaze often strayed across the vast raspberry patch in his direction. To her disappointment, he hadn't looked her way, at least not that she'd noticed, so she busied herself with the tasks at hand. To her surprise, he brought his dinner plate and joined her on a fallen tree fifteen yards from the cold campfire.

"Having fun?" He gave her the grin that never failed to stir her heart.

"Yes. And you?" Now that he'd joined her, she was enjoying herself.

Inhaling a deep breath, he gazed up at the sky, around at the tall pine trees and then at her. "I'm having the best time of my life." His gaze turned intense.

A giddy feeling stirred inside of her. "Glad to hear it."

He forked up a mouthful of potato salad. "This is your ma's recipe, isn't it?"

So much for good feelings. "Yes," she snapped. "My sisters and I always make it the same way."

"I like it. Tried-and-true." He did that funny waggle of his eyebrows, which for some reason irritated her further. "Like us."

She rolled her eyes. "Yep. That's us. Tried-and-true pals."

"Say, would you take a walk with me after we finish eating?" He tilted his head down the hill toward the creek.

Leaning away, she gave him a long look. "You know the rules. No unmarried couples going off together." Why on earth would he ask such a question?

"Ah, yes." Grinning, he scratched his cheek, as if he'd expected her answer. "Then how about a walk up the hill where everyone can see us?"

Something about his demeanor tickled her, and she giggled. "Why not?"

"Good. Hurry up and eat." He set the example by taking a big bite of his ham sandwich.

Once they finished their dinner, they carried their

plates to the creek, where the girls on dish-washing duty would scrub them clean for supper.

"Let's go." Tolley took Laurie's hand. At his touch, a pleasant buzzing rolled up her arm and swept over her neck. He tugged her up the hill from the creek and through the campsite, determination filling his expression.

"Tolley?" Micah called out from near the wagon.

Tolley waved at him. "We'll be right back."

Laurie gave her brother-in-law a questioning glance, but Tolley reclaimed her attention before Micah could respond.

Over the past month, Tolley had gotten used to the high altitude again after living at sea level for two years. But for some reason, he had difficulty breathing as he and Laurie reached the top of the hill. He'd carefully thought through his plan, but Reverend Thomas had almost ruined it by calling out to him.

"Here we are." He took hold of Laurie's upper arms and aimed her toward the summit of Greenie Mountain, pointing over her shoulder. "What a beautiful sight."

While she stared in that direction, he pulled the small box from his pocket and opened it. Going down on one knee, he held the ring out to her.

"Tolley, I don't see—" She turned as she spoke and then froze in place, her big blue eyes as round as saucers. "What are you doing?" With a nervous, uncertain laugh, she put one hand over her lips and bunched the other at her waist.

She was so beautiful. All of his planned declarations of devotion and promises to care for her faded from his thoughts, and he blurted out, "Laurie Eberly, will you marry me?"

Her jaw dropped. She blinked, and tears flooded her eyes. She didn't look at the ring at all, only at him. Which must be the reason his heart welled up and felt ready to pop right out of his chest. Was that love? He couldn't take time to examine his feelings. "Well? Will you?"

She nodded briskly, and some of those tears splashed in Tolley's direction. In the distance, he thought he heard a hubbub going on down at the campsite, but he'd look into that later.

"Go on. T-take the ring." Had he forgotten how to talk?

"No, silly." She held out her left hand. "You put it on me."

Shaking more violently than he ever had, he took the ring from the box and gently shoved it onto her long, slender finger. She shook, too, so he stood and pulled her into his arms. She lifted her lovely face to him, an expectant look beaming from her eyes. Noisy hoots and hollering sounded closer and closer, like a stampede coming up the hill, but he wouldn't for the world break this wonderful moment to look. Again his heart swelled with emotion.

"I'd like very much to kiss you, Laurie, but I think we've caused enough of a stir as it is."

She grabbed his face and planted a kiss right on his lips. "There. That'll stir 'em up a whole heap more." Her proper grammar dropped away just as her proper manners had. Tolley didn't mind at all.

Within seconds, they were surrounded by the entire party. Tolley tried to hold on to Laurie, but the fellas pulled him away and pumped his hand while the gals squealed and giggled, admiring Laurie's ring and giving her hugs and female kinds of congratulations.

Even Grace was in the thick of it, a big-sister smile on her pretty face. "I knew it. I just knew it."

Only Reverend Thomas stood back, not exactly frowning, but not joining in the celebration with the others. Tolley knew the minister would come around eventually. Hadn't he given his approval of Tolley last night, though not of this proposal? Besides, once the Colonel knew about the engagement, Tolley would be a great deal closer to getting *his* approval, which was far more important.

Seated behind Grace and Micah in the box wagon as the party wended its way down the mountain, Laurie snuggled under Tolley's arm. His proposal yesterday had shocked her, but the moment she saw him kneeling before her on the hilltop, ring in hand, she knew it was what she'd wanted all along. Knew she loved him more than words could express. She'd never been so happy.

She gazed up at his handsome face. Like all of the men on the campout, a two-day stubble covered his well-formed cheeks and strong chin. She reached up to touch the prickly dark hairs.

"Maybe I should let it grow." He grinned and tugged her closer.

"Go right ahead." She moved away a couple of inches from him. "Just don't expect me to kiss you if you do."

He tugged her close again. "You didn't seem to have a problem yesterday."

Her face warmed at the memory. She wasn't embarrassed for kissing him, however impulsive it had been. "That's when I learned I don't want to be married to a bearded man."

Watching only a few feet away, May and Georgia giggled, while Grace's chortle wafted back from the driver's bench. Even Thor, tied to the back of the wagon, whickered, probably in response to the human laughter. On the other hand, Micah gave her a sad smile over his shoulder.

Of all the twenty or so people on the excursion, only her brother-in-law hadn't congratulated them on their engagement. Why wasn't Micah happy for them? After he and Tolley spent time together and their talk appeared to help Tolley over some of his difficulties, she thought the two men would become good friends. Never mind. Soon they'd be brothers-in-law, and in time Micah would get over whatever bothered him. He was the most loving, forgiving person she'd ever met.

The journey home took most of the day. The campers arrived at the parsonage at suppertime and ate the last of the food they'd carried on the trip. Micah and Grace dispensed the buckets and boxes of raspberries, sending a good portion to those who'd paid others to do their picking and the rest to the needy. While Tolley took Thor to the livery stable, Laurie and May Bean carried their buckets of berries to the boardinghouse. They found Effie Bean and Mrs. Foster in the kitchen.

"Welcome home." Effie gave her daughter a hug. "My, look at those raspberries. We'll have to stay up late tonight making preserves so they don't spoil."

After Laurie and Mrs. Foster thanked her for helping out, she and May said their goodbyes and left.

"I'm so glad you're back." Mrs. Foster wore a worried look.

"Is something wrong?" Surely she hadn't heard about Laurie and Tolley's engagement. Even if she had, *surely* she'd approve.

Mrs. Foster clicked her tongue. "I do hate to complain, but…" She pointed to the ceiling over the kitchen sink, where water marks stained the white plaster. "Seems our new plumbing has sprung a leak."

# Chapter Sixteen

"**W**hat happened?" Tolley's excitement over coming home to Laurie diminished when he saw the water stain.

"We don't know." Mrs. Foster rubbed her cast. "We stopped using the facilities so it wouldn't get any worse."

"That's good." Now he wouldn't need to solve the problem tonight. He sat at the kitchen table and patted Mrs. Foster's hand. "Don't worry. We'll get the plumbers over here to fix it tomorrow." He'd have to tear up the beautiful mosaic tiles and the boards underneath to find the problem, but he was too tired to worry about it now. "Did Laurie tell you our good news?"

"Why, no." Mrs. Foster's expression lightened as she looked back and forth between them.

Laurie held out her left hand, pride and happiness shining on her beautiful face. "Tolley proposed, and I accepted."

"Oh, my!" Mrs. Foster behaved much like the females on the camping trip. She gripped Laurie's hand, admired the ring, shot a pleased glance Tolley's way and gushed out all sorts of compliments and congratulations. "I just knew this was going to happen."

Tolley grinned broadly, probably looking foolish. He didn't care. One more important person in his life approved of what he'd done. Mrs. Foster's unconstrained happiness for them went a long way toward soothing his worries about the plumbing, even about Reverend Thomas.

Those pipes could be fixed. First thing in the morning, he'd see if the plumbers were available. If they weren't, he'd call in Adam. Together they'd conquer the problem, and he could tell the Colonel about everything when the time came.

"Now, you understand, don't you?" Mrs. Foster said. "This means you two must be even more circumspect than before."

"Ma'am?" Tolley returned his focus to the conversation.

"Yes, ma'am." Laurie nudged his arm and giggled. "She means we still need a chaperone here at the house."

For a moment, Tolley got lost in her smile and thoughts of wanting to kiss her, until she nudged him again. "Oh. Right. A chaperone."

Despite his tiredness, that night he had difficulty falling asleep. Between making plans for his new life with Laurie and worrying about the plumbing, his thoughts refused to be tamed. At last exhaustion— the good kind—took over, and he woke up the next morning refreshed and ready to conquer the plumbing problem.

At the hotel, Garrick informed him the plumbers were installing fixtures in the new wing, so Tolley found Adam at the livery stable and asked him to help. Adam arrived in the afternoon just as Tolley knelt on the bathroom floor with a hammer and chisel.

"Wait!" The younger man grabbed Tolley's shoulder with uncharacteristic firmness. "We don't need to ruin the tiles. We can go through the crawl space."

"Huh. Good idea. Show me what you're thinking."

"This way." Adam stepped out of the room and descended halfway down the back staircase, where he knocked on the wall underneath the bathroom's floor level. "We can make a hole right here, frame it in, put in a door, and if there's another leak, we can reach it with no difficulty."

"Hmm." Of all the ways to solve the problem, Tolley hadn't thought of getting to the pipes this way. "Good idea."

They spent the next two hours gathering the building materials and making the doorway. Once a sixteen-by-eighteen-inch section of plaster and lath was opened up, Adam crawled inside, lantern in hand, to find the leak. Meanwhile, Tolley prepared the opening for framing. As he scraped away wood chips and excess plaster, debris fell on the canvas tarp they'd laid over the steps.

Waving away the dust floating in the air, Laurie brought cookies and lemonade. With her came that bothersome cat. It jumped from an upper step into the hole and disappeared into the darkness.

"Pepper, come here, you silly boy." Laurie laughed, a musical sound Tolley loved to hear.

Adam crawled out through the hole. "Don't worry, Miss Laurie. I'll make sure he's out before we close it up." He sat on the top step and took a long draught of lemonade. "My, that's tasty."

"Did you find the problem?" Tolley ate his third cookie in less than three minutes.

"Yessir." Adam pointed into the dark space. "It's the best possible problem to fix because the leak is in the drainpipe joint. The sealer pitch the plumbers used didn't take. I'll get more from the Del Norte lumber mill. Once it's dried, everything'll be right as rain."

"As long as it doesn't rain inside the house anymore," Tolley offered, and they all enjoyed a good laugh. "We should probably nail a piece of canvas over the hole to keep the hot air and dust from coming into the rest of the house." He wouldn't add that he'd seen mouse signs on the floor inside the crawl space. He could just hear Mrs. Runyan screaming if she found a mouse in her bedroom.

"Good idea." Adam set down his glass and lifted an edge of the canvas tarp. "I'll take this out back and give it a good shake."

"Guess it's time to get Pepper out of there." Laurie stared into the opening. "Come on, Pepper. Come, kitty, kitty."

The only response was a soft "mernt" coming from a dark corner near the front of the house and then a rustling sound.

"Must be after a mouse. I'll get him, Miss Laurie." Adam set down the tarp and reentered the space to belly-crawl across the beams toward the sound. "Well, I'll be." When his muted words reached them, Laurie and Tolley shared a puzzled look.

"What is it?" Tolley would crawl in after him, but

his broad shoulders might get him stuck among the joists and beams.

Instead of answering, Adam returned, shoving a canvas bag in front of him. "Look what the cat found, probably drawn by mice chewing on this." Although not eaten clear through, the bag bore numerous bite marks. "Good Pepper."

As if happy to hear its name, the furry rascal scampered over Adam's back and head and down the staircase.

"Yeah, good kitty." First time he'd seen any value in having the cat indoors. He took the heavy, dusty bag, upon which the words "Denver and Rio Grande Railroad" were imprinted. "It must be the stolen payroll."

"But how did it get into Mrs. Foster's house?" Laurie asked. "Much less into a remote corner between the floors."

"That's what I'd like to know." Standing in the hallway above them, a very worried Mrs. Foster rubbed her injured arm.

"Why, that must be what the prowler was after." Laurie jumped up from her seat on the steps and put an arm around Mrs. Foster. "I'm sure there's nothing to worry about. The outlaws are either dead or in prison. They won't come back for the money."

"We'd better report this to the sheriff right away." Tolley helped Adam out of the hole.

"I'll go." Before leaving on his errand, Adam brushed at his hair and clothing, sending up another cloud of dust.

As she had before, Laurie waved away the powdery

gray substance so she wouldn't breathe it into her lungs. This would be a big mess to clean up.

"I don't understand." Mrs. Foster continued to stare at the bag. "No outlaws ever entered my home. When that horrid Dathan Hardison came to town in '81, back when Marybeth lived here before she married Rand, I wouldn't let him into the house. Didn't trust him from the moment I laid eyes on him."

"Hmm." Tolley appeared thoughtful. "Did you ever see Deke Smith?"

"Hardison's partner, the one who died in the cabin last winter?" At Tolley's nod, Mrs. Foster's forehead furrowed. "Not that I recall."

Tolley looked like he had an idea, but he didn't say anything, maybe because tears filled the elderly lady's eyes.

"I feel so foolish. So vulnerable."

Laurie tightened her embrace. "We needn't solve this now. The sheriff will help us figure it out." She viewed the mess on the floor. "Why don't you rest? Tolley and I have some work to do before fixing supper." She gave him a meaningful look, hoping he planned to help clean up the mess he and Adam had made.

"All right, dear." Mrs. Foster stepped toward her bedroom door. "Thank you."

"I'll shake this out." Tolley gathered the canvas, folding over the edges to contain the debris. "Then I'd better take this bag over to the bank so Nolan can put it in his safe."

Laurie understood his errand's importance, but she couldn't stop a thread of annoyance winding through her. He'd made the mess and now expected her to clean it up. Not the best way for her fiancé to endear himself to her. Maybe she should consult with Maisie and Grace. She'd heard them both talk about their husbands helping around the house.

"These banknotes are genuine." Nolan Means held each one up to the light of his kerosene desk lamp. "Of course the gold is, too." He nodded toward the pile of five- and ten-dollar coins spread out across his blotter. More gold coins remained inside the canvas bag.

"Adam, you found buried treasure." Tolley clapped his young friend on the shoulder. "You deserve the reward the railroad promised."

"I don't know about that." Adam's bemused countenance held no expectation.

"I do." Lawson chuckled. "I'll wire the railroad about it as soon as we get this money into the safe. Nolan, how much do you think is here?"

"If memory serves me, the payroll was about five thousand dollars." Nolan thought for a moment. "That amount includes what the Purvis brothers and Skinner took before parting company with Hardison and Smith, so this is likely considerably less. I'd guess the money in Hardison's bank account came from this payroll. No one has come to claim it, so I suppose I should close it out and include it with the rest. Do you agree, Sheriff?"

"Don't do it right away." Lawson scratched his chin. "Could be he came by it honestly and it belongs to his kin, if he has any."

Once they'd concluded their business and stored the money in the large safe, Tolley, Adam and Lawson left the bank. Adam headed home, but before Lawson could step off the boardwalk toward the telegraph office, Tolley stopped him.

"Mrs. Foster is pretty upset by this whole thing." He couldn't forget the stricken look on the dear lady's face and longed to reassure her. "She's positive Hardison never set foot in her house. But I'm wondering whether Deke Smith might've gotten inside somehow. Do you have a wanted poster with Smith's picture on it?"

"I do." Lawson beckoned to him, and they walked next door to his office. Inside, he rummaged through a messy lower cabinet drawer labeled Dead.

Having never noticed it before, Tolley shuddered. How horrible to have one's picture stored in a bottom drawer under such a stark label. If the Lord hadn't sent Reverend Harris to show Tolley a righteous path, he might have left that same legacy.

"Here you go." Lawson retrieved a wrinkled paper poster. "Look familiar?"

"Yep, that's him, all right. It's been four years since they tried to rob the bank, but maybe Mrs. Foster will recognize him."

"Be my guest. I'm not worried about it, but if she is, we need to set her mind to rest about whoever hid the money." Lawson scratched his chin, as he did when thinking over a matter. "I'm guessing the prowler at her house was either Jed Purvis or Heep Skinner trying to find it."

"I figured that, too."

The matter settled, Tolley took his leave of the sheriff and hurried back to the boardinghouse, entering on Mrs. Runyan's heels. The milliner gave him an indifferent glance before going upstairs.

No longer caring what the other boarders thought or said, Tolley continued down the center hallway to the kitchen, where Laurie bustled around preparing supper. "Smells good, sweetheart." He'd never called her sweetheart before, but now the endearment seemed to pop out of his mouth. "What are we having tonight?"

"No help, that's for sure."

He hadn't noticed the hunch of her shoulders, a sure sign she wasn't happy about something. "I need to talk to Mrs. Foster." He showed her the wanted poster and repeated his discussion with the sheriff.

"Yes, of course." Her demeanor quickly changed. "Please reassure her."

"I will." Pleased that she'd gotten past her mysterious upset, he hurried up the back stairs. As he passed the hole into the crawl space, he remembered it needed to be covered before he went to bed. But first things first. He knocked on Mrs. Foster's door.

"Come in." The poor dear sounded weary. He found her in her rocking chair struggling to knit in spite of her splinted arm. "Tolley, what did you find out?"

The room felt stuffy, so he left the door open and raised a window to bring in a breeze. As he had with Laurie, he explained his trip to the bank and sheriff's office. "Do you recognize this man?" He unfolded the poster and set it before her.

She gasped. "Why, yes, I do. Must have been three or four years ago. He was a tramp with all his belongings in a tattered knapsack. Came to the back door asking for food, so I gave him a sandwich. In gratitude, he made a few repairs around the house. I haven't thought about him since then. Why do you ask?"

"I think he used his access to the house to hide the money." With the mystery solved, Tolley had only to discover how Smith had accomplished it. If he figured things right, the bag had sat under Mr. Parsley's room.

He'd wait until the watchmaker went to work before he investigated.

"Tolley, my dear boy, sit down a minute." Mrs. Foster waved him to the straight-back chair near the door. "I'm so pleased you and Laurie will be getting married. I know this is something your father wanted for at least one of his boys." Her faded cheeks turned pink. "I suppose it isn't proper to discuss this because your brothers and the older Eberly girls found other loves and are happily married. But I believe the Colonel will be delighted for you and Laurie. Don't you think?"

"Yes, ma'am." Tolley chuckled. "My father's approval is a pretty strong reason for marrying her." Of course he did love her more than words could say.

"I don't suppose you've managed to fix the bathroom yet." Mrs. Runyan stood in the bedroom doorway. "Seems a pretty shoddy way to run a boardinghouse."

Tolley glanced at Mrs. Foster before standing so he could tower over the grumpy boarder. As he'd hoped, she backed away. "If I recall, ma'am," he growled, "you said bathrooms are indecent. Nevertheless, be assured the problem with the plumbing will be fixed in a few days."

"Humph." Mrs. Runyan spun around and returned to her room.

As mean as it sounded, Tolley couldn't wait to inform her about the rent being raised.

"Why, I've never heard of such a thing." Mr. Parsley stood and threw his napkin down on the dining room table. "Mrs. Foster, you simply cannot raise the rent on a whim."

"Well…" Mrs. Foster cast a doubtful look around the table.

Before the landlady could change her mind, Laurie spoke up. "Of course she can. And it's far from a whim. As we've shown you, she's supporting the two of you in high style, while you're both making plenty of money in your businesses. Do you give away your hats and watches without being paid? I think not."

Tolley gave her an approving glance. She'd warned him to keep quiet for fear he'd lose his temper. No need to insult the boarders.

"The very idea." In spite of her indignant tone, Mrs. Runyan kept on eating her raspberry pie. "I shall look into other accommodations first thing in the morning."

"As shall I." Mr. Parsley, apparently tempted by the dessert, sat down again and resumed his eating. "Don't think I haven't noticed what you two have been up to." He glared at Laurie and Tolley.

"Do you mean getting engaged in front of Reverend Thomas?" Tolley winked at Laurie. "Nothing questionable about that."

She smothered a smile. No need to gloat over their happiness when these two never seemed happy about anything.

After supper, Mrs. Foster helped her clear the table and then retired for the night. Tolley still needed to nail a piece of canvas over the crawl space hole, so Laurie busied herself washing the dishes. She hoped for some time alone with him in the parlor this evening. If the boarders complained, she'd play the piano, or at least sit on the piano stool instead of beside Tolley on the settee.

"Haven't you finished washing the dishes yet?" Mrs. Runyan entered the kitchen from the center hallway.

To Laurie's knowledge, she'd never before set foot in this room.

"Why, no, ma'am." Laurie smiled over her shoulder. "Would you like to help me dry them?"

Mrs. Runyan gasped. "Of course not. I'm a paying boarder, not a serving girl."

Laurie sighed to herself. What made this unpleasant woman so arrogant?

Suddenly solicitous, Mrs. Runyan stood by the sink. "I only came in here because I'm concerned about you."

"Concerned?" Laurie viewed her with suspicion. "About me?"

"Why, yes, dear." Mrs. Runyan glanced around the room as if searching for listeners, then spoke in a soft voice like a hissing serpent. "From the moment I saw that young man, I didn't trust him."

Heat filled Laurie's face. She refused to hear this unpleasant woman, who nonetheless kept talking.

"And now I have proof he doesn't care the least bit for you. He's only marrying you to please his father. I heard him say so to Mrs. Foster this evening before supper." Despite her declaration of concern, she gave Laurie a triumphant smile. "If you have a lick of sense, you'll hand back that cheap ring and never speak to him again." She marched from the kitchen.

*Not true. Not true.* Laurie repeated the words over and over in her mind as hot tears began to splash into the dishpan. Why should she believe a horrid woman like Mrs. Runyan? And yet, for all of her hauteur, Laurie had never known her to lie. Further, Mrs. Runyan couldn't have made this up. Laurie doubted the woman had ever heard the Eberly and Northam discussions about uniting their families. Jokes, actually. No one took the idea seriously, never put pressure on any of them to make such a marriage.

And yet...

With Tolley so desperate for the Colonel's approval, did he plan to marry her to gain it? After all, he'd never said he loved her. Had only said they were good friends, made a good team. Yet never once lifted a hand to help her with what he considered "women's work" the way her two brothers-in-law did for her sisters, while she'd done all she could to make his work on the bathroom easier. Shouldn't love make him more generous toward her?

Now it all made sense. Almost from the beginning of his return to Esperanza, he'd cozied up to her as though trying to worm his way into her heart. Well, he'd succeeded. She loved him more than she ever believed it possible to love a man. And yet, she refused to be leg-shackled to someone who couldn't return the same depth of feeling. If she wanted that sort of artificial marriage, she could find it in Denver. At least if those wealthy society men didn't help their wives, they provided servants to help carry the load. She'd do well to return to the city as soon as possible.

She exhaled a long sigh and stretched to get the kinks from her back. Maybe she was tired from the camping trip and coming back to resume her many chores here at the boardinghouse.

Yet in the back of her mind, she'd always feared this was Tolley's motivation. He wanted her to abandon her lifelong dreams so he could fulfill his own. His kind deeds for Mrs. Foster notwithstanding, he was still the selfish, thoughtless boy he'd always been.

The sounds of the piano being badly played came

through the kitchen door. Tolley sometimes did that when he awaited her in the parlor, as though impatient for her to finish her work so they could talk. Always before, she'd thought his clumsy playing charming. Now it seemed an insult to everything that mattered to her. If he'd simply helped her wash dishes, they could've talked all this time. She hurried to finish her work in the kitchen and marched through the dining room toward the parlor.

At the sound of the kitchen door swooshing open, Tolley spun around on the piano stool, his heart just about bursting with love for the lady marching through the dining room toward him. Except that she wore a fierce scowl on her pretty face.

He rose to greet her, but she pushed him into a chair and stood over him, her fists bunched at her waist.

"Did you tell Mrs. Foster you wanted to marry me to please your father?"

The rage and hurt in her eyes bewildered Tolley. Where had this come from?

"Yes, but—"

She slipped her engagement ring from her finger, grabbed his hand and slapped the ring into his palm. "I thought you'd changed, but you're still the selfish boy you always were."

She hurried from the room before he could gather his wits. What on earth just happened?

Numbly, he did his usual rounds of checking the downstairs doors and windows before dousing the lamps and heading up to his room. He used the back stairs, and as he passed Laurie's room, he could hear her crying. He'd never done well with weepy women.

In fact, his sister and the Eberly girls never cried much at all. But Laurie's racking sobs tore at his heart.

"Laurie?" He tapped on her door.

Mr. Parsley poked his head out of his room. "Do you mind waiting until I vacate the premises before you engage in—"

"That's enough!" Suddenly Tolley wanted to hit something, and Mr. Parsley's face seemed a handy target. Instead, the face of his Boston mentor, Reverend Harris, came to mind, along with some of his wise words from Proverbs. *Answer not a fool according to his folly, lest thou also be like unto him.* "Go back to bed, you old grouch." Under the circumstances, it was the least foolish answer he could manage.

While the man huffed with indignation, Tolley continued to his room, where he experienced another fitful night of thinking about Laurie. Could this be about her music, about teaching in Denver and giving concerts? Had she counted the cost of marrying him and decided giving up her dreams and staying in Esperanza wasn't worth the sacrifice? If so, then she'd simply made up an excuse for breaking their engagement.

All he knew for certain was that he loved her more than words could say, and he'd failed to tell her, failed to truly consider her hopes and dreams, just as he'd failed at everything else in his life. Yet none was as important as wanting to make her happy. For so long, he'd thought of her in a brotherly way and wanted to offer her a marriage of convenience. Yet sometime during these past weeks, that fraternal affection had grown into so much more. From the moment he knelt down on Greenie Mountain to propose, he'd realized how much he loved her.

Maybe tomorrow, if she would talk to him, he could sort this out with her. But in the morning, it was Effie Bean who prepared breakfast for the boardinghouse. Laurie had packed up and gone home.

# Chapter Seventeen

In spite of Ma's protests about taking care of her hands, Laurie went to the barn early on her first morning home to milk the cows, taking over Georgia's chore. After straining the milk and delivering it to the kitchen, she returned to the barn to muck out the stalls. The hard work couldn't keep her from sobbing every few minutes. *Honestly, what's wrong with me?* She'd never in her life been weepy. Of course she'd never been in love, either. Or had her heart broken.

Ma, Pa and Georgia respected her need for privacy, even though she couldn't bring herself to explain her tears. Still, their worried looks over meals caused her some guilt. To assure them all she'd survive, she began to talk about returning to Denver. What she hadn't figured out yet was what to do about Molly.

"I've written a letter to Professor Gronseth assuring him I'll be there in September," she said over breakfast. "Would someone please take it to town today?"

"We've all got work to do. This ranch won't run itself." Pa cut into a slice of ham on his plate. "If you want it to reach Denver in time, you gotta take it."

Laurie looked around the table to see Ma and Georgia studiously devouring their food. Was this a conspiracy to put her in Tolley's path? No, it couldn't be. After she'd accepted his proposal, she hadn't had a chance to discuss it with her parents. She assumed Georgia had blabbed the news to them, yet they didn't say anything. Of course, Pa had made his disapproval of Tolley very clear. Why weren't they saying something about the situation now?

"Very well, then. Ma, do you need anything from town?"

With the list in her pocket along with her letter to Professor Gronseth, Laurie saddled Little Bit and rode toward Esperanza. Maybe this was better than hiding at home. Laurie had slipped away from the boardinghouse in the night without telling Mrs. Foster. This would give her a chance to apologize. Of course she wouldn't discuss Tolley with her friend. If he happened to be at the boardinghouse, Laurie would simply refuse to talk to him. She hid her mare behind the house and, finding the kitchen empty, scurried up the back stairs.

"My dear." Mrs. Foster greeted her with a one-armed embrace. "I worried about you."

"Please forgive me."

Seeing the hurt in her friend's eyes, Laurie shed more bothersome tears, then ended up telling her about the breakup, although not the reason for it. No need to make Mrs. Foster feel responsible or to blame Mrs. Runyan for telling her the truth Laurie had always suspected.

"I'm so very sorry, my dear." Mrs. Foster sat down in her rocking chair and clumsily picked up her knitting. "I do hope you can work out whatever caused your disagreement. My own romance with the major endured a few ups and downs."

Laurie nodded politely. This problem would never be worked out.

"By the way, I have some good news," Mrs. Foster said. "Well, good and sad."

Laurie knelt beside the rocking chair. "I'm all ears. Tell me."

Mrs. Foster retrieved a letter from the nearby table. "This is from my son in Philadelphia. When I asked you to write to him after my accident, I had no idea he'd insist I move back there to live with him. Although I love my friends here in Esperanza, I cannot think of a happier place to spend my last days than with my son and grandchildren."

Laurie sat back on her heels. How would Esperanza cope without Mrs. Foster? What would her piano students do for a teacher? But Laurie mustn't try to keep her here, since she planned to leave herself. "When will you go?"

"As soon as possible. At least by September."

Laurie forbade herself to continue crying. "What will your piano students do?"

"My dear—" Mrs. Foster patted her hand "—you've taught them for weeks now. You can take my place here and at the church. Reverend Thomas tells me how inspiring your music is."

Laurie laughed softly. "He's my brother-in-law. He's required to say nice things about me." Mrs. Foster laughed, too. No need to remind her of Laurie's own imminent departure.

They chatted for a while longer before Laurie left. As she walked Little Bit toward Mrs. Winsted's mercantile, she considered what her own departure would mean. Several other ladies played the organ, so church on Sunday mornings would have music. But what of her students? What of Molly Starling and her exceptional talents? Laurie couldn't expect anyone else to teach the child piano lessons without charge, and no one else in town taught singing lessons.

As she waited for Homer Bean to assemble the items on Ma's list, she felt the letter to Professor Gronseth burning in her pocket. Even so, she couldn't bring herself to deposit it in the mail slot at the back of the store, where Mrs. Winsted served as postmistress. Too many questions remained about her future, not the least of which was how she'd live in the same community with Tolley Northam after their broken engagement.

The time had come for her to confide in her parents. Packing up her burlap bag of groceries, she mounted Little Bit and galloped home.

"It's no use, Effie." Tolley sat on the corner of the reception desk. "I'll pay you for the next month, but I'm closing down the office today."

Her brown eyes exuded sadness. "I'm sorry it hasn't worked out for you."

"If you need a job, I can pay you to help Mrs. Foster until she moves back East."

"No need to pay me." Effie waved away the idea. "If she needs help, my May and I can take care of her like we would any neighbor in need." She smiled. "Like you and Laurie have done."

At the mention of his lost love, Tolley felt a hot knife pierce his heart. While Effie set aside her knitting and did a bit more dusting and sweeping, he packed his law books into wooden boxes and placed his framed diploma and Colorado law certificate into his leather satchel. He held the door for Effie as she left and then paused to look up at his shingle. Some lawyer he'd turned out to be. Not a single person had even mentioned his occupation, much less needing his services. He upended one of his empty boxes and reached up for the sign.

"What are you doing there?"

At the sound of George Eberly's gruff voice, Tolley almost fell off the box. What would the old man say to him? Holler at him for hurting Laurie? He'd already beaten himself up enough. What more damage could anyone else do? Sadly, it would be deserved. He stepped down from the box and faced Laurie's father to take his medicine like a man.

"Afternoon, George." He tried to sound nonchalant, but his voice broke. "I'm removing my shingle. Might try to find another town where I can hang it." Someplace where no one had heard about what a cad he'd been.

"Huh." George stood there, fists at his waist. "You mind doin' a little job for me before you go?"

Tolley stared at him, jaw dropping. "Um, you mean a legal job?"

George grunted out a laugh. "Sure don't want no illegal one."

Tolley gave him an awkward grin. "No, of course not." Unable to move, he stared at the old man.

"You gonna do this for me?" George waved a hand toward the open door.

"Yes, of course. Please come in." Tolley grabbed the box and hurried inside. "Come on back to my office."

Once they were seated on opposite sides of the desk and Tolley held a pencil and a tablet in front of him, he nodded to George. "What can I do for you?" Simply saying the words sent a little thrill through his middle. His first law case!

"Want to draw up my will." George pulled some wrinkled papers from inside of his shirt. "I've got the particulars written down here, what goes to whom and so forth. Need you to sort it out and put it in legal jargon so I can sign it. Can you do that?"

"Yessir." Tolley smoothed out the page. The awkward handwriting suited a man whose thick, muscled fingers had been shaped by a lifetime of ranch work. "When do you need this?"

"Any time before I die." He chuckled at his own joke.

Tolley responded with an uneasy laugh. He continued to stare at the page, but none of the information registered in his brain.

"Now, about Laurie."

Tolley's head shot up. "Laurie?"

"Yep, Laurie. Poor gal's heartbroken. Said you proposed so you could get the Colonel's approval." He picked at a cuticle. "That true?"

Tolley's heart ached as he remembered her racking sobs several nights ago. "I can't deny it would be one benefit to our marrying, but—"

"You mean to tell me you believed all that foolishness all these years when we joshed about a marriage between our families?"

Tolley gulped. In truth, he *had* believed it. Still did. Maybe George didn't entertain the notion, but the Colonel had long made his ambition clear when he tried to force Nate and George's oldest daughter, Maisie, into marriage. But Nate fell in love with Susanna, and Maisie and Doc hit it off from the moment they saw each other.

Somehow Tolley managed a shrug. "Truth is, sir, I love Laurie. Not that I deserve her, but—"

"Why don't you go tell her?"

Annoyed by the question and the attitude behind it, Tolley sat back and glared at the man across from him. "Because you told me to stay away from her."

"Huh. Guess I did. Well, I'm rescinding that order. You proved yourself a worthy man by facing those outlaws, risking your life to save those young'uns. Then you go and build a bathroom for Major Foster's widow so she don't need to tote water for her boarders."

Why was it always about something he'd done, either good or bad? Why couldn't he be accepted "just because"? He already knew the answer. As Reverend Harris had told him, only God gave unconditional love.

"Besides," George continued, "in spite of me expressing my disapproval of you, you went ahead and proposed…even after Micah advised you not to."

A shiver ran down Tolley's spine. Who else knew about the mess he made of his brief engagement?

"Hey, Tolley." Nate's voice echoed through the bare office from the reception room.

"Back here." Glad for the interruption, Tolley stood to meet his oldest brother, whose dusty clothes indicated he'd been working hard at the ranch.

"Hey, George." Nate shook hands with the older man. "Don't mean to interrupt anything."

"You ain't." George sat back like he had all day.

"I'll be quick because I have to get back and help

Rand with moving hay. Tolley, Mother sent me to invite you home for supper tonight. Can you make it?"

Knees suddenly weak, Tolley dropped back into his chair. "Yes. Of course. Is everything all right?" Had the Colonel died? No, he couldn't have, or Nate would be grieving instead of grinning.

"Everything's fine. Rand and I are moving our families back to our own houses tomorrow afternoon after church, and Mother wanted one of her big family suppers before we go." He gave Tolley a big-brother smile. "The Colonel is sitting up these days, and she says it's high time he finds out you're home. Doc says he has to be in bed at seven, and no visitors are allowed after that, so be sure to get there before then."

Not only was he invited to a big family supper, but he finally got to see the Colonel. Tolley swallowed a giddy laugh. "Tell her I'll be there before six." He eyed George, who wore a pleased smile, and suspicion crept in. "You have something to do with this?"

"Me?"

From the way George blinked and sat back, Tolley felt certain he hadn't conspired with his family. Yet he dared not trust this invitation entirely.

Nate and George took their leave, and Tolley locked up his office, leaving his books and papers behind. Tomorrow would be soon enough to begin work on George's will.

So he'd finally get to see the Colonel. He could hardly take in the idea. While he wouldn't be able to tell his father about a Northam-Eberly marriage, at least he could say he'd taken on his first case as a lawyer. That should be important enough to earn some approval from the old man, even if his client was the Colonel's old friend.

But as he helped Mrs. Foster with a few chores, spruced up his appearance, fetched Thor from the livery stable and headed south toward Four Stones Ranch, he considered his conversation with George. He wanted to see his father, but he needed to sort things out with Laurie first. It pained him to think of her being heartbroken because of him. Whether or not she agreed to marry him, he must make it up to her before another day, another hour passed by…even if it meant delaying his visit to the Colonel to another day.

Instead of proceeding south on the highway, Tolley turned Thor onto the lane leading to the Eberly ranch, his heart thumping faster the closer he got to the attractive two-story house.

*Tolley!* From her upstairs bedroom window, Laurie saw him coming down the lane. He stared her way, so she ducked behind her white lace curtains.

"What's the matter?" Georgia lounged on Laurie's bed reading *Pride and Prejudice* for maybe the hundredth time. The child was such a romantic.

Laurie started to say *nothing*, which would get her nowhere with any of her meddlesome sisters. "It's Tolley, and I don't want to see him."

"Of course you do."

"No, I don't." Laurie chewed her thumbnail. "Maybe I do."

"Well, then." Georgia abandoned her book and sat Laurie down at her dressing table. "Let's fix your hair." Side-by-side in the mirror, they almost looked like twins. Georgia fussed with Laurie's dark red curls, a near copy of her own. "Are you going to wear this?" She picked at the upper sleeve of Laurie's white shirt-waist. "What about your blue calico?" She went to the wardrobe and rummaged through Laurie's dresses.

Letting her sister fuss over her gave Laurie time to think. She didn't know for certain why Tolley had come, but she did know she needed to apologize to him. After pouring her heart out to her parents, they'd advised her to give him a chance to explain what he'd said to Mrs. Foster. They reminded her she'd always worked hard to please them, so shouldn't Tolley be permitted to please his father? Even so, she wouldn't agree to marry him—if he still wanted to marry her—unless she could be certain he loved her as much as she loved him.

Georgia stood back and surveyed her work. "You're quite beautiful, if I do say so myself."

It was a joke among the sisters, who all bore a striking resemblance to each other. "Why, thank you."

Georgia gave her a little shove toward the door. "So go, silly."

Laurie felt a ripple of nervous excitement inside her chest. This could end up being the best day of her life...or the worst.

Hat in hand, Tolley stood in the Eberlys' parlor, too nervous to sit while he waited for Laurie. The moment she descended the staircase in the hall, he forgot every word he'd practiced to say to her. She was so beautiful. That blue dress lit up her bright blue eyes and made them sparkle. Her ivory cheeks bore a hint of pink. Behind her, Georgia grinned like a monkey.

"Afternoon, Laurie."

"Afternoon, Tolley." Laurie waved a hand toward the settee. "Won't you be seated?" She cast a dark look over her shoulder. "You can go, sister."

With a giggle, Georgia sauntered down the hall toward the kitchen. When her footfalls ceased, Tolley had a suspicion she'd stopped to listen to this conversation, but he couldn't be sure. Despite Laurie's instructions, he remained standing until she sat.

"Pa told me you're going to supper at Four Stones. Don't you need to be there before the Colonel's bedtime?"

He shrugged. "Seeing you is more important."

That brought a smile.

"Laurie, I—"

"Tolley, I—"

They both laughed softly.

"You first," he said.

"All right." She appeared to gather her thoughts. "I should've let you explain what you said to Mrs. Foster. After all, we've always joked about it."

"A joke with some truth to it." Tolley wouldn't deny it. "But that doesn't mean I don't love you. I do. I'm just clumsy figuring out how to say it." He gulped before continuing. "And if you'll have me, I'll do everything in my power to see your dreams come true. We'll go to Denver, and while you teach and give concerts, I'll set up a law practice."

Her jaw dropped, and she batted those dark red eyelashes at him. "Tolley, you want to be a rancher. How can you give up your dream?'

"Laurie, I love you with all of my heart. Without you, there isn't any dream worth having."

Tears shone in her eyes. "That's the sweetest thing

you ever said to me." She sniffed into a handkerchief. "What about your family? Your father?"

"What about a man leaving his parents and cleaving to his wife, as the Bible tells us to do?" He waggled his eyebrows at her, which brought the desired laugh. "So, will you marry me?" He reached into his pocket for the box holding the ruby ring.

"Not until three things transpire."

His heart hiccoughed. "Which are?"

"You hurry over to see your father and get that all settled."

Somehow he'd make it through the ordeal. "And?"

"We have a serious discussion about what determines men's work and women's work."

He grimaced. That would be tough to work out, but he'd make the effort. "And?"

Her smile had never been sweeter. "You stay here in the San Luis Valley with me so I can teach music to my wonderful students."

A riot of emotions clogged his throat, and he could only nod. Finally, he managed, "Sounds good to me." He slid off the settee onto one knee and held out the ring. "Laurie Eberly, will you marry me?"

She offered her left hand. "Tolley Northam, I will."

Once he placed the ring on her finger, he pulled her up into a warm embrace, kissing her for all he was worth. He heard some female giggles and a manly chuckle coming from the hallway, but right now, he surrendered to the happiness exploding like fireworks in his heart.

The ride to Four Stones Ranch was both too short and too long. Tolley had been in Esperanza for almost two months, but it seemed every bit as long as the two years he'd spent in Boston. He'd asked Laurie to come with him, but she'd insisted he needed to do this alone. She was right, of course, as she was about everything. How he loved her. But now he must concentrate on resolving his lifelong problems with his father—if the Colonel was up to it, of course.

Tying Thor to the hitching post behind the house, he walked past Mother's kitchen garden, where an abundance of vegetables flourished. While the aroma of roast beef wafted on the air and stirred a mighty growl in his stomach, his heart hunger roared the loudest.

"Tolley!" Mother met him in the kitchen and reached up to hug him, while his niece and nephews wound themselves around his legs.

"Hey, hold on a minute. Gramma first." After embracing Mother for several moments and kissing her cheek, he gazed into her eyes, seeing only love there. How he'd missed her loving warmth, which had gone a long way to balancing the Colonel's coldness while he grew up. "Now you little rascals." He squeezed Lizzie, Natty and Randy in turn.

Once the little ones seemed satisfied with his hugs, they dashed back to their games. Tolley heard a hubbub in the front of the house, but he couldn't barge into it without preparation.

"How's the Colonel?" Did Mother understand the meaning behind his question?

She reached up and caressed his cheek. "Well enough to sit in his favorite chair in the front parlor. But before you see him, I must tell you something."

His insides quivered. "Yes, ma'am?"

Her eyes misty, she sat him at the kitchen table.

"I was wrong about the cause of your father's stroke. When you arrived, it had just happened, and even Doc still needed to make his diagnosis. I was the one who thought it was you, and I was afraid he'd get worse if he saw or even heard you. Doc honored my wishes, but he explained later that he'd been warning your father to slow down. He said overwork was the likely cause of the stroke, not your homecoming."

Tolley swallowed a lump in his throat. He hadn't expected this.

"Do you want to see him?" Mother stood and moved toward the door.

"Yes, ma'am." On shaky legs, he walked through the swinging door and the long dining room to the front hall, stopping in the double doorway into the parlor. Looking gaunt but with good color, one side of his face sagging slightly, the Colonel held court as he had through the years. Tolley's brothers and their families sat around talking. Voices ceased when they saw him.

For a moment, the Colonel looked bewildered, perhaps by the silence. Then his gaze fell on Tolley. For what seemed like an eternity, the old man looked at him as though trying to figure out who he was. Then a tiny smile lifted one side of his lips.

"Tolley." He garbled the word, but not as a drunk man would. "When did you get home?"

Tolley glanced at Mother, who stood beside him.

"We didn't tell him you were here," she whispered. "And I'm sure he's forgotten you were coming."

"So he doesn't know…"

"He knows nothing that's happened since you returned."

"C-come over here, son." The Colonel raised one shaking hand.

Desperately swallowing his violent emotions, Tolley stepped across the room and shook hands with the man who'd never before called him "son." The man whose eyes now glowed with the love and acceptance Tolley longed for all his life. He hadn't done anything to deserve it, but there it was nonetheless. What amazing work of God had happened here?

With surprising strength, the Colonel tugged on Tolley's hand, bringing him down onto the chair Rand vacated. "T-tell me about Boston."

With the room still quiet and all eyes on him, Tolley knew what he must say...and not say. He briefly recounted his years at Harvard, his friendship with old Reverend Harris, his receiving a law degree and admittance to the Colorado judicial system. The Colonel nodded through it all, his eyes filled with interest. After twenty minutes, he seemed to grow weary, and Mother announced it was time for him to retire. Nate and Rand started to lift him to carry him upstairs, but he asked them to pause.

He gazed at Tolley with unconditional love, love like the Lord's. Or so it seemed. "Welcome home, son."

"Thank you, sir." Tolley couldn't manage more. He hurried outside to lean against Thor. He hadn't wept for years, but the tears felt mighty close right now. He gazed upward where the first stars began to twinkle against the pale evening sky. "Thank You, Lord."

"Tolley?"

He hadn't heard Laurie arrive until he felt her comforting hand on his shoulder. He tugged her close, and she snuggled comfortably in his arms.

"I couldn't stay away." She smiled in her beautiful way. "Is everything all right?"

Talking around the clog in his throat, he told her what had transpired. She did him the favor of releasing happy tears he couldn't permit himself to shed.

"Oh, Tolley, I'm so happy for you. It seems the Lord was working all this time. I only hope your father's changes stick."

"Me, too." He brushed away a stray tear still on her cheek. "Even if they don't, I'm beginning to realize who I am and what I'm supposed to do."

"And that is?"

He gently kissed her sweet lips. "Marry you. Love you. Take care of you." He thought for a moment. "You know, Esperanza still doesn't have a lawyer, and Four Stones Ranch seems to be getting along fine without me. What would you say to us buying Mrs. Foster's house and living in town?"

"*I* was going to suggest we buy Mrs. Foster's house and live in town."

"Were you now?"

"Sure was."

"I like your idea best of all." He pulled her close for another kiss...until he felt something tugging on his sleeve.

"Uncle Tolley." Lizzie stood beside them, an adorable grin on her sweet face. "Gramma says it's time for you to quit kissing and come eat supper."

Dining with the family felt like old times, only better. Lots of laughter. Lots of reminiscing. Lots of hope for the future. After clearing the dishes from the dining room table, Rand, Nate and Garrick instructed the womenfolk and children to leave the kitchen.

"We'll take care of washing the dishes." Rand pumped well water into the dishpan.

"You ladies have been busy here in the kitchen all day." Nate carried a pot from the stove to the sink and poured boiling water over the dishes.

Garrick scraped and stacked plates. "I'm sure you ladies have some wedding plans to make."

Laurie caught Tolley's eye and gave him a saucy grin, and he knew he was in trouble. If after a long day of working on the ranch, his strong, tough older brothers didn't think dishwashing was women's work, he wouldn't have any excuses for not helping her in the kitchen. And if his dandy brother-in-law Garrick, a wealthy hotelier who'd been raised with servants doing all of the work, didn't mind scraping dishes, Tolley couldn't refuse to join them. He snatched a tea towel from the rack on the cabinet door.

"I'll dry," he said, as though he'd done this every day of his life. From Laurie's pleased smile, he could see she understood.

## Chapter Eighteen

*August 1, 1885*

At the sound of Marybeth's organ music, maid of honor Georgia proceeded down the aisle of the overflowing sanctuary. One arm looped in Pa's, Laurie followed her sister, wearing the white satin and lace wedding dress Maisie and Grace had worn for their weddings. Down front, Tolley awaited her, looking more handsome than she'd ever seen him in his black suit, white shirt and silver-and-turquoise string tie. Seated beside him in a wheelchair, Colonel Northam served as best man.

Laurie shed a few happy tears, not only because she would soon be married to the man she loved but also because of the new relationship between Tolley and his father. Whatever caused the Colonel to be so hard on his youngest son seemed to have vanished like smoke in the wind. Perhaps during his convalescence from his stroke, he'd sorted out the matter and chosen to let bygones be bygones. Tolley still couldn't talk to her about it without choking up.

Once Laurie and Pa reached the front, Pa handed her over to Tolley, and they both faced Micah. From the moment her minister brother-in-law said, "Dearly beloved, we are gathered together in the sight of God and these witnesses," to the moment he said, "I now pronounce you man and wife," Laurie was in a daze. Finally, she heard Micah say, "You may kiss your bride." Tolley pulled her into his arms and kissed her until she was dizzy. *And* until the congregation laughed and applauded. Even proper Mrs. Foster, seated on the front row with Laurie's family, smiled her approval.

Seemed the whole town had forgiven Tolley's youthful missteps. After Pa pronounced his will written to his satisfaction, many other folks enlisted Tolley's services. He now had more legal work to do than he could keep up with. It'd all have to wait until they returned from their honeymoon.

Tomorrow, Laurie and Tolley would accompany Mrs. Foster to Philadelphia and then proceed on to Boston to enjoy the historical sights and to visit the pastor who'd made such a difference in Tolley's life. Laurie wasn't eager to say goodbye to Mrs. Foster, but she looked forward to returning to Esperanza and making her friend's former boardinghouse her own home. In the meantime, Effie and May Bean would care for Tolley's new best friend, Pepper the cat.

The wedding party moved from the sanctuary to the reception hall, where a beautiful cake, a masterpiece created by the hotel's Chef Henrique, graced the refreshment table along with strawberry punch and coffee. Fred Brody made preparations to take the wedding pictures, and Laurie and Tolley moved to their places in front of his camera. After the first flash of magnesium powder in the lighting pan illuminated the scene and the click of the lens caught their images, Mrs. Runyan and Mr. Parsley arrived at the hall in a flourish and hurried to congratulate them.

Mr. Parsley sidled up to Laurie and Tolley. "You don't mind if we share your reception, do you?"

"Share it?" Tolley looked as confused as Laurie felt.

"You see, Bridget agreed to be my bride. We just now returned from Alamosa, where we became man and wife."

The milliner gazed at the watchmaker with nothing short of adoration. "It's true. I am now Mrs. Griffin Parsley. Surely you won't mind if your photographer takes our picture, too?"

Laurie and Tolley traded one of their special looks, and then burst into laughter. As always, the former boarders wanted the best services without paying the price.

Shaking his head, Tolley said, "I don't think—"

Laurie nudged him in the ribs. "Of course we don't mind." After all, with so much happiness awaiting them, they could afford to be generous, even to free-loaders like the Parsleys.

His eyes filled with love and good humor, Tolley gave her a quick kiss. "Of course we don't mind."

*October 1885*

The light, powdery snow falling on La Veta Pass dissipated as the Denver and Rio Grande train descended into the San Luis Valley. Although Tolley had never known such happiness as he'd enjoyed on his honeymoon these past two months, he couldn't stop the fluttering in his stomach over returning to Esperanza.

Beside him, Laurie gasped softly as the panoramic view of the Valley came into sight. "It's so beautiful."

An old fear crept into Tolley's thoughts. "Do you wish we were going to Denver instead?"

She gazed up at him, shaking her head. "Not at all. I was thinking how wonderful it was to be coming home. I don't know why I ever thought I wanted to live in Denver. Everything I've ever truly wanted is right here and always has been." She leaned against his arm in her delightful way, causing her fancy hat, purchased in Boston, to go askew. Which made her look all the more adorable. Her eyes sparkled, reflecting the blue-green of her traveling dress and the silver and turquoise necklace he'd given her for a wedding gift.

*You think anyone will be there to greet us?* He couldn't bring himself to ask her the question, not after his shattering disappointment last June when he'd stepped down onto an empty platform at the train depot. Instead, he bolstered his fragile emotions with the reminder that, once the train had departed, Laurie had greeted him that day, and she'd been his dear companion almost from that moment on.

They didn't speak for the rest of the journey, not even when the train stopped in Alamosa to unload and load passengers and cargo. From the way Laurie clung to him, he had a feeling she understood his trepidation, as she always had. He should tell her he had no expectations of his family, despite a joyous wedding celebration and warm send-off for the honeymoon. The send-off could have been as much for Mrs. Foster's departure as for Tolley and Laurie's.

The train chugged into Esperanza, hissing out white steam from the engine's undercarriage. From their seat near the front of the Pullman car, Tolley couldn't see the platform. Wanting to hold off disappointment, he lingered while the other passengers disembarked. Finally, he could wait no longer, especially since his beautiful bride kept nudging him toward the door.

"It'll be fine." She reached up to kiss his cheek.

"As long as you're with me, it'll be fine."

He stepped down from the car and held out a hand to her. Behind him, a hubbub broke out, and he turned to see a massive crowd. Nate and Rand held up a banner which read, "Welcome home, Tolley and Laurie." Surrounding them, what appeared to be the entire Northam and Eberly clans cheered.

In a daze, he drew Laurie into the crowd. He kissed Mother first, of course. Shook hands with his brothers and brothers-in-law. Kissed his sister and five sisters-in-law on the cheek. Three of them had new babes in their arms. He embraced his other nieces and nephews. Shook hands with George Eberly, who slapped him on the back like a long-lost friend. Then he came to the Colonel, who still required a wheelchair, but whose face had fleshed out and whose eyes had brightened with their former intelligence over these past two months. Tolley hesitated. Should he reach out to shake his hand? Before he had to decide, the old man reached out to him. Grasping Tolley's hand, he pulled him down into an awkward embrace.

"Welcome home, son, daughter." He looked beyond

Tolley and winked at Laurie, whose eyes were suspiciously moist. "Bartholomew, I have a legal matter I need you to tend."

And that was when Tolley knew he truly had come home.

\* \* \* \* \*

*If you liked this story, pick up these other*
**FOUR STONES RANCH** *books*
*by Louise M. Gouge:*

*COWBOY TO THE RESCUE*
*COWBOY SEEKS A BRIDE*
*COWGIRL FOR KEEPS*
*COWGIRL UNDER THE MISTLETOE*

*Available now from Love Inspired!*

*Find more great reads at www.LoveInspired.com.*

Dear Reader,

Thank you for choosing *Cowboy Homecoming*, the fifth book in my Four Stones Ranch series. I hope you enjoyed the adventures of my hero, Tolley Northam, and my heroine, Laurie Eberly. If you read *Cowgirl for Keeps* (Love Inspired Historical, July 2015), you already know why Tolley struggles to find himself and earn his formidable father's approval. And now at last, two offspring of the central families of my series have fallen in love and found their very own HEA.

My series setting is the beautiful San Luis Valley of Colorado, where I lived for many years. In case you're wondering, I don't have definite proof that any 1885 Valley settlers installed indoor plumbing in their homes. I do have lifelong Valley resident Emma M. Riggenbach's history, *A Bridge to Yesterday* (High Valley Press 1982), in which she writes about Monte Vista, Colorado, the inspiration for my series, and some of the uses of the natural artesian water in the area.

If you enjoyed Tolley and Laurie's story, be on the lookout for more stories set in my fictional town of Esperanza. Can you guess who my next hero or heroine will be? Who would you like to see have his or her own happily-ever-after?

I love to hear from my readers. If you have a comment, contact me at:

http://blog.Louisemgouge.com. (You can also sign up for my occasional newsletter there.)
https://www.facebook.com/AuthorLouiseMGouge/
Twitter: @Louisemgouge

Blessings,
*Louise M. Gouge*

COMING NEXT MONTH FROM
**Love Inspired® Historical**

Available May 9, 2017

## THE NANNY'S TEMPORARY TRIPLETS
*Lone Star Cowboy League: Multiple Blessings*
by Noelle Marchand

After being jilted at the altar, Caroline Murray becomes the temporary nanny for David McKay's daughter and the orphaned triplet babies he's fostering. But when she starts to fall for the handsome widower, can she trust her heart?

## HER CHEROKEE GROOM
by Valerie Hansen

When lovely Annabelle Lang is wrongly accused of murder after rescuing him, Cherokee diplomat Charles McDonald must do something! To save their lives—and their reputations—Charles proposes a marriage of convenience. But will this business proposition turn to one of true love?

## AN UNLIKELY MOTHER
by Danica Favorite

When George Baxter, who is working undercover at his family's mine, finds a young boy who's lost his father, he's determined to reunite them. Caring for the boy with the help of Flora Montgomery, his former childhood nemesis, he instead discovers hope for a family of his own.

## THE MARSHAL'S MISSION
by Anna Zogg

Hunting a gang of bank robbers, US Marshal Jesse Cole goes undercover as a ranch hand working for Lenora Pritchard. But when he discovers the widowed single mother he's slowly falling for may know something about the crime, can he convince her to tell him her secret?

---

# Get 2 Free Books,

*Love Inspired* HISTORICAL

## Plus 2 Free Gifts—

### just for trying the Reader Service!

"Why can't Miss Caroline be our nanny?"

All the grown-ups froze. David's eyebrows lifted. Had his
darling daughter just said "our nanny," as in she'd consider
herself one of Caroline's charges?

Caroline recovered from her surprise. "I'm sorry,
sweetheart. I couldn't."

Maggie's eyes clouded. "Why not?"

"Well, I'm not going to be here very long for one thing.
For another, I've never been a nanny before."

"Maybe not," Ida interjected. "But you certainly seemed
to have a way with the triplets. I can tell from the quiet in
this house that you finally got them to nap. Besides, we
wouldn't need you for long. Only until this nanny David's
trying to hire can get here."

"Ma, Miss Murray is here to visit her family, not work for
ours. It wouldn't be right for us to impose on that."

"Of course we wouldn't want to impose, Caroline, but your
family would be welcome to visit here as often as they want."

"Oh, I don't know." Caroline touched a hand to her throat

as she glanced around the kitchen. Her gaze landed on his, soft as a butterfly, filled with questions.

Did he want her to help them? The answer was an irrevocable no. Did he need her help? His mother's meaningful glare said yes. When he remained silent, Ida prompted, "We sure could use your help, Caroline. Couldn't we, David?"

He swallowed hard. "There's no denying that."

Caroline bit her lip. "Well, I'm sure my brother and sister-in-law could spare me now and then."

"We'd need you more than now and then." David offered up the potential difficulties with a little too much enthusiasm. "You'd have to stay here at the ranch. The triplets need to be fed during the night."

Caroline bit her lip. "What about the piano?"

David frowned. "What about it?"

"Would y'all mind ever so much if I played it now and then?"

Ida grinned. "Honey, you can play it as often as you want."

"In that case…" A smile slowly tilted Caroline's mouth. "Yes! I'd be happy to help out."

Maggie let out a whoop and reached for Caroline's hands. Somehow Caroline seemed to know that was her cue to dance the girl around the kitchen in a tight little circle. Ida sank into the nearest chair with pure relief. David opened his mouth to remind everyone that he was the man of the house with the final say on all of this, and he hadn't agreed to anything. Since doing so would likely accomplish nothing, he closed his mouth.

*Don't miss*
**THE NANNY'S TEMPORARY TRIPLETS**
*by Noelle Marchand, available May 2017 wherever*
*Love Inspired® Historical books and ebooks are sold.*

www.LoveInspired.com

LIHEXP0417